Joe Haldeman is the author of nine other books and numerous short stories, novellas and articles. A graduate of the University of Maryland in astronomy and physics, he received his M.F.A. from the University of Iowa. He and his wife live in Florida.

Also by Joe Haldeman:

THE FOREVER WAR
MINDBRIDGE
ALL MY SINS REMEMBERED
INFINITE DREAMS
STUDY WAR NO MORE

Joe Haldeman

Worlds
A Novel of the Near Future

Futura
Macdonald & Co
London & Sydney

An Orbit Book

First published in Great Britain in 1982
by Macdonald & Co (Publishers) Ltd
London & Sydney

First Futura edition 1982
Reprinted 1984

ISBN 0 7088 80908

Grateful acknowledgement is made to Harcourt Brace
Jovanovich, Inc for permission to reprint a selection from
Complete Poems 1913–1962 by E E Cummings; renewed 1966 by
Marian Morehouse Cummings.

Reproduced, printed and bound in Great Britain by
Hazell Watson & Viney Limited,
Member of the BPCC Group,
Aylesbury, Bucks

Futura Publications
A Division of
Macdonald & Co (Publishers) Ltd
Maxwell House
74 Worship Street
London EC2A 2EN
A BPCC plc Company

This is for Kirby, finally.

you shall above all things be glad and young.
For if you're young,whatever life you wear

it will become you;and if you are glad
whatever's living will yourself become.
Girlboys may nothing more than boygirls need:
i can entirely her only love

whose any mystery makes every man's
flesh put space on;and his mind take off time

that you should ever think,may god forbid
and(in his mercy)your true lover spare:
for that way knowledge lies,the foetal grave
called progress,and negation's dead undoom.

I'd rather learn from one bird how to sing
than teach ten thousand stars how not to dance

—e. e. cummings

Worlds

1 ✦ Worlds apart

You can't know space unless you were born there. You can get used to it, maybe.

You can't love the surface of a planet if you were born in space. Not even Earth. Too big and crowded and nothing between you and the sky. Things drop in straight lines.

But Earth people do visit space and Worlds people do visit Earth. Always to come back changed, sometimes leaving changes.

2 ✦ The Worlds

The world didn't end in the twentieth century. It did take a beating, though, and through most of the next century the psychic scars of the recent past were a prominent part of the human landscape; more prominent, perhaps, than present wonders or future hopes.

Many people, though not a majority, thought that the only real hope for the human race lay out in the Worlds, the orbiting settlements whose population, by the eighties, was approaching a half million. It looked as if the Worlds gave humanity a place to start over, clean slate, unlimited room for expansion. It looked that way from the Worlds, to most people, and from the Earth, to some.

They were called "the Worlds" for convenience, not as an expression of any significant degree of political autonomy or common purpose. Some, such as Salyut and Uchūden, were simply colonies, with populations that were still loyal to their founding countries. Others owed their first allegiance to corporations like Bellcom or Skyfac or, in one case, to a church.

There were forty-one Worlds, ranging in size from cramped little laboratories to vast New New York, home to a quarter of a million people.

New New York was politically independent, at least on paper. But after forty years of exporting energy and materials, it still owed huge debts to the United States of America and New York State. It had looked like a sound long-term investment back in 2010, since smaller-scale energy farms like Devon's World (then called O'Neill) were making fortunes. But then came cheap fusion, and New New could barely charge enough per kilowatt-hour to keep up interest payments. Two things kept the settlement in business: foamsteel and, surprisingly, tourism.

New New started out as an asteroid named Paphos and a philosophy called "economies of scale."

Paphos (its real name was 1992BH) was a small asteroid whose orbit brought it, once each nine years, to within 750,000 kilometers of Earth, about a half million miles. It was a nickel-iron asteroid, which meant it was made of nearly pure steel.

Two hundred and fifty trillion tonnes of steel is a prize worth going after. In 2001, an orbiting factory intercepted Paphos and latched on to it. For the next nine years, hundreds of carefully calculated nuclear blasts warped its orbit, bending it in toward Earth. In 2010, it slid into a geosynchronous orbit—a new star hanging still in the skies of North and South America, unblinking, brighter than Venus.

The bombs that had steered it were "shaped charges," and so did double duty, excavating the planetoid while moving it. When Paphos arrived at its new home, its middle had been scooped out, providing a hollow where people would eventually live. It had been made to rotate much faster than any natural planetoid, spinning to provide artificial gravity on the inside.

The megatonnage that brought Paphos into orbit and started it spinning had been donated by the United States (scavenged from obsolete weapons left over from the previous century's arms race), in return for perpetual "most favored nation" status. One percent of New New York's mass would supply the United States with steel for a thousand years, and it would be the only country that didn't have to pay duty.

They sealed off the open end and filled the hollow with air, soil, water, plants, light; landscaping the interior into a combination of carefully planned wilderness and manicured parkland. Then the people started to come. Miners at first, with huge mole-machines that chewed steel out of the solid metal ground beneath the growing grass and forest. The steel was worth its weight in money to any country or corporation that was building structures in orbit. Normally, ninety-nine percent of the cost of building materials was launch expense. New New York could transfer steel to any orbit for pennies, via slow solar-powered tugs.

After the miners had been tunneling for a year or so, the construction crew came in, to make city of the corridors and caverns. Like its namesake, New New York was to have a Central Park—more literally central in the case of New New—to provide a place of greenery and open spaces for people who would live most of their lives in metal caves.

✦ ✦ ✦

The cheap fusion that had undermined the energy market also made space travel accessible to the merely wealthy. Tourists came to strap on wings and fly (effortless along the zero-gravity axis) or to sit for hours in the observation domes, lost in the terrible wheeling beauty. Honeymooners and others came to consummate themselves in weightlessness, which is wonderful unless you start spinning, and to enjoy the extravagance of paying two thousand dollars a night for a small room in the Hilton. Oenophiles scrapped their life savings to come up and sample the wines that were never exported: the Saint-Émilions, the Châteaux d'Yquem and -neuf-du-Pape that had no vintage years because every year was the same; every year was perfect; the wine of the century down to eight decimal places.

The tourism worked both ways, of course. Nearly

every man, woman, and kiddo on New New wanted to see Earth. Balance of payments forbade it for all save one in a thousand.

Marianne O'Hara was one of the lucky ones. Depending on how you look at it.

3 ✦ Families

Unlike most of her contemporaries, O'Hara was not obsessed with genealogy, so she didn't know anything about any ancestors beyond her great-grandmother, who was still alive and in fact also lived in New New York.

She had to learn, though, facing *menarche* and the prospect of taking a mate. The prevalence of "line families" in the Worlds could generate a lot of relatives. They joked that before you went on a date, you had to check a computer to see what degree of incest you were liable to commit. O'Hara was fourth-generation Worlds, and was related to six different lines, three of them because of her grandmother, who in her time had been a one-woman population explosion.

Various families' records went back to a striking red-haired woman who had left a bad marriage and Prussia in the late nineteenth century and came to America. This woman married a blacksmith in Pennsylvania and they had seven children. One son went to wicked Chicago and made his living, eventually, as a courier of money and sometime pickpocket. He was good at both trades, and at being in the wrong place at the wrong time, and was machine-gunned to death, which was not an unusual way to depart, for a young criminal in Chicago. He'd left a son in a prostitute, who left it in an orphanage. The son was encouraged by a gaggle of nuns, and eventually became a stodgy professor of Attic Greek. He had a daughter (the Prussian woman's red hair coming back) who through a curious sequence of emulation and rebellion wound up with a doctorate in biochemistry, in a specialty that required some work in orbit. In orbit she had a bastard daughter. This daughter stayed in space, joining the New New York Corporation, and eventually became the great-grandmother of Marianne, who would take the name O'Hara.

✦ ✦ ✦

Her mother was annoyed at Marianne for choosing the name O'Hara. A girl-woman usually chose her name to honor someone; they didn't even *know* anyone named O'Hara. She said she'd picked it because she liked the sound (and it did sound better than "Marianne Scanlan," her root name); actually, she had pored over lists and lists, looking for one best name, until she had lost all power of discrimination.

The night before her menarche party, her body full of private outrage, her head foggy with the drugs that would precipitate fertility, she'd looked at the reading list for her course in twentieth-century popular novelists, and honored John O'Hara because he was near the middle of the alphabet, so she'd never be at the end of a line.

Did her mother have a tin ear, to name her Marianne in the first place? No; at the time of her birth, her mother's name had been Nabors. They didn't join the Scanlan line until Marianne was five, her mother all of seventeen.

Most of the people in New New belonged to line families; everyone who wasn't a groundhog was at least related to a line. The custom had its roots in America, just before the turn of the century, born of taxation and sexual freedom.

Line families first became widespread in New York, where inheritance taxes could gobble up as much as ninety percent of an estate. One way around this was to redefine your family as a corporation, with everybody on the board of directors. A best-selling book explained the simple legal process.

The State retaliated by proving in court that a corporation whose board was entirely blood-related had to demonstrate that it had not been set up purely for the avoidance of taxes. This generated a loud chorus of outraged editorials and pious pronouncements by temporarily out-of-work politicians. Another best-selling book, complete with tear-out forms, explained that the simplest way to get around the new law was to effect a merger: join forces, on paper, with some family that was not related to you.

At this time America was enjoying a return of sexual permissiveness, so a lot of the joining was done on beds as well as on paper. There was also a fashion for communal living, which started in rural areas but was widely embraced in cities—especially New York—when it was shown that a corporation of tenants could make a landlord very cooperative. The term "line family" became common in California, where members of these consensual corporations took the same last name; the custom moved east, and up.

In the Worlds, as on Earth, line families encouraged both nonconformity and rigidity. Over a couple of generations, experiment would become habit would become tradition—and if you don't like it, why don't you go start your own line; all right, I will.

For instance, the Scanlan line was made up of three-mate marriages called triunes. Triunes occasionally interlocked to form larger units, but that was considered racy. The Nabors line was less formal. In general, young men paired up with older women and young women with older men, with frequent changes of partners. That Marianne's mother was only twelve when she gave birth did not raise any eyebrows. But when it turned out that the father not only was not a Nabors, but was a groundhog as well, mother and child were unceremoniously disowned.

To become a Scanlan, a person only had to be of proven fertility, and had either to find a compatible broken triune or to apply with two other fertile people (all three not to be of the same sex). Marianne's mother took the latter course: she applied with two men, her current lover and Marianne's father, who returned to his Earthside wife a week later, as had been prearranged.

Thus Marianne was a fatherless prefertile adjunct to a broken triune, with a mother young enough to be her sister (Scanlan women normally postponed children until their thirties). She was different, and the other children were not kind. The boys were unkind and bigger than she was, which might be one reason she delayed womanhood as long as possible.

When she did become a woman she was striking, rather than beautiful, with the genes that had come from Prussia two centuries before: thick dark red hair, eyes the color of copper, skin as pale as wax. People would stare at her.

4 ✦ Blood sisters

A menarche party is fun for everybody but the guest of honor. Old wine doesn't mix well with new hormones. Smug sympathy while your girlhood is being torn bleeding from your body.

O'Hara knew she was drinking too much wine, trying to wash away the acid taste of vomit. *That* had been because of too many pain pills. The cramps were still there, gentle pressure, waiting for the medicine to wear off. If she sat still she imagined she could feel meat growing, shoving up beneath her boyish nipples. But she couldn't sit still; no position was comfortable for long. And she couldn't stand up without feeling nauseated. She had moved the party outside, upstairs into the park, which had helped for a minute. Now there was no place else to go. Except out the airlock. That sounded like an attractive proposition. She wasn't even bleeding yet, raped by stiff cotton. She would not cry. If one more woman tried to put her arm around her, she'd knock the bitch's teeth down her throat.

"My poor baby." Can't hit your own mother. "You're so pale. You aren't going to be sick again?"

"Thanks," she said through clenched teeth. "I'd almost forgotten."

"You really shouldn't drink so much wine, you know. It doesn't help."

"Mother. I always throw up at parties. Nerves. I'm all right now. Once always does the trick."

She smiled uncertainly and cocked her head at her daughter. "I can never tell when you're being serious."

"Never serious. Morose, sometimes. Never serious." She swallowed hard and blew her nose. "Boy. Wish we could do this every year."

"Well, you brought it on yourself. You know what Dr. Johnson said." The gynecologist had been after her for five years. The longer you put it off, the more it was going to hurt. Finally, approaching seventeen, she had to menarche or face real trouble with her pelvic girdle later on.

"Dr. Johnson knows as much about this as I know about peeing standing up."

"Oh, Marianne."

"It's true; he's never told me anything I didn't know. He just likes to poke around inside little girls."

"Don't be crude."

"Big girls, too."

"He's a nice man."

"Sure. Keeps his instruments in the refrigerator so they'll be nice and fresh."

She shook her head. "Poor girl. I know what you're going through."

Marianne leaned back and closed her eyes. "In a goat's gap, you do. You were twelve, weren't you?"

"Eleven. I was twelve when I had you."

"So don't call me 'girl.' In another five years I'll be twice as old as you."

"What?"

"Just help me up, would you?" She held out a weary arm. "I have to find the john."

"Are you going to be sick?"

"No. If you must know, I want to check and see if it's started yet." She minced away and muttered: "My glorious fucking womanhood."

5 ✦ Her misspent youth

When she was a girl, Marianne knew she annoyed some people and frightened others. It would be years before she made any conscious effort to put people at ease; until then, she was socially something of a monster.

She was single-minded and broadly talented. Under New New's merit-examination system, she was graduated from high school at age twelve; by fifteen she had baccalaureate certification in American Studies and World Systems. She earned medals in handball and gymnastics and played in the orchestra. Papers she wrote while a graduate student were published in academic journals in the Worlds and on Earth. New New's Academic Council gave her the rare opportunity to go to Earth for a year of postgraduate work.

Her mother, who had dropped out of school at the tenth-grade level, thought that Marianne was using her education as an excuse for delaying menarche, and she was not completely wrong. To Marianne, dating sounded like a boring waste of time and sex sounded gruesome. She knew that wasn't true for most people, but she also knew she wasn't *like* most people. So she exercised her legal right to put off adulthood.

For the first couple of months after menarche, Marianne had reason to wish they still did it the old-fashioned way. She cramped constantly and lost so much blood she had to have two transfusions. Her new breasts and hips ached from rapid growth and bumping into things. She felt clumsy and sore and messy and unnecessarily hirsute.

Once recovered from the transition, though, she went about becoming a woman with characteristic speed and thoroughness. She read all about it, of course, and asked innumerable embarrassing questions. She took a light academic load and kept an eye out for a likely-looking male. She found an unlikely one.

Students in New New, no matter how gifted, were not allowed to be passive beneficiaries of everybody else's labor. O'Hara was required to do agricultural work on Thursdays and construction on Saturdays. It was while slapping paint on seemingly endless acres of wall that she met Charlie Increase Devon.

The Devonites were the largest line family in the Worlds, though not too many of them lived in New New. They had their own settlement, Devon's World, which was sort of a cross between religious commune and brothel.

Like all Devonites, Charlie was a New Baptist. The only thing they had in common with old-style Baptists was that their initiation ceremony also involved water. They weren't even Christian; their theology could be described as Unitarian-on-Quääludes. They were nudists and body-worshipers. They had various interesting rituals—such as *se-marche*, when boys became men—that formed the nucleus for a large subgenre of ribald humor in the twenty-first century. They were promiscuous and often pregnant, both by commandment.

O'Hara was fascinated by Charlie. He was about the biggest man she had ever seen, heavily muscled from years of pushing steel, but he moved with uncanny grace. He was serious and quiet and not at all intelligent. Like all Devonites, he was completely hairless and always wore white; like most of them, he was a religious fanatic, in a quiet way.

They were total opposites, O'Hara being agnostic, intelligent, small, and not quiet. He seemed like a perfect man to start out with, since she did want sexual experience but didn't want to complicate her life with a love affair.

She might have been forewarned if her otherwise liberal education had included a few ancient Claudette Colbert movies ("you big lug"). They fell for each other, hard, even before they went to bed together, which was not long postponed. After he had gently initiated her into the glorious mysteries of friction and spasm, they clung to one another like the opposite poles of strong magnets.

It was not going to have a happy ending. Charlie had to start fathering children by age twenty-three (he was twenty-one when they met), or sin by omission, and although O'Hara's love was almost boundless, it could not encompass shaving her head and spending the rest of her youth manufacturing babies.

Of course, they tried to convert each other. Charlie listened to O'Hara's arguments with grave respect, but she couldn't penetrate his belief. O'Hara had less patience with Charlie's arguments, but after hurting him twice, she kept her mouth shut. Eventually, she agreed to go with him to Devon's World, even though the idea of a one-religion World gave her understandable premonitions of disaster. The only other one had suffered the fate of Sodom and Gomorrah.

6 ✦ Jacob's Ladder

Everyone remembers what they were doing on 14 March 2082, the day Jacob's Ladder came down.

World of Christ was an evangelical organization with a worldwide membership approaching a hundred million. In 2018, the hundredth anniversary of their founder's birth, they hired Martin-Marietta-Boeing to build for them Jacob's Ladder: a huge and beautiful space structure that combined the functions of church, monastery, and hotel. Most of the thousands of people who went there stayed for only a week or a month of praying in the ecstasy of weightlessness, suspended between the Earth and Heaven. A couple of hundred were especially blessed and lived there full time (which made them objects of intense curiosity for scientists concerned with the long-term effects of weightlessness, but WoX wouldn't allow them to be examined).

For economy, Jacob's Ladder was in low Earth-orbit, with a perigee of about 250 kilometers. This is why it came down. It had a limited capability for orbit correction, in case of atmospheric drag. A correction was applied on 13 March 2082, but somehow it was applied in exactly the wrong direction, elongating the orbit rather than circularizing it. This plunged the structure deeper into the atmosphere. It completed sixteen orbits, lower and lower, before it crashed flaming into the Indian Ocean.

If it had stayed aloft a fraction of a minute longer, the molten cathedral would have impacted on the Indian subcontinent, surely taking millions of lives. WoX spokesmen claimed this was evidence of God's mercy. They also claimed the disaster was a warning to sinners.

Their membership fell off drastically. They collected more than enough insurance to build another Ladder, but they never got around to it.

✦ ✦ ✦

The fourteenth was a Friday, so O'Hara was to have her weekly walk in the park with John Ogelby.

Deformed people were rare in the Worlds, but John Ogelby would not describe himself any other way: hunchbacked, bandy-legged, sticks for arms; he walked like a cartoon character and was barely a meter tall. He had come to the Worlds because low gravity was the best, safest anodyne for the constant aching in his joints, and because he suspected that a small world was like a small town: people got used to you and stopped staring.

He was well liked in the low-gravity engineering facility where he worked. He was a brilliant and careful worker, and had learned how to be affable in spite of a natural tendency to use his wit and deformity as a double-edged weapon. He did devastatingly grotesque imitations of video stars and political figures.

But he was wrong about this World being small. With more than two hundred thousand people, there was always someone seeing him for the first time, starting and staring. He got used to it, but could not stop noticing it.

So Ogelby was mildly surprised when he first met Marianne O'Hara. She didn't jump. She looked at him without staring, the way very old people sometimes did, and then walked over with a glass of punch—the bowl was obviously too high for him to reach—and spent the rest of the afternoon talking with him, with frankness and sympathy. She came up to look at his lab the next day, and they had dinner.

What developed was not exactly a love affair. Love can be driven by pity, and it can even be fueled by curiosity and a thirst for intellectual companionship, but that was not the case here. O'Hara was in love already, with Charlie Devon, and John's complicated strengths and weaknesses served to counterbalance Charlie's simple ones. The two men met once and liked each other cautiously, but Charlie privately could not understand how O'Hara could get used to looking at the hunchback, and John could not drive away the vision of Marianne lost in those strong arms. If you asked either of them, he would say that he was glad there was someone to give O'Hara what he could not (John would say "perforce").

O'Hara spent more time with John than with Charlie: playing games, exploring New New, incessantly talking and joking. Every Friday they met for lunch and a long walk in the park. John wasn't particularly comfortable there, but knew that if he didn't exercise in high gravity he would suffer progressive myasthenia and eventually be unable to leave the low-gravity section where he lived and worked. He was usually rather giddy on the Friday walks, because the pain pills made him light-headed.

He hadn't taken any pills this Friday, the fourteenth, and his knees and hips and curved spine throbbed with tiny pulses of fire while he waited at the outdoor restaurant. He was the only customer.

Marianne came briskly down the pathway, brushing out her wet hair, and started to apologize for having been held up at the pool's dressing room, but Ogelby cut her short with a voice that surprised both of them, a harsh croak:

"Have you heard about the Ladder?"

"Jacob's Ladder?"

"It's coming down." She furrowed her brow, not understanding. "It's going to crash. They can't save it."

"H-how?"

On the way to the lift that would take them up to Ogelby's flat, he told O'Hara about the incredibly botched correction maneuver; about the shuttles that had come up with emergency engines, too late. On its second pass through the atmosphere, the cross-shaped structure had picked up rotation and wobble; it couldn't be docked with. Many of the congregation had been killed when the satellite started rotating, the artificial gravity sliding them down to the ends of the cross's arms, then crushing them under a load of altars and statues and a boulder from Golgotha. The ones left alive first made a plea for help, then a dignified statement about the will of God, and then they cut off all communication.

While the world and the Worlds watched helplessly, Jacob's Ladder fell closer to the Earth each ninety minutes. The United States, Common Europe, and the Supreme Socialist Union argued over the morality of blasting the thing out of the sky.

Marianne and John sat silently, sipping coffee all day and into the night, watching his video cube and a jury-rigged flatscreen. The cube brought them Earth newscasts, and the flatscreen picked up signals from Worlds telescopes, tracking the Ladder as it spun and yawed over familiar continents and oceans.

On the fifteenth pass, it glowed cherry-red and made charcoal of two thousand martyrs. Calculations showed that it would come down next time, landing safely in the ocean. Missilemen locked up their systems and sat back in relief.

It was a terrifying sight, the spinning incandescent cross lighting up the night of Africa. Skimming in over the Laccadive Islands, its sonic boom broke every window and eardrum in its path. None survived long enough to notice the deafness. The Ladder hit the water at four miles per second, and detonated with ten thousand times the force of a nuclear weapon, and sent a high surge of steam-backed water rolling across the lowlands of Kerala. All but a few hundred thousand had managed to get to high land.

They watched the cube for several hours after the crash, as the true magnitude of the disaster slowly unfolded. Sometimes they were awkwardly arm in arm, Marianne holding John with uncertain delicacy.

"John," she said finally, "I've never asked. Do you believe in God?"

"No," he said. He looked at one ugly large hand and pipestem wrist. "Sometimes I believe in a Devil."

After briefly discussing the possibility of failure, they tried to make love, and it was the night's second disaster. After a year or so they could talk and even joke about it, and they remained fast friends long after Charlie had gone off to join a baby machine (his place in O'Hara's life was taken over by a rapid succession of men more characterized by variety than quality, Ogelby thought), and when she was on Earth O'Hara wrote more often to Ogelby than to anyone else, so long as she could write.

7 ✦ Licorice stick

O'Hara loved to play the clarinet. She had a thorough classical grounding—had played every boring note in Klosé—
because the clarinet had been her solo instrument for her
music degree. She even played in the New York orchestra
because she enjoyed losing herself in the complex har-
monies and rhythms of symphonic music and liked to be
around other musicians. But her real love was jazz: primitive American jazz—Dixieland, especially.

Her music library was dominated by tapes, flat-screen
or plain audio, of twentieth-century American jazzmen.
She often played along with them, and could do a dead-on
pastiche of, say, Goodman's solo in "Sing, Sing" or Foun-
tain's in "Swing Low." A friend who was good with electronics had made her a copy of "Rhapsody in Blue" with
the clarinet part filtered out; learning it had taken three-
hundred hours out of her seventeenth year.

An objective critic, and O'Hara was one by the time
she was twenty, would note that her playing was mechani-
cally competent and sometimes even brilliant, but she had
no particular personal style and no real gift for improvisation. It might have been different if she had had other people to play with, but no jazz musicians in New York were
interested in historic forms. The Ajimbo school, with its
sixteenth-note phrasing and weird clapping chorus, had

dominated jazz for a generation, in the Worlds as well as on Earth. O'Hara thought it was degenerate, obvious, and unnecessarily complex. other people might say the same of Dixieland, if they ever listened to it.

That was another reason to go to Earth. Chicago, San Francisco, old New York; they all sounded fascinating. But the place she most wanted to visit was New Orleans. To walk the streets they'd named songs after: Bourbon, Basin, Rampart. To sit on a hard chair in Preservation Hall, or nurse expensive drinks in crumbling old bars, or just stand on the sidewalk or in the French Quarter park and listen to old black men try to keep alive this two-century-old music. John Ogelby had been there (he was English but had taken a degree at Baton Rouge), and she made him talk about it all the time. She would go to New Orleans even if she could somehow foretell what was waiting for her there.

8 ✦ O brave new world/ That has such people in't

O'Hara didn't really want to go to Devon's World. She and Charlie both had a week of vacation coming up, and they'd discussed the possibility of going to another World, but it was Tsiolkovski she wanted to visit, or maybe Mazeltov. She had made a joke about going to Devon's World, and Charlie claimed he had taken her literally and bought tickets, nonreturnable. So she went along, grumbling, to experience Edward D. Devon's dream made solid, a World dedicated to the proposition.

Devon's World was the oldest large structure in orbit. Originally called O'Neill—a ninety-year-old oak tree planted by O'Neill himself survived—it had been home to some ten thousand workers involved in the manufacture of other large space structures. Out of minerals flung up from the Moon's surface they built energy farms, space factories, a large zerogee hospital, and other Worlds—thirty-two large structures and scores of smaller ones. But now its original purpose had been preempted by its children.

It was New New York that had forced them out of business. Foamed steel from the interior of Paphos was cheaper, stronger, and easier to work with than the aluminum alloys that lunar soil could provide. Devon's World still had a modest income from the manufacture of solar cells, for other Worlds, and some specialized products, such as large vapor-deposition mirrors.

But most of its workers, for generations now, had been lured to New New York. The New New York Corporation could afford generous relocation bonuses, high salaries, and profit-sharing plans, to save the cost of lifting men and women from Earth and training them to work in the hazardous conditions of space. Edward D. Devon and his New Baptists—who had seen the future and spent a decade in careful preparation—moved in as the workers moved out, in the most ambitious relocation of a religious body since Brigham Young's trek to Utah.

For Charlie, the trip was a pilgrimage. He hadn't been to Devon's World since his own semarche, ten years before. Marianne was going with the attitude of an anthropologist, a slightly apprehensive anthropologist: it was one thing to be in love with a sex maniac, and quite another to be locked up in a World with ten thousand of them. She brought lots of schoolwork, figuring to stay in the hotel and work ahead on her studies while Charlie used his divining rod on female coreligionists. She gritted her teeth and told herself she was not jealous.

As she should have foreseen, Charlie had other ideas. This was his best and last opportunity to convert her. She cooperated, out of respect for his feelings and to satisfy her own considerable sexual curiosity, and got much more than she'd bargained for.

In his holy book *Temple of Flesh*, Edward D. Devon had provided a spiritual rationale for virtually every sexual diversion, with only brutality and male homosex proscribed. Charlie seemed determined to start at the beginning and work through to the concordance.

O'Hara had to admit that Devon's World was comfortable, and beautiful—it had to be, considering that eighty percent of its income was from tourism (as opposed to eleven percent in New New)—but most of it was far too expensive for her and Charlie; prices reflected the small fortunes that groundhog tourists spent getting there. Charlie was able to get them space in a hotel that was a Devonite "retreat," and therefore affordable. A room in Shangrila, one of the World's two cities, would have eaten up all of their savings in a half hour.

Outside of the cities, the wheel-shaped World was mainly parkland, carefully manicured by an army of horticulturists. O'Hara admired its formal beauty but preferred the wildness of New New's park. She also found it disconcerting to have to step over and around people casually copulating on the path. Charlie primly pointed out that they wouldn't be doing it in public if they didn't want people to share their joy. O'Hara would just as soon have had them keep their joy to themselves.

The swimming pool was the worst. Acres of couples, and larger organizations, doing what came naturally (or with some effort). After much cajoling she joined Charlie there in public bliss, and was obscurely annoyed that nobody watched.

A bigger step was having sex with other people, which Charlie insisted was necessary. The people were invariably gentle and polite—once you got used to total strangers asking you to do things you'd never done even in your imagination—but she was surprised to find most of the experiences boring, because most of the people were boring. They seemed appallingly ignorant and smug. They had no curiosity about New New or even Earth, but could drone on forever about family, religion, sex, and jobs, in roughly that order. At least there was never any weather.

She gamely tried almost everything that Charlie suggested, and learned more from the failures than the successes. Some of the knowledge troubled her deeply.

The padded ropes. Charlie explained it to her and showed her the scriptural passage about it, about helplessness and trust. It seemed innocuous, if somewhat silly, but when Charlie started to tie her up she began to struggle, seized with mindless terror; she even bit him while he was trying to release her. She saw then that a large part of her love was self-love, pride in taming the beast, and the other side of the tarnished coin was fear of his huge strength.

Charlie made light of it, and even showed off the wound his "red Devil" had given him. But things changed, rapidly. Charlie was hard to find during the day and fell into deep sleep at night; O'Hara spent more time with her books, studying ahead of the assignments she had brought along. By the time they got aboard the shuttle for New New, they were distantly polite with one another. Two months later, Charlie emigrated to Devon's World, leaving her with confused memories and a disturbing fund of experience, some of which could get her a good job in Las Vegas, a city she had never planned to visit.

9 ✦ Sons of Judah and Prometheus

(From *Sons of Prometheus: An Informal History of the Deucalion and Janus Projects*, by John Ogelby et al., copyright © 2119 by Gulf/Western Corporation, New New York)

I'm John Ogelby and I was the one who introduced Marianne O'Hara to Daniel Anderson. Dan and I are both mudballers, though I was permanently committed to living in New New, and Dan had every intention of eventually returning to Earth.

Dan was on a research grant from Cyanamid International. He was a specialist in oil-shale chemistry, which made him quite valuable to the CC Section, where I was the token strength-of-materials man.

The CC stood for "carbonaceous chondrite," and to most Worlds people those two words spelled freedom. Our section must have been one of the most exciting—and excited—places to work in the eighties. Every test tube and caliper was heavy with destiny, yes, and the atmosphere was so clogged with Significance that Dan and I, the only mudballers, had to flee every now and then, to regain perspective. Talk about Earth and remember that there was more to the human condition than could be perceived inside a spinning rock full of slightly wonky people. Nice people, but wonky.

In retrospect, I can see that my attitude was short-sighted. But since nobody now will admit to having had that attitude, let me set it down here briefly. I could never resist a joke at my own expense.

Between the lunar mines and the bowels of New New, the Worlds would have had raw materials enough to increase their number a thousandfold or more, if all you needed for a World was a pressure vessel full of oxygen, shielded from radiation. But you also need organic material and water, and we suffered from a marked deficiency of those.

If the Worlds were ever to become a closed system, independent of Earth, they had to have an outside source of carbon, hydrogen, and nitrogen. Simply put, you burn the hydrogen for water; burn the carbon for carbon dioxide that plants will turn to food; plow the nitrogen into the soil so the food can have protein. Closed-system agriculture is not a hundred percent efficient, so it can't support a stable population, let alone an expanding one, without a constant infusion of these three elements.

There are three sources for these elements: the Earth, the asteroids, and comets, in decreasing order of handiness. Only asteroids of the carbonaceous chondritic type are useful, and most CCs are in damned difficult orbits. They found an accessible one, though, and named it Deucalion, and sent a bunch of unlucky engineers out to haul it in.

It was going to be a slow business, twenty-eight years. We couldn't use brute force, as was done with New New, because CCs are relatively fragile. One shaped charge and all you'd have would be ten million tons of dirt flying in every direction. So the first team set up O'Neill-type mass drivers at each pole, and settled in for a long, slow push—and died abruptly. It couldn't happen in a million years, a two-tonne meteor impact, but it did happen, and I was doubly glad I hadn't volunteered for that trip, or for any of the six replacement teams. Not that they would particularly want an SoM engineer who couldn't fit into a space suit.

Dan and I both thought it was a quixotic enterprise, a century or so premature. The Worlds were getting from Earth a constant supply of organics in the form of luxury food, which was a universally appreciated sign of status (and about the only thing you could buy, at least in New New). A well-aged Kansas City steak cost less than a day's salary. I had one almost every Sunday—with asparagus, by God, and washed down with a Coke. I never could abide fish, and a steady diet of New New's rabbit-chicken-goat regimen could turn an otherwise sane person to vegetarianism.

The point is, all that steak, asparagus, caviar, and whatnot went straight from the shuttle into the biosphere. Next year it would come back to you as curried-goat molecules (to cite my least favorite of New New's culinary abominations). All the Worlds were set up to recycle sewage and exhaled CO_2 into new food, and the Earth was supplying plenty of surplus organics to make up for inefficiencies in the system. To make food out of cold rock was going to take a whole new set of systems, expensive ones, and the end result was going to be yet more trout and Hassenpfeffer, and I would *still* be shelling out for steak. If there were some way to turn Deucalion into a cattle ranch, I would've been all for it.

So Dan and I were wrong. If everything operated as efficiently as hindsight, they'd have to scotch the laws of thermodynamics. But I was going to tell you about bringing the two of them together, Dan and O'Hara.

O'Hara and I were close friends, for reasons I did not care to examine too closely, and at this time of her life she was going through mates as if they were changes of underwear, so I thought it might be a friendly gesture to introduce her to Dan, in case there might be some chemistry there besides the oil-shale variety.

When our off-shifts and her class schedule finally

meshed, we met at the Light Head, a quarter-gee tavern one level down from my flat. I went there frequently, not only because of the light gravity, but because they usually had a few bottles of Guinness. It didn't taste anything like the Dublin variety, since it doesn't travel well, but it was better than the thin brew your ration book got you. And it made me feel biospherically virtuous, giving New New a couple of pints of water recycled from the River Liffey (at Trinity we always maintained that Liffey water suffered nothing in flavor and appearance by being passed through a kidney or two).

Dan came from old New York, which was where O'Hara would be spending much of her time on Earth. Since she was to leave in a couple of months, I thought she would welcome talking to him.

Well, we got off on the wrong foot. Dan and I were talking about the Deucalion project when O'Hara came in, and we were being slightly sarcastic. She took offense, and tried to argue the Worlds' case, citing as one instance the United States, which had to become independent of England before it could grow. An unfortunate argument, and I kept my silence, but Dan had to point out that Canada did quite well under the yoke of the Crown and had managed to avoid having two civil wars in the process.

That got O'Hara truly off, she being a local America expert and also young enough to believe that there were analytical answers to this sort of question. She compounded an interesting argument out of demographics, climate, distribution of resources, sectionalism, and God knows what else, which I was unable to evaluate (I've been to America, but only to study composite materials, not history). Dan wound up agreeing with her, and apologizing, though whether it was from the brain or somewhere south of that, I couldn't say.

O'Hara always was an odd person in many ways, but in this she was no different from anybody else: to lose an argument gracefully was a shortcut to her friendship. The rest of the evening was very cordial, not to say slightly drunken, and they left the Light Head arm in arm. For several days thereafter Dan showed up for work late and tired, and I dare say O'Hara probably missed a few classes.

(None of this is meant to condemn O'Hara's behavior. You must remember that this was the eighties, and sexual morality was much looser than it is today. A young single person with no line obligations was expected to "butterfly," lovely verb.)

Over the ensuing weeks I must admit I grew annoyed with myself for having introduced them, and was jealous of Dan for the O'Hara-time he stole from me. But if ever two people were made for one another, it was that pair. From that first night to the day O'Hara left for Earth, they were inseparable.

10 ✦ Chemistry lesson

O'Hara didn't like him at first. The Light Head is a fine little bar, but women are generally immune to its main attraction, a low-gee stripper. She was unreasonably annoyed by the way his eyes kept wandering, and said some outrageous things, to nail down his attention and John's.

So they spent a lively hour arguing, then a half hour conceding, during which Daniel's eyes didn't wander. O'Hara found herself liking him, and casually decided that she would try to lure him into her. He didn't take much luring.

It was a difficult, vulnerable time of life for her. She'd been just nineteen when Charlie left her, and hadn't had enough experience with such things to handle it gracefully. She was butterflying with grim determination, taking to bed almost anybody who could get there under his own power. By chance or her unconscious design, though, none of those men approached being her intellectual equal. Daniel Anderson did, and that was going to make a considerable difference.

By Devonite standards, Daniel would not have been considered a good lover. Their slang for men like him was "hard place": he had the minimum physical requisite but none of the skills they prized so highly. To O'Hara that was less a disadvantage than an interesting challenge. She enjoyed being good at things, and showing off her talents. So Daniel became the latest draftee into the platoon of men who indirectly benefited from Charlie Devon's religious upbringing.

He was the first one who didn't seem to be particularly impressed. Grateful, yes, and properly responsive to her ministrations, but from the beginning he seemed more interested in her brain than in the other organs. Rather than flattering her, this made O'Hara anxious. She had always taken her mind for granted.

But that was evidently what it took to make her fall in love. Intellectual combat: she searched out all of Daniel's most cherished beliefs and held them up to analysis, even ridicule; he gave it right back. They fenced and sparred and gleefully shouted each other down, and usually wound up in bed. It was an odd combination, pepper and honey, but they both responded to it. Within days, they had captured one another, and they grew ever closer during the two months she had remaining.

11 ✦ Leavings

"You've got to be sensible." They were squeezed together in the bed that took up a third of Anderson's small room.

"I know, I know." O'Hara sat drawn up tightly, chin on knees, arms wrapped around her legs. Staring at the blank wall.

"You're overreacting. There was almost no chance."

"Bureaucrats." O'Hara had tried to have her trip to Earth delayed six months, until it was nearer time for Anderson to go back. After eight weeks she got her reply: Denied.

"You can't pass it up. They won't give you another chance."

"They might. My record—"

"Your record will show that you were given the opportunity of a lifetime and refused it for the sake of a love affair. Drink?"

"No." Daniel inchwormed out of bed and squirted some wine into a cup.

"Mind?" He held up his weekly cigarette.

"Go ahead." The acrid smell filled the room quickly. To O'Hara it was exotic, but it made her want to sneeze. "I guess a lot of people on Earth smoke."

"Depends on where you go. It's illegal some places, like the Alexandrian Dominion. California." He set the cup on the bedstand and slid in next to her, pulling the cover up to his waist. "Try a puff?"

"No. I might like it." None of the Worlds grew tobacco. She slid herself under the cover, up to her breasts, and dabbed at her eyes with a corner of it.

"I don't want to see you leave, either."

"I'm glad you finally said that." There was an awkward silence. "Sorry. Unfair."

"All's fair."

She rested her hand on his thigh, under the cover. "Nothing is, really. First Law of the Universe."

"Philosophy." He blew a smoke ring.

"How long will it take you to finish that damned thing?"

12 ✦ Down to Earth

A rich tourist can get from New New York back to Earth in a little more than a day. Marianne O'Hara's trip was going to take two weeks.

Her goodbye to Daniel Anderson was as awkward and contrary to plan as such things always are. (John Ogelby had given her an avuncular kiss the night before, pleading that work pressure would keep him from seeing her off, which wasn't true.) She boarded the slowboat feeling sad and confused, and slightly ill from all the shots, and not thrilled at the prospect of two weeks of weightlessness.

Actually, her slowboat was a triumph of the electrical engineer's art. Its forebears, which had first made practical the transfer of large masses from high orbit to Earth, were *really* slow, taking months to spiral in.

The few dozen passengers and their life support system made up barely two percent of the huge vehicle's payload. The rest of the cargo was industrial materials that couldn't be made on Earth. Light and ultrastrong foamsteel girders from New New. Whisker matrices from Von Braun. Impossibly pure beryllium from Devon's World, tonnes of it, and exotic alloys from B'ism'illah Ma'sha'llah and Mazeltov. Each weekly flight involved an exchange of money equivalent to the gross national product of a small country.

The people riding on top were baggage, an afterthought. The accommodations and food reflected this.

O'Hara spent a lot of her time exercising. Three stationary bicycle contraptions that could be worked with hands or feet stood opposite the only window in the craft. Faced with the prospect of walking around for a year in Earth-normal gravity, she exercised her legs most. Also, being strapped on the bicycle was the only opportunity she had to sit down, that posture being unnatural in zerogee. She worked up quite a sweat, and got it back in the form of one liter of water per day, for washing.

She slept well, strapped up standing against the wall, and read a lot of books and magazines, and watched more cube than she ever had in her life, and became an expert in the art of the zerogee toilet. She kept to herself. There would be a year of being nice to strangers, groundhogs at that. Mudballers. Earthies. Must forget those words for the time being; must not bristle at being called a spacer. As if there were no difference between a Devonite and a Yorker.

For days there seemed to be no change in the appearance of the Earth: the same face she had seen all her life, as New New marched in lockstep over northern Brazil. Then Africa and Europe peeked over the edge, and the Americas began to slide away. Sere Asia over the vast Indian Ocean. One day there was almost nothing but water, the Pacific framed by little bits of Australia and Alaska. The globe began to grow, and eventually its rotation was perceptible from hour to hour.

A fat nuclear tug was waiting for them at the edge of the Van Allen belts, through which the ion-drive slowboat could not pass. They switched payloads. The outward-bound cargo was mostly hydrogen, food, acids, and a few economy-class passengers, including a dance troupe cursing their tightwad manager.

O'Hara and the others felt acceleration for the first time, a gentle nudge. They cruised into low Earth orbit—the globe now spinning dizzily below them, once each ninety minutes—and the passengers transferred to a small shuttlecraft (the cargo went into large cone-shaped crafts called "dumbos," which would be robot-guided into splashdowns near the purchasers of each load).

Even though she had taken the required tranquilizer, O'Hara felt growing excitement, along with a little apprehension. In space, almost all transportation is graceful and slow, not to say boring. She knew the shuttle would be fast and violent, though safe: only two had crashed in her lifetime.

She strapped herself in and waited. There was no countdown, just a steady growing surge of acceleration. From her window she could see the dumbos shrink away, then sweep out of her field of view as the shuttle tilted to present maximum area to the atmosphere, for braking. She was weightless again, no feeling of motion. Her window showed nothing but stars.

For long minutes nothing happened. Then the curve of the Earth rolled up, stopped, rolled back out of sight, making her a little dizzy. She had seen this on the cube a dozen times and wasn't scared at all. A high-pitched moan sat at the edge of audibility when the steering jets stopped blasting: the atmosphere slowing them down.

O'Hara might have compared the middle part of the trip to a roller-coaster ride, had she known what a roller coaster was. The craft rolled, pitched, and yawed with controlled violence. When the sky showed, it started taking on color: inky violet brightening to cerulean. The stars faded away.

They came in over the Florida coast to a vista of breathstopping and, to O'Hara, thoroughly alien beauty. The sun was low in the west, almost dim enough to look at directly, illuminating a spectacular array of high cumulus, crimson and gunmetal against a deepening sky. The ocean was almost black, studded with froth that the sun tinged red. The horizon had lost its curve: for the first time in her life the Earth was not just a planet, however special. It was the world.

From the shoreline to the horizon was a complicated maze of buildings and roads. If you could turn New New inside out and lay it down flat, it wouldn't cover one tenth part of what was unrolling underneath her, yet this was a small city, she knew.

It changed abruptly at the edge of the spaceport's territory. Swampland and scrub, mangrove jungle laced with streams and lakes. A wide, bridged river with a queue of huge barges carrying dumbos to be launched and refilled.

They were falling lower, impossibly low, and seemed to be gaining speed. An illusion, she knew, but she tightened her throat against crying out as the ground flashed by underneath and then they hit hard, bounced, and the tires were screaming protest; then braking rockets boomed, pushing her hard against the restraining straps, hard enough to hurt her hipbones and shoulders; then they were rolling, more and more slowly, to a quiet stop. Her eyes filled with tears and she started to laugh.

13 ✦ Three letters

John,

Where to start? You've been to the Cape, so I won't give you a travelogue. It gave me a chill, though, the spaceport's defenses. I counted ten of those offshore gigawatt lasers; there were probably more over the horizon. (Horizon! This damned planet bends the wrong way.) I wonder if they still work.

We took a subway to old New York, which only took a little over an hour, even though we stopped at Atlanta, Washington, and Philadelphia. Tempted to get out and see those places, but I guess there's time for that later.

I called the school when we got to the station (for some reason they call it Pennsylvania Station; Pennsylvania must be over a hundred kilometers away). They sent a woman to pick me up, an older woman who had emigrated from Von Braun after the crack-up.

A lot of New York City came down in the Second Revolution, but they must have rebuilt with a vengeance. Pictures can't do it justice, can't convey the size and intensity of it. I almost fainted when we stepped out on the street.

I suppose a lot of this wouldn't affect you, since London is bigger and older than New York. Humor me, though (you're so good at it).

Looking up makes me dizzy anyhow. It's the same

middle-ear problem you had when you moved to New New, but in reverse. I'm used to operating in a rotating frame of reference. But there's so much to look up at. The tallest thing I've ever seen was the lift tube in Devon's World. You could stand that up on any street here and not notice it.

We came up a long escalator and stepped out on 34th Street. I just stared (Mrs. Norris was ready for it and had me by the arm). Half the buildings are so tall their tops are above the cloud. The cloud, as Daniel warned me, is atmospheric pollution from the industries to the south. They keep it at the thousand-meter level with some sort of electrical thing, but it doesn't work perfectly. The air is thick and has a chemical smell, not too unpleasant. I don't even notice it anymore, after two days.

Mrs. Norris went to a stanchion on the sidewalk and pushed a button twice, calling us a cab. Do they have those in London? They're little yellow robot vehicles, most of them two-person size, some bigger. You get in and tell it your destination, and it computes the most efficient route for the prevailing traffic conditions. Theoretically, anyhow. Some of the students think they're programmed to maximize fares. I don't use them anymore unless I'm lost, which I never would be if the streets made sense.

In the cab we went by a little park in the middle of town, a war memorial built around the ruins of the Empire building. Empire State. It really looks shocking, all bare rusty skeleton. It used to be the tallest building in the world, not even a kilometer high.

That would interest you, for your strength-of-materials. It's easy to tell the post-Settlement buildings from the older ones, since they could only build so high without composites. And real estate is so dear the cheapest way to go is up.

We got to the school and my luggage wasn't there. Turns out it went to Rome, Italy, which everybody but me thought was hilarious. Mrs. Norris said I was lucky they didn't reshuttle it and send it back to New New. It's happened, at least to low Earth orbit.

My medicine was in there, though, and I broke out in hives during dinner. They cleared it up in an hour or so, but it was an ugly time. Triggered my period a week early. You can imagine how that cheered me up.

They brought my bags in after midnight, without any detectable apology. You mudballers.

All of us newcomers got a guided tour of the city yesterday. We got practical advice as well as tourist stuff. There are places you don't go at night and places you don't go, period. The crime rate here isn't much higher than in New New, per capita, but there's a lot of capita. And the crimes tend to be dramatic. Did they have wasters and wolf-packs in London? The wasters scare me more, because the wolf-packs don't operate downtown. They're people who go berserk, usually in crowded places, and start killing indiscriminately. Sometimes just with knives or whatever they can pick up; sometimes with real weapons. You can imagine what a hand laser could do in a crowded store. Last year one killed almost two hundred people at a subway stop.

(When they told us about that I remembered hearing it on the news, but it didn't make much of an impression at the time. I guess we expect groundhogs to do crazy things. I have a lot of prejudices to work on.)

Most of a whole street, Broadway, is nothing but a big meat market. Sex of every description, but somehow evil. Like Devon's World turned inside out. Yet prostitution is *illegal*. The guide said they tolerate Broadway because it contains it, makes it easier to control. One of the students told me it's been that way for more than a century, but he thought they tolerated it because it made payoffs easier, for politicians and police. It's big business.

The police are frightening. They're all men, big men. They look even bigger with the body armor, and you can't see their faces for the mirrored helmets. They're heavily armed. But I've talked to a couple of them, getting directions, and they seemed friendly enough.

So much of this place is so old (yes, I know where you went to school in Dublin was even older). The oldest thing I'd ever seen before was the sputnik in the park; maybe I'm too easily impressed. I've been walking around at random, usually alone, stumbling over history. I found Washington Square, where the Second Revolution started. Wall Street. Tiffany's and Macy's.

I made the mistake of riding the subway without a native guide. I never was good at maps, and the subway map looks like a plate of sūmen. Anyhow, I crossed over when I should have crossed under, so went north instead of south, and wound up getting out at 195th Street, which is one of those places you're not supposed to go even in daytime. I didn't go outside the station, which is above ground, but even so it was scary. Even with a pair of policemen on each side of the platform. There were strong young men loitering all around, too well-dressed, who never took their eyes off me, but otherwise everything was filth and poverty. Horribly crippled beggars and some who seemed to be diseased, perhaps dying—though both the city and the federal government have socialized-medicine programs. (Well, it's no secret that the hospitals are overcrowded, and it's hard to get a berth if you don't belong to one of the Lobbies in power.)

It is all so strange. I feel more alive than I ever have, but at the same time intimidated and frustrated that I only have a year here. I could spend a year in New York City—in the museums and libraries alone!—and not come close to seeing everything. Yet in a few months I'll be running desperately around the world, for a 75-day course in "cultural relativism." Then there's the rest of the States to see, and the two independent states, if I can get safe entry into them (though most people seem to think that Nevada is just a bunch of thugs and anarchists, and Ketchikan nothing but a racist farming commune). All the while studying. At least I don't have to write my dissertation until I get back to New New.

I've begun a diary but it seems inadequate. It feels like so little time here, I hate to waste it keeping records. On the other hand, there's so much input I can't trust my memory.

Must run. Give my love to Daniel and keep some yourself, Quasimodo.

Daniel dear,

Just a note to let you know I'm getting along all right. Will write in more detail after I've sorted out my impressions.

It looks as if I might as well have vowed a year of chastity, for all the bright prospects here. Most of the Worlds people here are stuffy academics. (Except for two Devonites, and I've had my fill of that particular dish.) The New Yorkers are, well, creatures from another planet. What about you? Going out every night with that little peeler from the Light Head? (Don't do it; that type is invariably frigid. Besides, she'd sag in high-gee.) Or did you think I never noticed the way your attention wavered when she was onstage?

New York City is all you said it would be, and more. All the little things you must have always taken for granted. Coins! My pockets are always full of them (doing wonders for my voluptuous form) and I can't add them up fast enough to tell whether I've been given the right change. Those miserable little aluminum dimes. Half the stores won't take them, and the other half shovels them at you in change.

But I'm loving it. Every day is a big vulgar epic. School starts tomorrow, and already I begrudge the time I'll have to spend studying. Though it will save money—at the rate I'm going, the hundred thousand they gave me wouldn't last four months (I could always get a good job on Broadway, with what Charlie taught me).

I hope your work is going well, and hope you'll eventually come around to our way of thinking as to its importance. Though I suppose this experience is going to make me less of a separatist. Or maybe more—I had a terrifying experience on the subway (went to 195th by mistake), and suppose there will be other shake-ups in store soon.

Wish you could be here to show me around. Maybe soon. Let me know how your rotation schedule works out; I may not be in the U.S. if you come back too soon. But love will find a way, as the salmon said.

I have a picture of you by my bed, the flying one you said you liked. Another picture when I close my eyes, that might embarrass you, but which has its uses. Love:

Charlie,

I just wanted to write and remind you that I'm not in New New anymore. I've come to Earth for a year, mostly school.

The address on this 'gram will be good all year, though I'll be traveling around. Yes, I'm living in old New York, and a stranger place you've never seen! It's something like Devon's World in its decadence (look it up, lazybones), but it's almost all buildings and streets. Do you remember the pictures we looked at? Well, they were taken on a "clear" day. You only get pictures like that after a hurricane.

I've seen the sun only once since I got here, and that was because a holiday weekend (Labor Day) closed most of the factories to the south of here. I think the sun was one of the things I liked best about Devon's World, and I wish we had it here.

I hope you're enjoying your line, and I'm sure they're all nice people. Have you started your first baby yet? I might have one myself, once they find a way for the man to carry it around the first nine months.

Your friend,

14 ✦ Diary entries

4 Sept. 2084.   First class day. Let me just set down my
schedule for the quarter:

M/W	Topics in Manage-ment	7:00–9:00 (p.m.)	138 Russell
M/W/F	American Literature Seminar	9:00	4579 Lindsey
	History of Ameri-can Business	11:00	447 Russell
	Religion in America	1:00	8006 Lindsey
T/Th	American Dialects and Creoles	10:00–12:00	7837 Lindsey
	Entertainment Sem-inar	3:00–5:00	2099 Lindsey
Sat	Entertainment "Laboratory"	varies	varies

The "entertainment laboratory" is intriguing. Find out
about it tomorrow. I guess we'll be going to shows and
things. Interview whores on Broadway.

5 Sept.   Last night a group of us went to a Vietnamese
restaurant. Strangest food I've ever had: squid (aquatic
mollusk) stuffed with ham and something else, with un-

identifiable spices. Only the fish sauce was familiar. The ham didn't taste anything like what John fixed for me last year, but it was all very tasty and hasn't caused me any trouble, yet.

They almost never eat goat or rabbit here, or anywhere else in the country. Mostly fish, pork, chicken, and beef. Dolores Brodie (who's been here for two quarters, from Mitsubishi) says it's the beef in their diet that gives them that rancid smell. Guess I'll stop noticing it about the time I start to smell that way myself. Will have to try some beef tomorrow. So dark and strong. Maybe they fix it better down here, though.

There are usually two "meatless" meals—they don't consider fish to be meat—in the morning and midday. More starch than I'm used to. Have to watch the rice and hominy.

The entertainment seminar doesn't look as if it will be all that entertaining. The professor (Marlie Gwinn) has that desperately serious attitude teachers get when they have to be defensive about the academic worth of their specialty. I'll write her a somber paper comparing sex on Earth with zerogee sex. That's entertainment. The laboratory might be fun, most of the time. Shows and old movies, demonstrations of dances and games, concerts, who knows what. Must remember *not to be entertained.* This is serious business.

I don't know whether the dialect/creole course is going to be worth much. Mostly historical, except for a few isolated groups of antitechs and illiterates.

I'm the only Worlds citizen in the management seminar. Also the only woman. Have decided not to be Machiavellian about it (though that's contrary to the spirit of everything I know about management); it would be easy to twist the discussion around to Worlds administration, since everybody seems curious about it, including the professor. But I'm here to learn about Earth models. Earth mistakes.

Don't know much yet about the business and religion courses. They're both big lectures, and the first day was mostly devoted to administrative details: goatshit about grades and attendance. Attendance! Are we children?

Interestingly, the American literature seminar is led by a German, Herr Doktor Schaumann. He's a twinkly old fellow with a dry sense of humor. The way he almost-hides his intelligence reminds me a lot of John; it looks as if the course is going to be Socratic-aggressive. Simple questions full of fishhooks. Meat and drink for someone who grew up in the New New system, naturally.

No Worlds people in that seminar, either. But they're an interesting bunch, predictably different from the business and management types. One of them, Benny Aarons, is a bushy poet who seems to be interested in me. I don't know whether or not to encourage him.

Daniel wanted me to jump right in, try to live a normal social/sexual life. But it's so damned complicated. I would really rather think about him than lay with someone else. And there's so much else to do. Still, I liked the way that Benny boy looked at me when he thought I couldn't see him. Maybe it's because I'm Worlds, though, rather than my fatal charm.

Mrs. Norris told me that Worlds women have a reputation for being easy sexual "conquests." Strange attitude on the part of Americans (and some other countries, too), that sex is more competition, testing, than playing and loving. Women are prizes as much as partners. I don't know yet whether to adapt to it or be stubborn. Learn more if I adapt, I suppose, but I've never been much of a compromiser. Maybe look at it as being an actor instead. Learn all the responses that an American woman makes unconsciously.

I don't know. It's nice to be deferred to, even if the deference is only to your slippery plumbing, but there's an ugly current underneath it. Rape. Ownership, selling yourself.

Maybe it would be well to start out with a poet. Isn't that cold-blooded?

6 Sept.   John called today, with Daniel on the extension, and we had a short but warm talk. They hadn't gotten my letters yet—paradoxically, it's cheaper to send letters to Florida for transmission, rather than beam them up from New York. They were probably still being sorted. Maybe they went to Rome. Crazy planet.

Decided to put off beef until my period's over. Feeling queasy, anyhow. Cramps no worse than usual but heavier flow than I've ever had before. Called the infirmary and they said it happens to everyone, whether they come from a low-gravity satellite or an Earth-normal one. Advised me to take iron, which I had already figured out. Maybe I don't notice the cramps so much because the rest of me is such a battleground: feet, legs, back, shoulders. I wake up every morning in knots. Dolores (who lives down the hall) says it only took her a couple of weeks to get into shape, and Mitsubishi is also 0.8 gee. So I do my creaky calisthenics every morning and slump to the shower; hot as I can stand it for as long as I can stand it. The water isn't metered, but it's "grey" water, New York's version of recycling. It's not drinkable and it smells, slightly of humans and strongly of halogens and soap. No tubs. Who would want to take a bath in soup, anyhow?

Reading Hawthorne and Poe for the seminar. Poe is easy and entertaining but Hawthorne (maybe a better stylist) is dense with religious mystery, hard to unravel. I'll have an easier time of it when we get to the 20th century. (And we'll probably spend a lot of time there, since it's Schaumann's specialty.)

The business and religion courses are NEA (National Education Association) packages, as are most beginning graduate surveys. It sounds good in principle: a different lecturer, in holo, for each topic. The lecturer is one of the world's authorities on the topic, chosen for teaching ability as well as expertise (they say it's the best job insurance an academic can get, to be an NEA designee). There's a live proctor—supposedly live, in the case of the religion class—

who is supposed to use the last ten minutes to tie the lecture in with the general run of the course, and answer questions. You can also ask questions of the NEA network via the keyboards in the libraries and dormitories, but that costs money.

Problem is that the only way you can stop a holo lecturer is to throw a brick at the cube (or at the proctor, maybe). It looked as if about a quarter of the business audience this morning was totally lost after the first ten minutes. It was a very rapid review of precolonial European mercantilism, and I suppose it would be very hard to follow if you had never had European history.

I'd better read the Hawthorne over. Want to make a good showing for Dr. Schaumann (or is it for Bushy Benny?).

7 Sept.   I went to a Worlds Club luncheon today, between dialects and entertainment, and it was interesting. Think I'll join, if only to help keep my perspective. I didn't get to really talk to anybody, since there was a speaker, welcoming all of us new people. How many were interested beyond the free lunch—good old familiar rabbit—it's hard to say. Find out at the meeting Tuesday night.

The courses keep slapping me with double-vision déjà vu. First there was *Scarlet Letter* followed by a religion lecture on Puritanism. Then the dialects class was about the myth of survival of Elizabethan English in Appalachian enclaves, and the entertainment class covered folk music of that area—including a slightly dreadful half-hour cube of an old woman torturing a guitar and droning incomprehensibly through her nose—with a fascinating explanation about how Elizabethan English survived, etc. etc. It's a conspiracy; they set up this whole university to convince me that I'm going mad.

8 Sept.   Miserable day. Last night I was ready for beef, and joined a group that was going to an improbable place

called Sam & Pedro's Tex-Mex Saloon. It was quaint. The decor and costumes were bogus 19th-century Western, straight out of the classic 20th-century movies. The only beef on the menu that I recognized was chili. It was good; the spices masked the beef flavor and weren't as hot as the curries I'm used to. Different, though. I started to regret it about 6:00 a.m.

I divided the morning between bed and toilet, with occasional forays to the phone. The infirmary told me to sit it out, very funny, and come down if it didn't clear up soon. Drink water. Called Dr. Schaumann and got the assignment for Monday (*Billy Budd* and *Tom Sawyer*, both of which I've read). Called the library and got the business and religion lectures piped in to my cube.

I tried to get the next couple of lectures in those courses, but they were "only available under special circumstances." Infuriating. They're afraid you'll sit down for eighteen hours and take a whole course. Never show up at the auditorium. What's wrong with that? On New New you pass or fail depending on your final exam or paper, even in most precertificate courses. Why do they treat us like this?

By afternoon my digestive system evidently decided it had successfully repelled all invaders, but I didn't feel up to going out with the rest of the floor to celebrate the Fridayness of it all. I studied for a while, and wrote to John and Daniel. Watched half of an idiotic sex farce on the cube.

The one nice thing that happened today was that Benny Aarons called. He offered to bring over his seminar notes, wondered if I had plans for dinner. I explained my position, horizontal, and we made a tentative date to have lunch at the zoo tomorrow.

On paper that looks rather aggressive, but he was actually sort of diffident and shy about it. I think I do like him.

Went down to the music room and did some scales and intervals, then was suddenly starving. Walked to the Vietnamese restaurant and had some rice with *nuoc mam*, as they call their fish sauce, and a couple of glasses of cold rice wine, and wrote this diary entry. Now bed.

9 Sept.   The zoo was fun but somewhat unsettling. It's in the Bronx, one of those areas where you only go in the day-time. When Benny showed up to escort me, he was wearing a long knife on his belt; at the zoo, most of the men and some of the women were similarly armed. The zoo was safe enough, Benny explained, but anything could happen in the subway station or on the street. I wasn't sure what good a knife would do against a waster or a wolf-pack, but it did make me feel a little safer to have even symbolic protection. The subway stop was almost as bad as 195th Street.

(It's against the law to go armed, technically, but the law's only enforced after the fact, unless a policeman thinks you're up to no good. Benny said he'd never used the knife for anything but woodcarving, and never planned to. But a couple of years ago a robber gave him a bad skull fracture, and he'd carried it ever since, outside Manhattan. He suggested I get one, but I'd feel ridiculous. I'd rather run.)

There were so many different kinds of animals I couldn't begin to record them all. Most of them were from other countries, exotic biomes like jungles and deserts. Some I'd never even seen pictures of, like anteaters and fruit bats (much too big!). What was really interesting, though, was the "farm zoo," where they have everyday agricultural animals. I petted a cow, big oafish maudlin ani-mal, which hardened my resolve to learn to eat beef. Never let sentiment interfere with diet. Bunnies are cute, too.

Their goats were much bigger than ours. I'd expected them to be smaller, with the gravity. Efficiencies of scale, I guess, as John would say. Their rabbits and chickens looked like ours. Benny was surprised I knew so much about them (groundhogs think the Worlds are just big cities in the sky). I told him he should spend ten years of Thursday afternoons scraping up after the creatures. Builds character.

(I saw a real groundhog. Benny asked why it made me laugh; I said it reminded me of a friend.)

He's not like most of the Earth men. He's polite but not deferential or condescending. Except for a funny observation at the monkey house, he never mentioned sex, even though we went back to his apartment after the zoo, to look over the seminar notes. It could be a diversionary tactic, of course, but I don't think so. He seems too open and simple. He reminds me a little of Damien (who also wrote poetry, I recall), and of New New men in general. I feel comfortable with him.

He lives in a tiny flat down by Washington Square, even smaller than my dormitory room; about the size of my room in New New. It was cluttered with stacks of books and files; he had a phone but no cube. When he let the bed down from the wall, it took up most of the clear floor space. (I clenched my knees at that, but it was the only place to sit besides his desk chair; he gave me my choice.)

After we'd gone over the notes, I asked whether I could see some of his poetry, and he said he'd rather wait until we knew each other better. He'd had a few of them published, but didn't like those anymore, and he politely refused to talk about what he was doing now that was different. He said that words you used up on air could never live on paper. Fair enough, I guess. He did show me some of his artwork, which looked more like an engineer's work than a poet's: meticulously detailed street scenes done in rigid pen-and-ink, with carefully graded washes. He said he only did it to relax, and occasionally pick up some tourist money.

He's lived in New York all his life; in this same flat since he was sixteen. He obviously has spent a lot of his money on books. Many of them weren't library printouts, but were actually hard-printed and bound. One whole shelf was taken up by antique books, bound in leather.

Besides selling his art, he picked up a little money tutoring and baby-sitting (lots of small children in his apartment complex), and he had a small scholarship from the city.

I haven't mentioned that he has a weird sense of humor and can juggle, four coins at once. He makes figures out of string, like cat's-cradles but more complicated. He's tall and skinny and always wears a hat, and never opens his mouth when he smiles, which is often.

I'm glad he didn't complicate my feelings by making any overtures. I would probably say yes and regret it, or no and regret it, or later maybe and worry about it.

10 Sept.   Reread the Twain and the Melville and went to the library to listen to exaggerated dialect samples, practicing the phonetic alphabet. I should have asserted myself when the advisor recommended this course. It can't possibly help me back home.

Ate a hamburger, beef, for lunch and waited for it to explode. Nothing happened. Though I'll probably dream about that damned cow tonight.

While at the library I made a copy of Brant's *Clarinet Concerto*, though my schedule hasn't settled down enough yet to plan regular practice hours. Played for a couple of hours before dinner. Two weeks on the shuttle didn't help my lip. (Dropped by a music store and bought a bamboo reed—ten dollars! It tastes bitter but has a more mellow sound than plastic.)

11 Sept.   The man who sits next to me in the management seminar is a federal policeman (FBI); he showed up in uniform tonight. It was a "field" uniform, light armor, and he was carrying one of those mirror helmets.

He explained that he had to go straight from class to an FBI class in night maneuvers. He's training for a field commission but also wants to get his M.M., so he can switch over to management eventually.

I sort of liked him before; now I don't know. He's a quiet man, but with the uniform his quiet has a dangerous, smoldering quality. Oh, he explained about the mirrored helmets: they protect your eyes against laser fire, beyond a certain range. I'd assumed the reason was psychological. The invisible man, machine-like, invulnerable.

His name is Jeff Hawkings and he sort of reminds me of Charlie. Same slope-shouldered hugeness, and with his close-cropped blond hair, he almost looks bald. Even bigger than Charlie, and more articulate, of course, and better educated. But I have a feeling their basic drives are parallel.

It does annoy me. Nobody's responsible for where he was born, all right; nobody has control over his early environment. But I get this definite radiation from Hawkings that he's totally in control, that I should be just quivering to slip between some sheets with him, that when he gets around to it he'll give me the signal....

Get ahold of yourself, O'Hara. Three weeks of abstinence and every man is a penis. Projecting your own need—no, it's not that simple. Earth men *are* different.

Well, there's always the Worlds Club meeting tomorrow. Latch on to a Devonite, for old times' sake.

12 Sept.   The club meeting was informal and comfortable. We met in the back room of the River Liffey, an old Irish-style pub (black stout on draught; John will be so envious). After a short and raucous business meeting, we fell naturally into small groups from each World.

There were ten others from New New. Being the most recent addition, I was quizzed for information and gossip. Even though they can't vote, they were interested in the upcoming elections. (I think Markus will be reelected; there are so many candidates for Engineering Coordinator-elect that it's anybody's game, though John thinks Goodman will at least get the engineers' votes, for his CC work. That's only one or two percent, though.)

The club meets on Tuesday nights because that's the

night of the weekly Worlds news broadcast. A half-hour of watching Jules Hammond drone on about balance of payments. Will I ever be nostalgic enough to look forward to that?

One of the men I slightly knew from highschool; he was in the form ahead of me, and we both played in the orchestra. He was percussion, though, on the other side of the room. I couldn't think of his name and, after having recognized him, didn't have any graceful way to ask him (being new, I was wearing a nametag).

I have a feeling that many of these people have no social life outside of the club. Must not fall into that trap; it is so comfortable, being with your own kind. I have to learn all I can about Earth people, especially Americans. The transition to separation and independence will come in my lifetime, and I will be involved, in administration if not politics per se. It won't be a smooth transition.

(Suddenly I'm reminded of Benjamin Franklin, who spent twenty years trying to avert a revolutionary war, living in England most of that time, eloquently explaining the Colonies in England and vice versa. He was a glib and charming genius, and he failed. What am I? What will I have to do? Sometimes—now, in the dark morning—I have an almost mystical certainty that I will be some sort of a pivot, and the more I learn of history the less I want to be caught in the middle of it.)

I drank a little too much and so walked back to the dormitory—about three kilometers—with two other women, one from New New (Sheryl Markham Devon) and one from Von Braun (Claire Oswald). The walk cleared my head and woke me up. So deliciously cool now. I think New New's planners made a mistake by choosing a constant subtropical climate. Too late to change, though, without importing a whole new ecology for the park.

New York's streets are spooky after midnight. Most of the cabs are garaged and there's almost no truck traffic, or buses. The slidewalks are all turned off. Half the people we met were police, and the other half were strange. A male prostitute made us a remarkable offer. Sheryl's reply left Claire and me helpless with laughing; the whore just stood there open-mouthed. She was only half-joking, I suspect.

All of the pedestrians were men, most of them drunk or zipped. A couple of them made me nervous, but Claire was armed and we were rarely out of sight of a police officer. (Sheryl wasn't armed but carried a spray can of Puke-O in her bag. She says it's a fine rape deterrent unless the wind shifts. Even then, if you have a fastidious rapist.)

Back at the dormitory I met Dolores (she was at the meeting but took the subway home) in the hall, coming back from the shower with her damp sleepmate Georges. I think it's a mistake to take up with someone from your own dorm, let alone your own floor. Convenient, though.

13 Sept.   I had it out with my advisor this morning and managed to drop the dialects class, substituting AmHist 507: "The Role of Sub-official Politics in American History." It should be interesting, mostly a history of the Lobbies before the People's Revolution. Spent the afternoon in the library, looking at last week's lectures and catching up on the reading assignments.

Becoming a real social animal. Had lunch with Benny and he asked me to go to a movie tonight, part of a free series of antique classics they're showing at the Student Activity Center. Unfortunately it conflicted with the management seminar. At the seminar I got to talking to Lou Feiffer and we discovered a mutual interest in handball, so we're going to meet at the gym tomorrow for a couple of rounds (he's smaller than I am and has a hard time finding partners). Big old Hawkings also plays handball, and said he might come watch. I can feel those blue eyes on my backside already.

Well, it should help get the kinks out, if I don't break my neck.

14 Sept.   My hand hurts so I can hardly hold the pen. I'll be a mass of bruises tomorrow.

I could almost cry. I'm good at handball—but not here! In the first place, the ball won't go where it's supposed to. I can compensate for the extra drop for heavier gravity, but the damned thing doesn't drift. No rotating frame of reference, no Coriolis drift. You can't unlearn a lifetime of instinct overnight. I misjudged every damned ball, finally had to quit.

In the second place, they play handball as a competitive sport. The idea is to make the other person miss it, not to see how long you can volley. Really bizarre.

Lou was sympathetic to my frustration, after I explained about compensating for drift, and he tried serving slow ones to me. That was even worse, of course, and that's how I got the bruises.

I was glad they have separate dressing rooms for men and women. I didn't feel like making small talk.

Jeff Hawkings was waiting with Lou when I came out; they asked if I wanted to go find a beer. Told them I had to study. I suppose they're both nice people, but I didn't feel like going through the strain of being polite. Feel like a broken bone.

15 Sept.   Mother wrote saying she was pregnant again. What will it be like, having a little sister or brother (she didn't say which) who's twenty-one years younger? Glad I'm not living at home anymore.

I wonder if she's just doing it for the allowance? Seems more trouble than it's worth.

Joanna Keyes, who lives down on the 36th floor, came up and visited for a few hours this afternoon. She's an undergraduate in politics and government, and an odd person but likeable. So intense. Very bright; she took the business course I'm in, last quarter (it's not normally open to undergrads).

She wanted to know everything about how New New is run—not just the formal business of overlapping cells and so forth, but also what goes on behind the scenes. Who runs whom, what should be voted on and isn't, where does the real power lie. I asked her similar questions about America and got some ferocious answers.

I've always thought the pre-Revolutionary system was more elegant, but it did concentrate too much power in the hands of one person. Keyes says that at least you knew who the man was then. The person who represents a Lobby in Congress is never the one who makes the real decisions; the real leaders are rarely identifiable and are never held responsible for their actions. If a puppet gets in trouble they sacrifice him and haul out another.

I don't doubt that that's true, at least some of the time, but it's certainly not the whole story. If a Lobby consistently acts against the public interest, its voting power dwindles away. Keyes says that's a cynical illusion: all the polls reflect is how much money a Lobby has put into advertising.

Well, that reinforces a cliché about groundhogs, that they sit around all day zipped, staring at the cube. But then who are all those people on the street? How do they manage to maintain a complex, technology-intensive society? Somebody must have some sense!

I think she's a bit myopic. No government works perfectly; any system attracts its share of crooks. In America and New New, at least they have realtime polling. Look at England, look at the Supreme Socialist Union. By the time the will of the people has percolated to the top, the situation may have changed radically.

But I like her. She has real fire, and asks hard questions. So many of my classmates are just hard-working drudges, in the business of getting their degrees.

She wanted to take me down to a little wine-house on Eastriver, but I have to do the class on Crane Monday (talk about drudges) and had better read some criticism or

Schaumann will nail me up to dry. I told her we'd do it some time next week; she said there are always a lot of interesting people there, political types.

It occurs to me that I'm too consciously "observing" people, like an entomologist (Keyes, Joanna; 150 cm. X 40 kg., swarthy, short black hair, burning black eyes, aquiline nose, boyish figure, styleless clothes, radical, cynic, witty, intelligent—and possibly interested in me for reasons other than politics. Which side should I wear the earring on?). Do the people notice?

16 Sept.   Spent all day in the library, after the entertainment lab, which was more folk music. The banjo is a queer instrument; I'd only heard it Dixieland-style, strummed. The man who played for us picked the strings individually, and very fast, though repetitive. He seemed to be daydreaming, not paying much attention to his fingers. The other soloist played the fiddle, and he was exactly the opposite. He stared down at the instrument with a fixed expression of amazement—am *I* doing that? He was a big fat man, with a white beard, and his fingers were so huge you would think he couldn't play anything smaller than a bass. He made sweet music with it, though.

Most of the management seminar was in the library's journal room, since our assignment was to analyze a couple of dozen papers on personnel selection, and they didn't come in until Saturday noon. The ones who could afford copyright just made copies and took them home. Hawkings and I were there all afternoon, scribbling away. So he has a saving grace: at least he's not rich.

17 Sept.   Waded through Crane and Crane criticism all day. He's a good writer but I have to keep looking up archaic expressions, especially the dialect: "Dere was a mug come in d' place d' odder day wid an idear he was goin' t' own d' place. Hully gee!" (It took me a long stare to figure out that last one was a euphemism for "Holy God!")

18 Sept.   I was a little nervous, but the Crane class went pretty well. Schaumann assigns each author to a student, in rotation (so I won't have to do it again for a month). The student gives a half-hour talk about the work and the author; then Schaumann takes over. You aren't graded on the talk. Schaumann says he teaches that way because he's lazy, but the real reason is to give himself insurance, providing both a dialectic base for his questions and one sure victim.

After religion I went down to Eastriver to meet Keyes. Eastriver is a small city in itself, built over the East River about twenty years ago by a group of real estate developers. The developers went bankrupt and the courts still haven't sorted out the mess. So the place has a temporary, unfinished quality to it. No big buildings; whole blocks of empty space. Some places the foamsteel construction of the bridge itself is only covered by safety gratings. You can watch the river traffic toiling by under your feet.

I met Keyes at a place called the Grapeseed Revenge. It sits in one corner of a building that evidently will someday be a warehouse, taking up maybe one-twentieth of the shell's volume. The acoustics are incredible.

No revolutionary cabal would dare meet in a place like this; it looks too much the part. The only light comes from a candle on each table. The chairs and tables are random mismatched castoffs. Huddled groups talk in low tones. I expected to see pictures of Kowalski and Lenin on the walls.

Keyes found me while I was still groping blindly through the darkness, before my eyes adjusted to the candlelight. She led me to a table (an old door on legs, actually) and introduced me to three friends.

One of them did look like a revolutionary. His name was Will, no last name or line name offered. His face looked small, framed by an unruly cloud of hair and beard; he was slight, bony, quick-moving. He was wearing laborer's overalls (but when I asked what he did he said "sit and think"). The other two were students, Lillian Sterne and Mohammed Twelve. They treated one another with casual affection, like long-time lovers. Lillian is small, blond, and pale as a Yorker; Mohammed is big and black. He was surprised, and pleased, that I knew how important the name Twelve was in African history. His great-grandfather's brother. That was a bloody time.

I went through the same sort of quizzing that Keyes had done, mostly from Will. He was didactic and hostile, but intelligent. When he talked, all the others listened carefully. He was obviously used to leading.

I'm afraid I was guilty of coloring my responses—not really lying, but feeding him what he wanted to hear, pushing him. For instance:

Will: Suppose one or both of the Coordinators were dishonest—

Me: They're politicians.

Will: Right. What stops them from making vast personal fortunes from import and export?

Me: Ten billion dollars a week goes through their hands.

Will: And they have the final say as to suppliers and customers, on Earth.

Me: They oversee the Import-Export Board.

Will: I wonder how much someone would pay for, say, the franchise on oxygen.

Me: Hydrogen; we make our own oxygen. They'd pay plenty, I'm sure.

And so forth. What I didn't say was, for instance, no actual money changes hands for hydrogen; it's a straight barter with U.S. Steel. There's no doubt a Coordinator could skim off millions—but what could you do with it? Count it? You'd have to go to Earth or Devon's World to spend it, and people would probably find out, since ex-Coordinators automatically join the Privy Council. They'd miss your vote.

(The idea of personal wealth certainly distorts Earth

politics—what an understatement—but I don't suppose our system would work with billions of people.)

It was interesting, though. You don't meet many real political dissidents in the Worlds; too easy to go someplace else if you don't like it at home (it strikes me suddenly that there is more political variety in the Worlds than the Earth has had for a century). The Grapeseed Revenge is the quietest bar I've found in New York, by far, and the cheapest. Large glass of drinkable wine for three dollars. I'll take Benny next time.

19 Sept.   The new politics course is interesting. The stodgy old Lobbies evolved from a bunch of real pirates—I knew that from University, but it's fun to go into the actual details of blackmail and bribery. American history is so rich with nasty treasures!

Watched Jules Hammond at the Worlds Club meeting again. Checked my pulse; still not thrilled. Meeting shifted to Wednesday next week, for the elections.

Claire Oswald told me I should be careful about the company I keep. She's on Keyes's floor, and Keyes is not the most adored person there. Dolores added that the Grapeseed might be watched, and I am after all an alien.

Maybe I should take Hawkings there instead of Benny. See if he says hello to anyone.

20 Sept.   Small world, as they say on this big world. Benny goes to the Grapeseed all the time. Has met Will, doesn't like him. Was going to ask me to go there, once he was sure I'd be "comfortable."

I kidded him about being a poet and political at the same time; he said he was an unacknowledged legislator of his times. That must be a quote I'm supposed to know.

We had dinner at the dormitory machines and went on down to the Grapeseed. It's pretty crowded at night. Will wasn't there, for which I was doubly glad, but Lillian and Mohammed were; we sat and talked for a couple of hours.

They're a beautiful couple, not only because they look so arresting together. They've only known each other seven months but fit like gears meshing.

They talked about emigrating to Tsiolkovski. I tried to talk them out of it. It's such a joyless, hard place. They keep expanding without ever consolidating, trying to make life comfortable. Maybe I just lack pioneer spirit.

It's unlikely they'd be acceptable, anyhow. I don't think they'll pay your way up unless both of you have a skill they need. Mohammed is in philosophy, ethics. Lillian's a double E, electrical engineering, but she's also Jewish. Not a believer, she says, but it would still be a mark against her. They don't like conflicting loyalties.

I did tell them about the Mutual Immigration Pact. If they could get up to New New, or any other World, and become bona fide citizens, then Tsiolkovski would have to take them. Not with open arms, though. Every World needs somebody to shovel shit, and that's exactly what they'd do for the rest of their lives.

I didn't convince them, but maybe I planted a seed. I'd love to see them in the Worlds, but not Tsiolkovski. Not smothered under the blanket of a grey old revolution.

I got the feeling that there's something going on that I don't know about. Maybe Dolores's warning made me a bit paranoid. But there was something in the way that Lillian and Mohammed and Benny looked at each other. Maybe it's because Benny was so serious. Just a feeling.

One of Poe's stories, "The Purloined Letter," claims that the best place to hide something is to leave it in plain sight. Maybe the Grapeseed Revenge is full of revolutionaries.

It was after two when we left, so Benny and his conspicuous knife accompanied me home. We had a cup of tea in my room; talked about the James and Fitzgerald readings. He was his old self, witty and animated. I was sort of expecting a sexual overture—inviting one, maybe—but nothing happened. Maybe Benny's homosexual, or celibate.

Maybe I'm not the most ravishing creature in the World, I mean world. (Have to go reread Daniel's last letter, for confidence.)

21 Sept.   Didn't mention that before I met Benny yesterday I talked to Hawkings and Lou, at the seminar, and they suggested that I try out some sport that doesn't involve trajectories—if I learn how to play handball or volleyball here, I'll just have to start all over again when I get home.

Hawkings suggested fencing. (He was appalled to find out that I didn't know how to handle any kind of weapon; I'm afraid I laughed out loud.) There's a beginners' group that meets every Thursday morning, so I went down there today.

They do two kinds, sport fencing and self-defense. I'm sure Hawkings had the latter in mind, but it looks too rough to be fun. I bruise too easily.

It's awkward at first. The postures and steps seem artificial, clumsy. But it is exciting—I've never played a competitive sport more physical than chess—and the more advanced beginners look as graceful as dancers. It's a real workout, too, which is what I'm interested in. Hard on the ankles, though.

We moved into the twentieth century in entertainment seminar today, still doing music. Listened to a couple of hours of jazz, rock, blues, and so forth. Never mentioned Dixieland.

26 Sept.   Haven't written for several days because I've been in the hospital. Hard to write now.

Thursday night a man attacked me in front of the dorm, as I was coming home from dinner. Right in front of the stairs.

He came up behind me and squeezed a hand over my mouth, and put a knife to my throat. He told me to drop my bag, and he kicked it away.

He cut the waistband of my slacks and pulled them down, then pulled down my underclothes, and I bit him, hard. When he pulled his hand away I screamed. I didn't feel him stab me in the buttock. He wrestled me to the ground and I kept screaming. He banged my head against the sidewalk, twice, forehead and face, then grabbed a handful of hair and jerked up. I was still screaming when he tried to cut my throat; both dormitory doors burst open and six or seven people came charging down the stairs. They tore the man off me and I just lay there slowly fading, while they scuffled with him. A woman turned me over and put my head in her lap, and I vaguely heard a siren over the ringing in my ears.

The next couple of days are a blur of anesthetics and tranquilizers. Inventory: broken nose, slight concussion, three broken teeth, dislocated shoulder, superficial (!) knife wound below the chin, deep puncture wound in the left buttock, bruises and scrapes all over.

He really wanted to kill me. I think he wanted to kill me *first*, and then rape what was left. I can't imagine such an animal. Whenever I think of him my heart wants to explode with rage. And fear. They say he's in "grave" condition, from the beating he got from my rescuers. I hope he dies. I really hope he dies. I want to go home.

27 Sept.   Feeling better. They closed all the wounds and put in new teeth the first day, but have been holding me for observation and therapy. I guess the therapy's working; I haven't cried all day. For a while it was hours at a time. Maybe I've lost the knack.

I don't know much about the therapy because most of it's under hypnosis. A doctor talks to me every morning, checking me. He admitted this morning that there's a drug involved in the interview (one of my wake-up shots). I knew there was; it makes me babble.

Benny came by a couple of days ago with my books. I

sent him away too abruptly. I didn't want him there when I started crying, and I didn't especially want the company of any male. That's over now.

Lots of visitors today. Keyes came over and we commiserated about the shortcomings of the male race. We changed the subject when Benny showed up (they know each other, not surprisingly), and we played cards for a while, before they had to go to class. Lou and Hawkings showed up together, on their way to the seminar (Lou left me a tape of Monday's session, and said he'd make another one tonight). Hawkings had checked with a friend in the New York Police Department, who said the man was probably responsible for five rape-murders over the past two years. They wouldn't know for sure unless he regained consciousness, to be questioned.

Dr. Schaumann came in after dinner (Benny had told him why I wasn't in class) and probably did me more good than the therapist ever would. He was all grandfatherly and comforting, but at the same time he was armed with ruthlessly pragmatic philosophy. You were lucky enough to survive, but now you have to realize that it's within the man's power, living or not, to keep hurting you for the rest of your life, unless you vigorously deny him access. It's like being struck by lightning (something I'd never thought to worry about); you're not responsible for it happening, but you *are* responsible if afterward you're afraid to go outdoors. No amount of rationalization or sympathy from others can alter the fact of your responsibility. He even kissed me. His mustache smells of pipe tobacco.

They let me stay up to watch the elections. Markus was reelected as Policy Coordinator and announced that he planned to step down after five years. Good thing; fifteen years is plenty. Wouldn't do to have his coordinator-elect die of old age, in office.

The new Engineering Coordinator–elect is a woman named Berrigan, a park service engineer. I vaguely remember her name. Didn't study the candidates this time, since I knew I'd be on Earth. My new floor rep to the Privy Council is Theodore Campbell, whom I had for a disastrous course in algebra some ten years ago.

Yesterday I wrote that I wanted to go home. I guess Schaumann talked me out of it, obliquely. I won't let this planet beat me.

28 Sept.   Back at the dormitory. Everyone is so solicitous, I feel like getting a disguise.

The rapist is dead. By judicial order. The police traced down his address and searched his flat. They found five vials containing five scraps of dried flesh which matched the parts excised from the victims of "Jack the Raper," as he was called by one subliterate journal. The DNA matched the victims'. Since he had once been convicted of a sex crime, and was under indictment for attacking me, the police were able to get a court order reducing his MedicAid status to Class C. So they pulled the plug on his life support system, saving the State electricity, twice. I feel confused about it. Could he have been cured? If he were, would I want him walking free? If they had given me the plug, would I have pulled it? I suppose I would.

Maybe it's the State disposing of him as casually as swatting a fly. Maybe it's just that he never knew he was being punished for hurting me.

There were long and interesting letters from Daniel and John waiting for me. The discovery of CC material on the Moon might be one of the pivotal events in Worlds history. Mudball news never mentioned it.

15 ✦ Black gold on the Moon

O'Hara:

I'm sure Dan has written you about this, but maybe not in much detail. He's probably the busiest person in the section right now, and loving it.

You know the polar-orbiting Lunar Prospector satellite? Probably not; it hasn't done anything new in half a century. It was built to analyze absorption spectra from the lunar surface, to draw a map of mineral deposits on the Moon. One thing we looked for, hoping against hope, was a carbonaceous-chondritic "infall"; a CC meteorite remnant that we could mine for carbon, nitrogen, and hydrogen.

We didn't really expect to find one, because the temperature of the explosion when a meteorite hits the Moon is enough to decompose a CC rock. All of the precious stuff evaporates into space.

Well, they decided it was time to refurbish the Prospector, since we have much more delicate sensing and analysis tools now. Technically, it belongs to Devon's World, but since it was no longer functioning, we claimed it as salvage. That was fine with them, of course, since if we found anything, we'd have to use their mining and launch facilities, at standard royalty.

The Prospector found an anomaly that seemed worth investigating. It turned out to be a strip of CC gravel, about two kilometers wide by two hundred long. It was evidently the result of a low-velocity impact of a large CC meteorite that hit the surface tangentially, a glancing blow that shattered it into millions of pieces. Most of the chunks are on the order of a centimeter wide (mostly buried in the dust), though there are a few boulders a meter or so wide scattered around.

All we have to do is rake the stuff up and haul it to the mass drivers. There's more than ten thousand tonnes of it, easily accessible.

What this means is that we can scale up our CC decomposition factories a thousandfold, and have them running smoothly long before Deucalion comes in.

It doesn't mean independence from Earth; ten thousand tonnes holds about 250 tonnes of carbon and 1300 tonnes of water, and only about thirty tonnes of nitrogen. (Some people think there might be many similar gravel fields, though.) The main thing is that we'll be able to run the factories at the same rate of materials flow as we'll need when we start dismantling the asteroid.

It is exciting, even for an old mudballer like me. Everybody in New New is galvanized, understandably. Lots of smiles and spontaneous laughter. You should have seen the chaos in the Light Head the day they made the announcement. I had to take my Guinness and go home (thanks for telling me about the River Liffey; it makes my stout taste flatter).

I'm glad you decided to drop that language course. The only person around here who has any dialect, to my ear, is Dan, and you seem to understand him pretty well. Are you going to replace it with anything, or just take a lighter load?

Well, tomorrow we go out and vote. Big surprise: it looks as if I'll be on the Privy Council, as Representative-at-large from External Systems. As you probably know, there's a technicality that requires two candidates for Rep-at-large. Eugene Knight has agreed to be my "stalking horse." The sole item in his platform is that he proposes to replace all the air in New New with hydrogen cyanide, as an experiment in terminal ecology. Well, he gets my vote.

Seriously, the Privy Council isn't too bad, but I'm already on the Import-Export Board, so there's two days a week out the lock. I almost hope that Goodman doesn't win Coordinator-elect. He wants me to be in his cabinet. When would I ever get any work done?

You've been gone over a month and Dan tells me you haven't picked up any of those degenerate Earth boys yet (see, no secrets). What's wrong with our little butterfly? Gravity got your hormones?

Privately, listen to Uncle Ogelby, I think it would help Dan's peace of mind if you told him you were getting your ashes hauled (bet you've never heard that one), even if you aren't. Although I doubt that he's said anything to you, I know he's afraid you're going to work yourself into a pressure situation and suddenly fall for some groundhog because he presents a metaphorical shoulder at the right time. Don't tell me you've never done it before, daughter. Remember the parade that followed Charlie?

Maybe I'm talking out of turn, but I don't think so. Dan treats you too gently. As a lover should, I suppose.

I better transmit this before I lose my nerve. Feel free to write back that my advising you about sex is like you advising me about crystalline lamination. Love—

John

16 ✦ Seduction of the innocent

30 Sept. 84

Daniel dear,

I know it must have been an ugly shock to you, getting my letter about the rape right after sending your letter exhorting me to go out and butterfly. I also know you've tried to call me at least twice. Forgive me for being "out." I never was any good on the phone, even for something simple.

I didn't keep a copy of my letter, but I'm afraid it was a little hysterical. Subsequent therapy and some kind friends calmed me down.

Let me save you the cost of a call and answer the obvious questions. One: Yes, I'm all right physically. He gave me a severe beating, but the hospitals here have a lot of experience with that sort of thing. Two: No, he didn't make any sexual contact with me, unless you count stabbing me in the butt. He didn't have time, even though I was pretty well unconscious; a half-dozen students grabbed him and kicked him to a pizza. He died. I'm glad. Three: Yes, I do feel uncomfortable and ambiguous about men and especially about sex. Or is it the other way around. Anyhow, Four: Yes, I'm going to take your advice. I will write you about it honestly, as we agreed.

Tell Uncle Ogelby that crystalline lamination obviously causes senility, and that I can haul my own ashes in a pinch. Much love—

O'Hara

2 Oct. 84

Daniel dear,

I didn't have to give too much thought to deciding who my first earthman would be. There are a few who have expressed interest (including one woman), but none of them appeals. I set my sights on a poet whom I shall call Byron.

Byron and I have a class together, study together frequently, and have gone out occasionally, to eat or drink or sightsee (he's a native New Yorker and enjoys playing Native Guide). He spent a lot of time with me while I was in the hospital, chatting and playing cards. He is gentle, intense, political, intellectual, and bushy. He has a sense of humor that John would describe as wonky. In all the time we've spent together, he's never once made an advance, never mentioned any girlfriends or boyfriends, and seems about as close as you could get to being aggressively nonsexual. Now I know why.

I asked him over last night to study. Dressed for action and plied him with wine. For a couple of hours he deflected all of my hints, so I finally dropped subtlety and asked him right out to spend the night, sleep with me, do the beast with two backs.

By then he wasn't surprised, of course, but he seemed almost resigned, then embarrassed—he blushed—and he stammered out an explanation, saying he'd never talked to anybody about it.

He's an old man of 25, but had had a total of only two (consummated) sexual experiences. One with a woman, which was devastating, and one with a man, which was little short of rape. His few subsequent forays into the sexual arena were absolute functional failures, and he had been celibate for the past four years.

I have to admit I felt out of my depth. I hadn't expected to be the therapist in this little encounter. I was ashamed with myself at having pushed him into sharing the painful confidence, and for once in my bigmouth life I was at a loss for words.

He rescued me with a light joke, though, and wryly volunteered his services, so long as I would agree to expect absolutely nothing. We talked a long time about it, I revealing my past in all its sordid (by Earth standards) variety, and then spent a sweaty couple of hours.

As you might imagine, it wasn't exactly a night of a thousand delights, since Byron has all the self-control of a bunny in heat, and knows absolutely nothing about a woman's body, and it wasn't the time or place to begin teaching him. But I know a thing or two thousand about men (and am modest besides) and was able to surprise him with his own recuperative powers. I didn't fake any response myself, which I felt would be too manipulative, and couldn't fantasize myself into anything, because I was too worried about him.

(Which from the point of view of my own needs was probably the best thing that could have happened. I never once thought about the proximate motivation for seducing the poor boy, and I think managed to solve my own problem, obliquely, by addressing his. Isn't that a terrible cliché? Things become banal by being true, though.)

Anyhow, when I woke up this morning he had his scratchy beard on my breast, and was wearing a childlike smile in his sleep. I left him a note and had an amphetamine breakfast, to get me through the morning classes (the class we have together meets at 9:00 a.m. on Mondays, but I decided to let him sleep through it).

So I have come to terms with it. The rape was not at all a sexual act, and wouldn't have been even if he had entered me. It was violence, pure and simple. Not simple. We found that the man had killed and raped—*in that order*—five women in the past, and what he did to them was so brutal that I can't bring myself to put it down on paper. But it doesn't have anything to do with Byron (had to erase his real name there), except that his homosexual experience was spoiled by cruelty, and it has even less to do with you.

Speaking of yourself, I daydreamed about you all day and so have virtually nothing in my notes about Hemingway, Eli Whitney, and Methodism. The night with Byron was somatically unsatisfying, but it did reawaken an overpowering itch I've been scratching away at by myself for a month.

Sorry, old groundhog, I can feel your ears getting red. But I've made an exhaustive study of masturbation over the past few weeks, and I would like to share with you my findings: it is quick and easy and you don't have to clean up your room beforehand. I would do it right now but I have a late seminar and can't afford to be more tired than I already am. If I take another 'phet I'll be up all night, and be out of phase with the rest of the world for a week. (That's how dull and rationalized my so-called sex life has become.)

So I will bow to your wishes (and John's) and stop keeping my hands to myself. Whether I'll continue the tutelage of my pet poet, I don't know. See if he's still smiling, the next time I see him. Love—

Marianne

17 ✦ One-sided conversation

—Hello, no vision.

—Oh, it's you.

—Two new friends, maybe. Let me call you back later.

—Endit.

(A half-hour later he walks into a bar he knows will be crowded and noisy at this time. He nurses a drink until 2:47. He goes to the public phone and punches the number that is appropriate for that day and hour.)

—Will here.

—We have a probable and a possible. Probable is the poet type I mentioned last time. He's somewhat conspicuous, but that does have its uses. The other is a woman from New New York—

—New New York, the satellite. She—

—I know. Not to get deeply involved; not to find out too much. Her sympathies might be valuable some day. She seems politically disaffected with her home government and realistic about American politics.

—Yes. . . .

—She's a student at NYU. American Studies and something else.

—I don't know. It's usually a year. That would be

enough time for what I have in mind. . . . Oh, one complication. She's a friend of the poet's; I think they're sleeping together. For the time being, we shouldn't bring him in any deeper than she goes.

—No, she was brought into the Grapeseed by one of my fourth cadre, second level. A female who lives in the same dormitory.

—No, the poet, well, they met outside. He's been coming down for a couple of months. It's—

—I know. But it doesn't seem suspicious.

—Trust me, I'll feel them out a little more. The poet seems clean but it's hard to check up on her.

—Sure.

—If you can do it without any fuss. Her name's Marianne O'Hara, line name Scanlan. She mentioned living on the, uh, fourth level, which is a voting region. . . .

—Presumably. But the University records could be forged.

—Can't see it. If she's acting she's too good for them to insert at this level. And why would they do an insert who was an alien and a priori a temporary resident?

—Barely possible. Anything's possible. If you want, I'll hold off until you check.

—All right.

—No, we lost one last week. Cab accident, didn't look suspicious. So now we stand at one seventy-eight, with fifty-four at the expediting level.

—We do indeed. Endit.

18 ✦ Death and tariffs

O'Hara went to the next Worlds Club meeting armed with the information John had passed on to her. Most of the people knew that and more.

"They could have kept it secret," a man from Mazeltov complained. "That's the trouble with you Yorkers. You stay in too-close touch with Earth."

"Where would you peddle your metal," a man said, "without our marketing and shipping arrangements? Build your own slowboats and shuttles?"

"I'm not talking about economics," the Mazeltov man said.

"What *are* they talking about?" O'Hara asked Claire. "What secret?"

"The lunar CC material. It's all over the papers, haven't you heard?"

"But I haven't seen a thing. I've known about it for days!"

"Didn't use to be news," Claire said, looking through her bag. "Not until the Lobbies started twitching.... Guess I left the paper at home."

"I'll get one." O'Hara went into the main restaurant section of the Liffey and put a dollar in the *Times* machine; punched up "Space." It dropped twenty pages and flashed for another fifty cents. Usually you got two pages and change. O'Hara bought the rest and scanned the pages as she walked back to the meeting room.

The Senate was in an uproar. U.S. Steel was calling for a unilateral boycott of Worlds goods and services, and they had a lot of support.

Tomorrow night there was going to be a prime-time referendum: "Resolved: That all exports to the Worlds be halted until new agreements, guaranteeing long-term economic interdependence, can be reached between the United States and the Worlds, together and severally."

She sat down across from Claire and leafed through the pages. "It's out-and-out blackmail."

"Not really," Claire said. "Just good politics; better to do than be done to. Unusually farsighted."

"I was going to say 'premature.' Don't they know that this is really just a test?"

"But you do have to admit that we would pull our own boycott, eventually. Once we could live off Deucalion."

"Twenty years or more."

Claire shrugged. "Farsighted."

The man from Mazeltov sat down with them. "Claire, you're in systems engineering, right?" She nodded. "How long can we hold out?"

"I've been thinking about that. It depends on what you mean by 'we.' Your world and mine, Von Braun, will start to feel it in a couple of months. Larger systems are more resilient to shock; Devon's World could hold out for years. New New York could go twenty years, probably, with careful birth control. If you add selective euthanasia, they could keep the World running for centuries."

O'Hara looked thoughtful. "Twenty years."

"You see? They aren't really being precipitate. Just cold-blooded."

"What about a larger 'we'?" the man said. "New New could export food and water; they've done it before."

"They did it for Braun when I was a baby," Claire said. "What do you think, Marianne?"

"That was an emergency. I don't know." She sipped her beer. "There's another political aspect to it, that the U.S. has to be thinking of ... not just maintaining imbalance of trade. It looks as if they may be trying to push us into unity." She glanced at the paper. "That's why the phrase 'together and severally.' "

"There are worse things," the man said.

"It would be a disaster." O'Hara sighed. Old argument. "We'd be a suburb of Earth forever. Just another country." The Worlds did have a loose organization, through the Import-Export Board and various unanimous agreements concerning immigration and noninterference. But there was nothing resembling autonomy except for a mutual orneriness toward Earth.

There was an awkward moment of silence while everybody decided not to run around that track again. "Speaking of other countries," O'Hara said, "what about Common Europe? Are they cooperating?"

"Europe"—Claire nodded—"Supreme Socialist Union, and the Alexandrian Dominion. Japan has pledged to import nothing and limit its launches to bare life support for its two Worlds. The Pan-African Union is officially neutral, but their only launch facility is Zaire. They're in bed with Germany. We do have Pacifica on our side, and Greenland, I think."

"Who couldn't launch a sputnik."

"But it works both ways," the man said. "What happens to all the high-tech countries' economies? They need our energy and materials."

"Maybe not so much as we'd like to believe," Claire said. "At any rate, they have plenty of food and water."

✦ ✦ ✦

For once, all of the Worlds Club waited for Jules Hammond's newscast with anticipation.

Both Coordinators were guests on the program, and

they outlined a course of action (nobody considered seriously the possibility that U.S. Steel's referendum would fail). They were going to offer a horse trade: rather than a mutually absolute embargo, New New and Devon's World would continue to export electricity—not a small thing, since the satellites supplied about ten percent of the Eastern Seaboard's power—if the Lobbies would agree to supply the Worlds with enough hydrogen to offset normal daily loss, which would be about one shuttle flight per week.

It was an interesting move, especially so for having been done in public, prior to the referendum. A half billion cube-staring groundhogs knew that, if the Worlds did embargo energy, that missing ten percent was going to come off the top: their own comfort and leisure. Just for hydrogen enough to make a swimming pool's worth of water.

Various things weren't said. For instance, the amount of hydrogen requested was the amount lost in a normal week, but most of that loss was due to industrial processes that would largely stay dormant during a boycott. So the Worlds would actually be storing a surplus of water, in case of seige.

Leaving the solar power stations on would not be particularly altruistic, either; they are totally automated and require only sunlight as a raw material. It would be more trouble to turn them off than to leave them running.

One thing that would not be broadcast for a while was that a hastily gathered committee of experts in nutrition and agriculture had been able to assure the Coordinators that there would be no starvation, so long as there was an excess of water. People would have to revise their diets. But if it came down to fish sauce and rice, New New alone could feed practically everybody in the Worlds.

The Club stayed on until closing time, arguing, wondering, worrying. When O'Hara got back to the dormitory, there was a message light blinking for her. Daniel had called six hours before, urgent, and left a prepaid return guarantee. She punched up his number and eventually heard his sleepy voice.

"Anderson here, no vision."

"Daniel, it's me!"

The screen lit up to show Dan in his absurd pajamas. "Jesus, sweetheart, where have you been? I called till midnight."

"Worlds Club meeting; lots to talk about."

"Shit. I should have called you at that restaurant. Look, I've got to make a decision fast."

She nodded at his image. Four dollars a second, he nodded back at her. As often happens because of the time lag in transmission, they both spoke simultaneously: "Well—" and "Well?" That was good for an eight-dollar chuckle.

"Cyanamid has closed up shop here completely; they're calling all of us back, tomorrow. Today."

Her voice broke with excitement. "Then you'll be home in . . . a week or so?"

"That's the decision." Another expensive pause. "I may be home right now."

She frowned slightly. "You mean—"

"John says he can get me citizenship in five minutes. I, I want to do it. But . . . I also want you, and now."

"So come on down with Cyanamid and then go back to New New next year, with me. I'm sure they'll pay your way; even if they didn't—"

"That's just *it*, Marianne! I'm the only specialist in oil-shale chemistry here. They need me now more than ever. And with the embargo they won't be able to get anyone to replace me. You've always told me how important this work was; now I feel it, too, maybe even stronger than you can."

"Wait . . . what are you saying? You want me to help you make this decision? Or just approve of a decision you've already made?"

He looked almost ill. "I don't know."

"Not fair." She was thinking furiously. "Look. The embargo can't go on that long...."

"Don't bet on it. From here it looks like it may be years—" Dan's image disappeared in a swirl of rainbow static. It coalesced into that of a man wearing a Bellcom operator's uniform.

"I'm sorry; we're having some transmission difficulty, apparently because of solar activity. Please try again later. Your money will be refunded."

"That was a collect call."

"Then your caller will have his money refunded."

"How do you know it was a man?" she said sweetly, and thumbed it off. Then, on impulse, she punched up ten digits.

A bald woman in a Bellcom uniform appeared on the screen. "Directory assistance, Devon's World. May I help you?"

"Sorry. Wrong number." Solar activity, in a pig's ass.

Daniel dear—

I'm sorry I was such a bitch on the phone last night. It was a confusing, difficult day and I was bone-tired.

You are obviously right. Doubly right, in view of the political situation. But even without the current troubles, it would be ultimately best for us for you to stay in New New and become a citizen. It's where we both belong.

In fencing, they keep telling us "Fence with your head, not with your heart." I should apply that more generally.

Love,
Marianne

19 ✦ A few words from Benny

This is the 15th of October. No entries for the past several weeks, old Journal, because I've been trying to sort out my feelings toward Marianne O'Hara; trying to divine her feelings toward me.

The second part, I fear, is easier. She sees me as a friend whom she can help. Little more. (Surprising how difficult this is to write!) She is accustomed to being casual about sex and, I suspect, enjoys showing off her expertise.

All of which confounds and delights me. To discover passion so late, and through such a bizarre vehicle. I am obsessed with her. But I dare not put the name "love" to it. Even if the first sight of her in the morning makes my heart stammer.

It's strangely appropriate that she isn't beautiful. She has a more rare quality, concentrated in her expression: striking, magnetic, charismatic. The first time I met her I found it difficult to keep from staring; I've seen that struggle a thousand times since, with friends and strangers. She is aware of this quality, of course, but will not discuss it. For me it seems most intense when she is off guard, reading or watching something distant. Her face then takes on (bad pun) an otherworldly calm, which I only yesterday identified with a painting: Botticelli's Venus. And she Benny's Aphrodite.

She was attacked, and badly injured, three weeks ago. I visited her several times in the hospital. The first time she was brusque, almost rude; later she said she was trying to get rid of me so I wouldn't see her crying. I would give a great deal to see her cry. Or do anything that showed a break in control. She has the soul of a compassionate machine. Bitter Benny. You know she isn't like that with everyone. I wonder what she is to Daniel, the man she left up in New New York? Or to that Devonite she says she loved so terribly. I don't even know what she is to me, not honestly. All I know is that I haven't written a poem in weeks that I didn't tear up immediately.

> There once was a harlot from space
> With a very remarkable face,
>> Whose nethermore part
>> Could break a man's heart
> With a taste of its tiny embrace.

Still haven't. Can't tear this page out, though, or years from now I'll wonder what I had to hide from myself.

Trying to be honest: the bitterness is a predictable refraction of thankfulness, indebtednes that can never be discharged. I could have gone through life a eunuch. She gave me new life and all I can do is amuse her.

(She does laugh well. Last night I caught her off guard, juggling two of her shoes and a piece of candy. When I got them going good and fast I told her "Watch closely . . . I'm going to eat one of these.")

Maybe there's no room in my life right now for poetry, dominated as it is on one side by this nervous passion for Marianne, and on the other side by ever more complicated politics. I have felt for some time that the Grapeseed Revenge was more than simply a watering hole for hairy grumblers. Now I know for sure.

There's been a great deal of angry rhetoric over the Lobbies' boycott of the Worlds. As if the threat of starvation were not a time-honored aspect of American foreign trade policy. I got so weary of hearing the same things shouted over and over that I began playing devil's advocate, defending the Senate's righteous actions against those piratical colonies (that's not a popular word at the Grapeseed). Marianne was entertained by my ranting, but we had to make a hasty exit, or leave aerially.

Throughout my act, the strange fellow who calls himself Will—that's metonymy, not contraction—sat impassively, with a tired smile. Later that night he called. He said he had enjoyed my bit of comedy, and from it had deduced that I might be one who preferred action to empty argumentation. If so, would I meet him and some friends at such-and-so corner; please repeat it and don't write it down.

It happens that I *do* prefer words to action, of course, but I couldn't help being intrigued. I went to the place at the time specified. After waiting twenty minutes I gave up and walked away. A woman I'd never seen before caught up with me and asked me to follow her. After a confusing subway ride, we wound up on the other side of town. She left me at the door of a tenement and asked me to wait a few minutes, then knock. She left. I was beginning to enjoy it, the comic-opera aspect, but almost walked away myself; if they had a realistic reason for all the mystery, I would just as soon not get involved. Some great poetry has been written in prison, but I don't think I want to put my own skills to that test.

Before I could knock or not-knock, the door opened of its own accord. A soft voice bade me come in. It was a large room with only one person in it, standing behind the door. He (I say for convenience) led me wordlessly to a table in the middle of the room. He was hooded and wore shapeless black fatigues. His tenor voice could have been male or female. He sat me down on a hard chair and sat himself across from me, then from a drawer took a polygraph plate and a clipboard. Did I mind being asked a few questions? I asked him what would happen if I gave the wrong answers. He said I'd given him one already. I was suddenly comforted by the weight of the knife on my belt; glad I'd unsnapped the retaining strap when we'd gone down to the subway.

I put my hand on the plate and he asked me a number of remarkable questions, to calibrate it. They all had to do with my private life over the past couple of days: trivial things like what I'd had for lunch, whom I'd met when, and so forth. So I'd been under surveillance.

Then he quizzed me about possible government affiliation (except for a couple of months in the Boy Scouts, I was clean) and then about my political beliefs. I don't think he liked all of my answers; he wanted a reflex radical.

After a few minutes of this he got up and led me—reluctantly, I thought—up a flight of stairs, where he rapped on a door and left without a word.

The man who answered the door startled me. He was blind, with a bugeye prosthesis. Not many people are born blind and rich. He asked me if I was Benny, and shook hands, smiling.

There were three other people inside, all about my age, sitting around on shabby hotel furniture. The blind man said his name was James, and he introduced the others: Katherine, Damon, and Ray. Offered me tea. When I asked where Will was, he stiffened and said that some of these people didn't know Will.

We talked for a while about generalities, uncomfortably, people pointedly avoiding any talk that had to do with their personal lives. James noticed my puzzlement and said they were waiting for one more.

There was a knock at the door and James sat for a few seconds, then got up and answered it. It was Marianne. . . .

20 ✦ Welcome to the party

After the absurd questioning downstairs, and the hide-and-go-seek nonsense that preceded it, I was ready to tell Will he could stick it, and leave. Then I got two sudden shocks.

The man who opened the door was blind, with huge surgically implanted lenses set in his eye sockets. I'd read about them, but of course had never seen any, not in New New.

The second shock was Benny. When I saw him sitting there, I thought for a moment that it was all an elaborate joke. Nobody was laughing, though. The blind man introduced me to everybody, saying "You know Benny, of course." Benny gave me a funny look and I gave him one back, I guess.

The blind man, James, fixed me a cup of tea. "For the benefit of the two new people, let me outline what we do here."

"Does this outfit have a name?" Benny asked.

"No." Since his lenses were fixed in place, James had to turn his whole head to look at you. The effect was riveting, machinelike. "We use various names for various purposes. Sugar?"

"No, thanks." He stared at the teacup as he brought it over to me.

"It all sounds very mysterious, I know. Let me try to

put your minds at ease." He sat down and looked at Benny. "We do nothing illegal, at least not beyond the level of misdemeanor."

"I once got arrested for littering," the woman, Katherine, said.

James nodded slightly. "Handbills. We are a pressure organization, Benny. We write letters, organize rallies, use cube time, and so forth. On another level, we gather information about the government and analyze it, in hopes of eventually building an accurate picture of the country's actual power structure."

"Then why all the secrecy?" I said. "It seems to me you'd want publicity instead."

"Mostly insurance. It's true that we could operate in the open now, though we could expect a certain amount of harassment. Conditions may change, though—the government becoming more oppressive or, perhaps, our tactics becoming more extreme.

"In essence, we do have a public side, since many of our members belong to other organizations with ambitions similar to ours. We are not shy of using them.

"We cover a rather wide ideological spectrum, but we are basically libertarian and humanitarian. We believe that the government exercises too much control over individual freedom, and does it in ways that most people are powerless to resist. We want eventually to establish a truly representative form of government, with strong controls on its use of the broadcast media as tools for mass conditioning."

That struck a chord. The commercials on the shows that preceded the Worlds boycott referendum were scary. Subtle and powerful.

"But why me? I'm not even a citizen of this planet."

"That's exactly why. Your objectivity, and experience with other political systems. For your own part, you might consider it a trade; I understand that you plan on politics as a career, once you leave Earth. What you learn here, helping us with our analysis, can only help you later on. Also, the people you meet might prove valuable contacts, eventually."

"If you get into power," Benny said.

He swiveled. "Some of us do have political ambitions, of course. I think most of us are only interested in seeing the present system replaced by one more responsive to the actual needs of the electorate."

"You're planning a revolution," Benny said.

"Not actively," James said.

"Where would we get weapons?" The short man, Ray, bustled across the room to fill his cup. "You can't fight a modern army with knives and homemade bombs."

"Not every state has New York–style laws."

"Sporting weapons," Ray said. "Rifles and shotguns. Sorry, you can fight without me."

"Well, there's always Nevada," Benny said. "You can buy anything from a hand laser to an atom bomb there."

"But you can't get it out," James said. "The border guards are—"

"If you can buy an atom bomb, you can buy a CBI man." I was a little surprised to see Benny talking this way.

"You seem to have given the matter some thought," James said.

He shrugged. "Revolution is inevitable. Whether anything will come of it, I don't know. It may depend on how prepared we are."

"If you had proper organization," I said, "and the support of most of the people, you might be able to do it without sophisticated weapons. That's how the Vietnamese won."

James laughed. "Looks like we've recruited a couple of fire-breathers."

"Theory's cheap," Ray said, and James gave him a sharp look. "If it did come down to fighting, would you do it? Would you kill people?"

"I don't know. The situation has never come up." Benny touched his knife, probably an unconscious gesture.

"I suspect I could kill if somebody was trying to kill me. Of course, it wouldn't always be that way."

Ray nodded, apparently satisfied. James shook his head, microscopically. (Suddenly I visualized what the world must look like to him when he shakes his head or nods.) "I, for one, hope it can be done without violence. None of you is old enough to remember the Second Revolution. I was ten. It was a terrible time."

"And look what it accomplished," Katherine said. "You men. How can you even think of ... doing that again?"

The fourth man, Damon, had been sitting silently, alert. He was tall and black. "Katherine. We all would prefer reform to revolution. But we can't proscribe violence as a possible final resort. It is the State's last resort against us."

"Which they will only use if we provoke it," she said.

"Please," James said, "this is all familiar ground. Shall we get on with the week's business?"

Katherine reported on a rally and petition drive, which she had organized but didn't take part in physically. Ray had been in Washington for the past couple of days, where he had cultivated the friendship of the man who took care of the Senate's steam room. He'd learned nothing beyond the level of idle gossip, but the man obviously could be an important contact some day. Damon had just come back from two weeks in Ketchikan, where he had tried to make contact with a group of non-Separatists, without any success.

Finally, James asked whether Benny and I might be willing to do some work for the organization.

"What happens if we say no?" Benny asked.

"Nothing drastic. We would ask that you not tell anyone about us, and of course we would watch you for a while. Or you may just want some time to think about it; that's all right, too."

"Tell me what it is you want."

"Well, we want to take advantage of your writing skill." He opened a briefcase and handed Benny a thick envelope. "This is stationery with the letterhead of the 'Committee of Concerned Citizens,' which has no members other than yourself. Be careful to handle it in such a way as not to add fingerprints to it. The fingerprints on it belong to the Swedish printer who made up the stationery, and the paper itself would be difficult to trace: it was made by an Italian firm that's been out of business for twenty years."

"Sounds like you want a ransom note."

He smiled. "Not quite. . . . Write on a Praktika or Xerox machine; they print with stabilized burners that don't vary from machine to machine."

"There's one in the Drama library."

"Good. We need seven letters, to senators whose votes are crucial to S2876, a bill having to do with public disclosure of corporate income taxes. There's a shit-sheet on each senator, with at least one fact that would be embarrassing if it were given to the media."

"Blackmail?"

"Not if you word the letters correctly. Willing to try?"

Benny shrugged. "Okay."

"Good. Send me copies at the address on the envelope. You'll find the senators' home addresses inside; it would be well if you mailed from Grand Central or the main P.O." He turned to me. "Marianne, how's your statistics?"

"Math is my worst subject."

"But you can program?"

"Of course. I'm not illiterate."

"Good. This is a fairly simple job." He handed me a folder with two sheets of paper in it. "We're trying to verify consensual links between various supposedly antagonistic Lobbies. We're fairly sure the links exist, with the result that the same people stay in power no matter which way an election goes. What you'll be doing is pairing up voting records, trying to find suspicious correlations."

"Sounds interesting." It did, as a matter of fact.

"Keep track of the computer charges; I'll reimburse you in cash. You, too, Benny."

The meeting lasted another ten minutes, with Damon and Katherine getting new assignments. Benny and I left together; the others were going to follow at staggered intervals. We took the subway.

Benny looked inside the envelope as we swayed crosstown. "I'm Lloyd Carlton," he said. "Three-fifty Madison Avenue. Good address."

"What do you think?" I talked just loudly enough for him to hear. There were several others in the car.

"About the organization? I don't know, not yet. I'd like to know how much they didn't tell us."

"You were talking pretty radical in there."

"Trying to kick something loose."

"You almost succeeded with Ray, I think. Katherine wasn't too impressed. 'Revolution is inevitable,' eh?"

"Only if they interrupt the World Series."

21 ✦ Behind the scenes

After the others had left, the blind man sat alone, reading. A door opened silently and Will stepped in. "Interesting?"

"Except for the diagrams."

"Not the book, those two new ones."

"Ah. Yes, they were interesting. I think we'd better keep a tag on Benny for a while."

"No problem. How about O'Hara?"

"I'm bothered by her necessary lack of commitment. We'd better keep her well insulated from the expediting level. Benny, too, until she leaves."

"True. Want to go upstairs?"

He got up. "No harm in being early."

When the elevator came, Will inserted a key and pushed the button marked "Penthouse."

"MacGregor thing set up?"

Will nodded. "Tonight, if everything goes smoothly."

They stepped out into the penthouse suite. There were five people sitting around a long table. Four of them were cleaning weapons. They saluted, right fist striking chest, and the two men returned the salute.

Katherine looked expectantly at Will. He nodded. "Tonight." She finished assembling the palm-sized oneshot laser, put it in her purse, and left.

Will walked along the wall, running his fingers down

the stocks of the dozens of long guns racked there: lasers as well as gunpowder and CO_2 weapons. At the end of the rack, he picked up a practice rifle and aimed it at the man-shaped target across the room. The target had light-sensing devices at head and heart. Will squeezed off five shots in rapid succession; a bell rang five times.

James smiled, took a long-barreled sniper's rifle off the rack, and sat down to disassemble it. He was the best marksman in the room.

(The next morning's papers would report that Senator William MacGregor had died in his sleep, of a cerebral hemorrhage. They wouldn't mention that he wasn't sleeping alone, or that the hemorrhage was caused by a point-blank laser blast to the base of the skull, or that there was a printed manifesto pinned to the blood-soaked pillow.)

22 ✦ A tangled web we weave

20 October.   While I was finishing up the program for James's group, my favorite FBI officer walked into the computing room. I told him I was working on a project for my Lobbies class, which gave me a little thrill. Marianne O'Hari, girl spy.

Hawkings had a short program and was finished by the time I got mine printed and bound, and we went out for coffee. Keeping the conversation safe, I mentioned next quarter's Cultural Relativism tour—and was surprised to find that he's going on it too! He's been saving up money and leave-time for a couple of years.

Really mixed feelings about that. It will be nice to have somebody familiar along, and I like Hawkings well enough, for an American man. But I can imagine what he'd think about Will and James's activities. (Actually, his reaction wouldn't be simplistic, since he is an intelligent and politically "aware" person. But I don't think he'd have a sense of humor about blackmailing senators.)

After coffee, we went to the gym, found partners, and fenced for an hour. He did self-defense style, two weapons, and his partner didn't have a chance, from the one bout I watched. I lost all four of my own bouts, and managed to lunge into a stop-thrust and get stuck in the armpit, which still hurts. I'll never be really good at it, but it is fun and lets off steam. Afterwards, I sort of wished they didn't have separate showers for men and women. He looks so much like Charlie—do I miss him, in spite of everything? Maybe my body misses his body. Maybe I miss looking at naked men, or showing off my resistible secondary sexual characteristics.

I stared at that program for hours, and haven't come up with any consistent pattern. I think the pattern does exist, but I'm just not a good enough mathematician to isolate it. Maybe James will have me shot.

I'm tempted to throw the whole business out the lock. Interfering with the politics of a foreign country. Foreign planet. They could put me in jail.

Though I suspect they wouldn't dare, so long as I personally don't do anything blatantly illegal. It would be too good a news item. The U.S. claims to be a bastion of personal freedom. In fact, though, the civil disobedience laws of most states are so broad that they can arrest you for saying that the president of General Motors shits daily. And you can spend a long time waiting to come to trial. Will claims that there are tens of thousands of political activists rotting in jail.

What I'll do is confront James directly, and tell him that I refuse to do anything either illegal or public; for this, he has my cooperation and silence. It *will* be valuable, seeing American politics from the underside.

21 October.   Entertainment lab was a fascinating backstage look at a Broadway play. We went to the Uris Theatre, where they're doing a revival of the 1998 musical *Chloe*. We got there at nine, and watched all the preparations for the 1:30 matinee; then watched the show from the orchestra pit—there being no orchestra, since the music was all old-fashioned electronics. It's a supposedly funny

story about suicide. I think a banjo might have pepped it up.

Jeff Hawkings asked me out to dinner tonight. Life certainly does get complicated. I told him I had to pound the books, which was true, since I have to give the class on Steinbeck Monday. I had planned on eating out, sudden craving for pasta, but to keep my conscience clear I just got eggs and toast out of the machine. How can they make eggs and toast that give you indigestion?

Steinbeck won't be hard, since I spent a week on him a couple of years ago in that "Tools for Social Reform" seminar. And having survived the Crane class helps.

Grapeseed tomorrow with Benny.

22 October.   First snow of the year, of my life. I made Benny walk with me to the Grapeseed, even though it was sloppy and cold. The stuff is beautiful. Pictures don't do anything. It's the feel of it on your face and the crisp smell of the air. It gets on your eyelashes and doesn't melt for a while.

Benny brought up the idea that our "inner circle" with James may be far from the innermost circle. He described the system of interlocking cells that the Communist party used in the United States last century, where no one knew the identity of more than a few other party members. It sounds logical.

I told Benny I didn't think I wanted to go any deeper. There's enough potential for trouble at James's level. He agreed, outwardly, but was thoughtful.

The Grapeseed was more crowded than I'd ever seen it. Bad weather is good for bars, I guess, especially bars that specialize in conversation. They were serving hot buttered rum, which sounds great but tastes like someone had taken a drink and stirred it with a fried chicken leg.

Will showed up but was quieter than usual. When he was more or less alone with Benny and me, he explained that a friend of his had just died, evidently by her own hand. It was Katherine, who had been so aggressively non-violent at the meeting. She poisoned herself, with barbiturates and alcohol.

I've never understood that. I guess I've never been depressed enough, not even after the rape ("sexual battery," but it will always be The Rape to me). I can accept voluntary euthanasia, at least intellectually, and am glad that New New offers it as an escape hatch, in case some day I'm very old and in constant pain. But I can't imagine existential pain so great that a person my age would take her life. A square meter of earth, Dostoevski said; if all you had was a square meter of earth to stand on, and nothing around you but impenetrable fog, living would be preferable to dying. Did Katherine know something he didn't?

Wish I hadn't seen *Chloe*. Ghastly memory now.

23 ✦ Insect, repellent

No percentage in not being friendly to a man I'll be traveling with for ten weeks. Before the management seminar, I asked Jeff whether he'd be free for dinner Tuesday. I think he tried not to act surprised. He probably thought my refusal Saturday was a dust-off. I'll take him to that nice Italian place in the Village.

The seminar was interesting enough, employee selection and training. The class was going down to "our" bar afterwards, but I had to pass it up. Still haven't really caught up in religion, after the stay in the hospital, and playing spy takes up time.

Benny met me outside the classroom, the first time he'd ever done that. Said he'd walk me back to the dormitory.

We didn't say much on the way to the subway, trying to keep our footing on the icy sidewalk. When we got to the dorm, I asked Benny whether he'd like to come up for tea. He hesitated, then said yes.

Upstairs, I started for the hotplate, but Benny caught my arm. "Let's take a shower together."

I just stared at him. He stared back with a look that had to do with neither hygiene nor sex.

He kept the same queer expression as we undressed and got towels. Walking down the hall, he held my arm in a grip that was almost painful. There was nobody else in the shower room. Benny turned one up full force and hauled me inside.

He held me close and whispered, "We don't dare talk in your room."

"Aren't you carrying this—" He cut me off with a violent shake of his head.

"I'm not being paranoid. This morning I couldn't find a book, looked high and low, finally looked under the bed. I found a bug."

I didn't understand. "Are you zipped? There are bugs everywhere."

"Not a bug bug," he whispered harshly. "An electronic one—microphone and transmitter and battery. Size of your little fingernail."

"How in the world would you recognize—"

"Christ and Buddha, don't you ever watch the cube? You can buy them over-the-counter at Radio Shack. Somebody's eavesdropping on me, probably you, too."

"You think it's . . . James?"

"Or Will. If it were the government, I wouldn't've found the bug with a microscope."

"That's terrible."

"That's only half of it. The first half is Katherine."

It took a second for the name to register. "The suicide."

"The one who died. I thought I saw her Friday night, the day before she died. You know I had to go to Washington."

I nodded. He was part of a show in a gallery there.

"Thought I'd take the red-eye, save a couple of bucks. Went down to Penn to catch the two a.m. Going down the escalator to the train, she was coming up. She had a wig on, but no way you could disguise that nose."

"Sure it was her?"

"I sort of half waved, then caught myself. She saw me and looked away."

"What are you driving at?"

"Don't you see? James gave her an assignment in Denver. Remember? And here she is, sneaking in from Washington at two in the morning. And the next day she's dead."

"My God."

"You see? It's too much of a coincidence. It's possible, just possible, that she did commit suicide. Not likely."

I held him more tightly. "Somebody found out she was . . . working for the government."

"A counterspy, double agent, whatever. What probably happened was, they had somebody following me, checking me out. Saw her, reported . . . maybe she was under suspicion anyhow. They force-fed her some pills and washed them down with booze."

"The Times said there was a suicide note."

"Right. In her typewriter."

The door to the shower room slammed and I felt a chill down my back, under the hot water.

"What are we going to do?" I whispered.

"Right now? We—" I put my hand over his mouth. A man was using the urinal. There were only three men on this floor, and they were all closer to the other john. My heart was banging.

"Sammy? Is that you?"

The urinal flushed. "Maintenance," an unfamiliar voice said. I held on to Benny with my teeth clenched and eyes squeezed shut. Then the door slammed again.

"Was that the maintenance man?"

"I don't know. I've never talked to any of them. Benny—stay with me. I'm afraid."

He stroked my shoulder softly. "I don't think we're in any danger yet. They don't have any reason to suspect that we think they're anything other than they said they were."

"You left the bug where it was?"

"Of course. And you should do the same if you—no. Just assume there *is* a bug, in your room somewhere. Don't bother to search."

"You will stay with me tonight?"

He kissed me. "Sure." If there was a bug under my bed

that night, it heard nothing more erotic than two people staring at the ceiling.

It was a good idea to keep my diary as loose sheets. After Benny left in the morning, I removed all the pages that referred to any of this spy stuff, tore them up, and flushed them away (after retyping the innocent parts). I decided I might keep a separate diary if there were some way to absolutely hide it.

24 ✦ Apparent and absolute magnitude

The organization that O'Hara and Benny have made contact with is neither small nor without a name. Of the people they've met, only James is aware that he belongs to the Third Revolution (Katherine also knew the name, and was willing to die for it, though that happened in a way she had never foreseen).

The FBI is aware of the 3R, and is concerned. They have dossiers on over twelve thousand members and suspect there are some fifty thousand more, protected by the tight cell system. They are wrong by an order of magnitude: the Third Revolution claims over six hundred thousand Americans and resident aliens (including one from outer space). About one out of five operates at the "expediting" level, which is mostly target practice and weapons drill. Fewer than one in five thousand is aware of the actual size and strength of the organization, which has over a million small arms stashed around the country, and tonnes upon tonnes of high explosive, made into standardized bombs, for sabotage. And two nuclear devices, one permanently sealed under the subway tracks in Washington, three blocks from the Lobbies' Office Building.

Of the very few people in Washington who are aware

of the true danger presented by 3R, one is the FBI's second-in-command, who is also 3R's first-in-command.

The 3R's attitude toward America would have been easily understood by the soldier of the previous century who said, "We had to destroy the village in order to save it."

25 ✦ Diary of a spy

(The following entries written in tiny script on cigarette papers, hidden between two pieces of cardboard that formed the bottom of a box of tampons. She got the trick from the Marquis de Sade.)

29 October.   I gave my report to James last night, same place as the first meeting. He seemed interested and sympathetic, as were the others, and agreed that there might be a pattern, which a better mathematician could extract. ¶Benny was too nervous. I hope they don't suspect anything. He gave his report and was warmly congratulated. James had already seen the letters, of course. The bill comes up for "second reading" next week, and we'll find out then whether the letters had the desired effect. ¶The meeting was subdued because of Katherine's death. Damon, who shared her faith, said a short prayer in Arabic. It was grotesque. Did James kill her? Damon? ¶I gave my "ultimatum" to James, and he accepted it without question. He said he would do the same in my position. Toward the end of the meeting I felt lulled. That's dangerous. They seem nice people, full of concern and social consciousness. One or more of them are capable of putting a bug under Benny's bed and, probably, killing a person for being on the wrong train. I'm frightened but also fascinated. Only seven weeks before the quarter's over, and I can escape to Europe without arousing suspicion. But Benny?

30 October.   Benny and I discussed possible stratagems. He's even more scared than I am, with good reason. Talked for hours and wound up where we'd started. ¶He raised an interesting, possibly hopeful, point. The bug might easily be left over from the previous tenant. Benny knows that she was a small-scale drug dealer. So either the police or her wholesaler could have been eavesdropping on her. ¶Also, Katherine. All I really knew of her was her intensity. Alvarez, in *The Savage God*, says that every suicide "has its own inner logic and unrepeatable despair," and for some reason that sounded like Katherine. Maybe she wasn't the woman on the escalator. It's a big city, full of unrelated twins.

6 November.   I really don't know. Benny and I are trying to convince each other that it's just paranoia. The meetings are innocent enough on the surface. Nothing's said that would raise an eyebrow at the Grapeseed. But there's so much goatshit mystery around it. Today a stranger sat down across from me at lunch and struck up a conversation. When the other person left he said he had a request from James: would I be willing to give a speech to a small group, comparing the state of civil liberties in the Worlds with those here. I told him what I'd told James. Nothing public. He said it would be only about forty people, and very private. I agreed to do it. ¶In fact, I'm looking forward to it. It won't be what he expects.

12 November.   It's a good thing I had my notes together. Less than a day's warning for the speech (Damon gave me the message, at Grapeseed). ¶The speech was less interesting than the reactions. The old-fashioned communists didn't like what I had to say about Tsiolkovski. The ones who leaned toward conventional People's Capitalism were alarmed by the distribution-of-wealth system in Devon's World, as, I suppose, were any fellow atheists. (Well, it

doesn't really alarm me, but I don't consider myself anti-clerical. A job is a job.) ¶Will was there, but he didn't say anything. I wonder about him and James. Who is whose boss, or are they equals? As far as I could tell, they didn't even say hello. ¶Benny wasn't there (I talked the speech over with him, but he wasn't invited) and neither was anybody else I knew but James, Will, and Damon. From the atmosphere of the crowd (it was more like sixty people than forty) I got the impression I was talking to a group of leaders. Love to know more about the structure of the group, and the actual size of it. But when I tried to bring it up last meeting, a real chill dropped.

13 November.   A woman in my religion class dropped a note in my lap on the way to her seat. "Take care not to recognize me." Well, I didn't. She must have been at the talk last night, but I was nervous in front of a room full of strangers, and rarely looked past the first two rows.

17 November.   Will came to my room tonight, and we talked for a couple of hours. He was more relaxed than I have ever seen him. ¶The main topic under discussion was the need for secrecy and his concern that I shouldn't misinterpret the group's motivation for it. There are conservative elements in almost every Lobby, even the labor Lobbies, that would love to have a libertarian "whipping boy." (Which is odd in the perspective of my own reading of American history, which strongly associates libertarianism with conservatism. Terms change as attitudes evolve, I suppose. Jefferson was a libertarian but owned human slaves.) ¶Most disturbing was his assertion that there is some group, small and highly secret, that is practicing "waster politics"—assassinations and pinpoint sabotage—which is being covered up by the government. He couldn't reveal his source and offered no proof, other than the fact that a lot of politicians have died very young recently. He also

pointed out that no competent electrical engineer would accept the authorities' explanation for last week's blackout in Boston (that goes along with what I heard at Worlds Club Tuesday). These assassinations have all taken place in Washington, where the government virtually owns all news media. Will believes the group must indeed be part of the government, perhaps a powerful Lobby, perhaps even a clandestine arm of the FBI or CBI. If his aim was to reassure me, he accomplished the opposite. Two nameless groups to be afraid of now, instead of one.

26 ✦ A weighing of parts

If all poets had Benny's capacity for enjoying alcohol, literature would be an easier course of study. There wouldn't be as much of it.

We spent Wednesday afternoon at a wine-and-crackers place near the Russell building, willing to pay a little more to get away from the being-watched feeling we got at the Grapeseed. The wine wasn't remarkable, and I wasn't drinking much anyhow, with management seminar in the evening. I had one glass out of the first liter, and Benny finished the rest in less than an hour. Which wasn't unusual; it took that much to relax him.

He was in one of his odd manic moods, though, and the wine might as well have been tea, for all its apparent effect. It had been more than a month since the Washington show, and he hadn't spent half of what his drawings had brought in.

He signaled for another liter. "Can you imagine? Any idiot with a drafting board and a steady hand could do that."

"Come on, Benny; I couldn't. And I've got the steadiest hand at this table. Currently."

"Nope." He held a hand out in front of me, palm down. While I was trying to frame something to say, a silver five-buck emerged slowly from between the first two fingers. He rolled it down his knuckles, flipped it and caught it. "Want to try?" He held it out to me.

"Seriously, I'll have to go to class in a while. You don't want one of these characters to walk you home."

We were almost two blocks from Broadway, but most of the people were orifice-peddlers of some gender, with their usual retinue. "Might hire one," he said.

"What?"

"To walk me home, spacer. Some of them'll do anything for a price."

"Just keep it down to four liters. It bothers you, doesn't it."

I could hear his brain grinding out some non sequitur about the wine or the whores. Instead he nodded and said quietly, "That gallery called today. They want twelve more."

That was twice as many as he'd sold in October. "That's wonderful—"

"When I said no, they offered to drop their commission to fifteen percent."

"You still refused?"

The waiter brought the wine. Benny touched the flask but didn't pour himself any. "It's not art."

That was true, as far as I could tell. Good decoration, though; I had one on my wall. "So what is baby-sitting?"

"Baby-sitting, I can read. Besides, I'm good at it."

"You're good at drawing, too. How long would it take you to do a dozen scenes?"

"Two days, maybe three. A week if I was lazy."

"Three months' income for a week of work? You're a lunatic!"

He laughed and poured us each a glass. "I think you've just put your finger on it. Must be that cultural perspective James admires so."

"You can't get out of it that easily. You're being a prima donna and you know it. You need the money."

"No, I don't. I need the self-respect."

"What's so denigrating about using your hands, crafts-manship?"

"Nothing!" He drank half the glass, and refilled it. "I'll still do some drawings. And I'll go out on the Square, as usual, and set them up on a rack, maybe do some juggling, sell them to people walking by."

"For a tenth what the gallery pays."

"Less than a tenth. But listen ... you should've been there. They had this poster up, big doleful picture of me, puffed-up biography with all these embarrassing reviews, rising young poet who may become—nobody bought those drawings as art, or even as craft. They bought them as sim-ple curiosities, maybe investments. People who can drop a couple of thousand bucks like a handful of soybeans, just for—"

"That's just it! They can afford it; it might as well be you who takes it."

He waggled a finger at me. "That doesn't sound like a good communist talking."

"I'm *not* a communist."

"Excuse me." He took a drink. "You live in a state—"

"A World."

"You live in a world where the state, the world, owns all the capital and gives you room and board, and an allow-ance, and little trinkets like trips to Earth if it thinks you need them. To me that sounds like 'From each according to his abilities, to each according to his needs.'"

I tried to keep my voice steady. "I meant communism, Earth-style. Not Marxism. But we don't have that, either. Marx couldn't have foreseen the kind of isolated economy you get in a space settlement."

"All right, Marianne." He took my hands in his warm ones. "If we see something that takes in oats at one end and gives out horseshit at the other, and you say it's a Buick, well, *I* say it's a Buick, too."

I resisted the impulse to pour the jug of wine in his lap. "You have such a poetic way of putting things. But don't condescend to me."

"You were condescending to me."

"I'm sorry if you think so. But I think you're confused."

"Now you're getting warm." He released me and finished his glass, and sat back with a thoughtful look. He was composing. "I am confused, but not about that. Anyone who sees clearly sees chaos everywhere. Art is a way of temporarily setting order to confusion. Temporary and incomplete; that's why we never run out of new art. Anyone who comes to the tools of art without that sense of confusion is an invader."

"That's not really fair."

"Nothing against dabblers," he said quickly. "Cheaper than psychotherapy. But supposedly serious artists who think they know, *know*, what a human being is and where he stands in relation to the universe, they're nothing but hacks. Propagandists for false values."

I filled his glass to shut him up. "Even if that's true, it doesn't apply to your drawings. It would apply if you were writing jingles for commercials or something. But you've said yourself that you don't take the drawing seriously. You're a dabbler yourself."

"There you have it. I do them to relax and don't care to keep them afterward. It pleases me to give them to friends; it amuses me to give them to strangers in exchange for an occasional dinner or a few days' rent. This gallery deal amounts to doing it for a living."

"Well? It would be an easy living."

"All right. You enjoy screwing, and you're good at it. Why don't you get a low-cut dress and join those slits at the bar? One night a week, and you'd go back to New New York with twice what you brought here."

I gripped the edge of the table and took a deep breath.

"But you only give it to friends," he said softly. "And your friends do appreciate it."

Before I could decide whether to wound him—he was no better at analogy than at sex—I heard someone tapping on the window next to us and looked up. It was Hawkings; I waved him in.

"Be on your best behavior, now," I said. "This is that FBI agent I told you about."

"Jesus! Does this place have a back door?"

"Don't be silly," I whispered.

"Nothing silly about healthy paranoia. Don't you think there's some small chance we're being watched?"

"They don't have an army. But even if we are, there's nothing suspicious about Jeff passing by on his way to class—"

"But then there *is* something suspicious about our being here."

"So speak clearly. We don't have anything to hide."

He rubbed his throat. "So why do I feel this noose, tightening around my neck?"

"Anxiety reaction. Shut up." Hawkings had stopped at the bar before coming over, and was bringing a liter of wine. For all his cool detachment, he was always polite and considerate. That was welcome now.

I dragged a chair over for him and made introductions. "I've never met a poet before," Hawkings said. "What have you published?"

That was the right question. Usually people asked, "Have you published anything?"—to which Benny would reply, "No, I just *call* myself a poet."

Benny told him the names of his books. "Haven't written much lately. It comes and goes."

He nodded. "I have to admit I don't envy you. It must be a very uncertain way to live."

"More certain than yours, I think. At least in the sense that no poet ever was killed in the line of duty."

Hawkings smiled. "I could take issue with that. It seems to me that the death rate for poets from suicide is rather high."

"Touché." Well, at least they had found something in common. Morbidity.

"I don't actually encounter very much violence. It's mostly footwork and paperwork. There are scuffles and threats, often enough, but it's not serious. In four years, I've only been fired at once."

"Safer than the subway," I said.

"You shot back?" Benny said. Hawkings nodded. "Did you kill him?" He nodded again. "I don't know if I could live with that."

"Well, you're not trained to." Jeff's voice was quiet and dry, classroom style. "It was almost purely reflex. It wasn't even an FBI matter, technically."

His brow furrowed as he poured himself half a glass of wine. "I was snooping around a warehouse, after hours, but with a warrant. Some burglar had picked the same night.

"The place was brightly lit. I walked around the corner of a stack of crates and this man was standing there, about three meters away, with a pistol pointed directly at me. If he'd taken a moment to aim, he would have killed me. Instead, he started blasting away in my general direction. He got off four or five shots, two of which struck me, before I could draw and fire."

"And you did take time to aim?" Benny said.

"Not at three meters, not with a laser."

"Were you hurt badly?" I asked. He'd never mentioned this to me.

"Technically. Chest and abdomen. But I stayed conscious long enough to call for a floater. My heart stopped twice on the way to the hospital, but once I was there I was out of danger. You know how good they are at that sort of thing."

"I do indeed." I tried to match his dispassionate tone.

"But that's when I decided to go back to school and get out of field work. Just another fourteen months."

"I don't suppose they were quite as, ah, efficient in trying to save the burglar's life," Benny said.

"No, they just left him for the meat, for the morgue floater. That's not as callous as it sounds. Science can do wonders, but they haven't yet figured out how to unscramble an egg."

I shuddered. "Can't—"

"It doesn't bother you?" Benny said.

"Should it?" He sipped his wine carefully, looking at Benny over the rim of the glass. When Benny didn't say anything, he added: "I know he didn't grow up wanting to be a burglar; I know he didn't spend years in school studying how to shoot FBI agents. I know that it was a complex of social pressures, perhaps social injustice, and plain bad luck, that led him to that warehouse.

"And it was plain dumb bad luck that he saw me first. If I'd seen him, I would have taken a picture, then let him finish his work and leave; I was after bigger game. Still, when he pulled that trigger he committed suicide. If there's a moral dimension to his death, it starts and ends there."

"I take it you're saying you don't think there *was* a moral dimension," Benny said.

"Not insofar as it concerned him and me. I am what I am and he was what he was; if we replayed that scene a thousand times, it could only have one of two outcomes. Depending on whether he could kill me before I could clear my weapon." He looked at me. "There was no moral decision on my part. Both of his effective shots had hit me before I pulled the trigger. I would like to meet the person saintly enough not to kill under those conditions."

Benny poured himself another glass of wine. He was speeding up, which sometimes meant he was going to get funny.

"I follow your logic, but I don't think I would see it that way. Haven't you ever wondered about his family, for instance?"

"What about my family? My stepmother had a nervous breakdown. One of my line sisters said she'd never speak to me again if I didn't quit the Bureau. She hasn't.

"I don't even know if he had a family. I'm a policeman not a social worker." He pointed at the knife on Benny's belt. "That's no nail file. Doesn't wearing that declare your willingness to kill?"

"Not to myself. Maybe to a potential attacker—I never wore one until I got hit a couple of years ago. But it's just a bluff."

Hawkings smiled slightly. "You can't say that for sure until the next time you run into a hitter."

"I'll concede that. But I think I know myself." I resisted the impulse to point out that he'd just been trying to convince me that that was not possible.

"You should carry one, too," Jeff said to me. "Even if it's just for show. And you know enough fencing to help, if you did have to use it."

"I've got a can of Puke-O in my bag." I'd had it when I was raped, though. "Can't we talk about something more unpleasant?"

I did manage to steer the conversation to more mundane regions, and it moved into politics soon enough. Benny was very restrained, understandably, but Jeff was surprisingly critical of the government, even to the point of bitterness.

After about a half-hour we had to go on to class, leaving Benny with his wine. The freezing air was wonderful after the stuffiness in the bar, and a few flakes of snow whirled around in the traffic breeze.

"Are you always such a radical, out of uniform?"

He hunched his shoulders under the heavy cape. "Well . . . I was exaggerating a little. Trying to put him at ease. But the Bureau doesn't much care about an agent's politics so long as they're just opinions. I can't join any political groups, of course, not even a Lobby."

"Not even a Lobby? How can you vote?"

"You didn't know that?" He looked at me oddly. "We can't. Police and soldiers don't vote, except on local and nonpartisan referenda. Soldiers, not even those."

"But how can they do that?"

"Well, it's not the law, it's the mechanics. If you don't belong to a Lobby, you can't register approval or disapproval. At least I'm a resident citizen of New York, so I can vote on garbage collection and so forth. A soldier can never be a permanent resident of any state or city, no matter how long he lives there. He can make his opinions known in the annual census, but that's it. It's unfair, but I think the logic behind it is clear."

When I didn't say anything, he went on. "After a revolution, the people who get into power are pretty conscious of the forces that brought them there, and if they're smart, they'll do something to make sure the tables don't get turned. People's Capitalism, before the Second Revolution, mainly appealed to the lower middle class; you know about that."

I thought back. "Because of inflation. It gave them the same sort of safeguards that the upper classes enjoyed."

"That's right. And it's the lower-middles who run the military and the police forces. The people who *command* may belong to the upper classes, but their orders aren't worth anything if the sergeants and privates won't follow them."

We queued up for the Tenth Avenue slidewalk. "That's why it was such a short war. All the stirring rhetoric aside, Kowalski had all the guns, long before the Fourteenth of September. When the private soldiers and noncommissioned officers joined the general labor strike, it was all over. Even though it took a month for Washington to fall."

"So the Lobbies didn't want the same thing to happen to them; all right, I can see that." He took my elbow and we stepped on the 'walk together. "And I can see that disenfranchising the military would be a kind of insurance—but how could they get away with it?"

"It takes a close reading of the history of the first few months after the Revolution to see it. Watch for ice, here."

We moved to the right and stepped off; I slid a half-meter but kept my balance, with Jeff's help.

"That was a confusing time, anyhow. Step by step, the measures seem logical and innocuous—remember, the Lobby system didn't spring full-born from the forehead of Kowalski; there were some months of martial law, and then about a year of hybrid chaos.

"At first, it looked as if they were protecting the general public by not allowing the soldiers to unionize, which didn't seem so outrageous, since they hadn't been allowed to before. And they laid down an effective smokescreen by lionizing the military and police, and giving them liberal social benefits. It's still about the most secure job you can get.

"When the smoke cleared, though, we were a highly honored bunch of citizens who somehow couldn't find any appropriate column on the voting machine."

It was bright and warm inside the Russell building. We stopped alone in the foyer to brush off snow. "But you still have all the guns," I said.

Jeff smiled and put one finger to his lips.

27 ✦ Diary of an ex-spy

4 December.   Too brazen. Somebody got into my locked room today and left a note on my desk: Meet us at 8:00 p.m. Tues. usual place, tell B. ¶My nerves are about to snap. Ten days left in the quarter, papers and exams piling up, and now this. I quit.

5 December.   Lunch with Benny and told him I had had enough of James's bunch and was pulling out. He had some good suggestions. ¶Benny is in too deep to simply walk away. Not only the letters, but another thing he says he can't tell me about. He says that he's tempted to turn informer, go to the FBI with what he knows. But doesn't think he knows enough to make it worth the risk, especially if what we fear about Katherine is true (he didn't talk like this until we were out of the restaurant, walking through the park). ¶He says that if worse comes to worst, a friend of his has a small farm in South Carolina, where he could hide. Shave off his beard, get new papers, start over. I told him I thought he should do it now. I think they're capable of anything.

6 December.   The meeting went smoothly. I followed Benny's advice and tried not to let my anger or fear show. Very mundane: I was nearing the end of the quarter and ac-

ademic work has to take precedence; then I would be traveling for more than two months. I would use that time to "order my priorities" for the rest of the year. ¶That I'll be in and out of New York the third quarter, on field trips to various cities and states, didn't discourage James. He thought that might be useful.

7 December.   I have a feeling I shouldn't leave this cigarette-paper diary in storage with the rest of my things. If they can get into my room, they can get into my locker downstairs. I certainly can't take it with me, crossing dozens of borders. I was going to ask Benny to keep it for me, but decided he doesn't need any more trouble. I'll hide it in the library, back where they keep the old bound periodicals. *Time* magazine, 100 years before my birthday.

28 ✦ Get up and go

Surprise, Benny showed some common sense.

I turned in my last paper, comparing the evolution of Earthbound Devonites with those in orbit, and set about the serious business of enjoying New York for a few days. I met Benny at his apartment.

He'd finished up his classwork a few days earlier. When I went into his room I was surprised, and pleased, to see the drawing table unfolded, and several of his street scenes in a stack, matted and ready for display. On the board, he'd just started inking in a drawing of the old Flatiron Building, with sketches and flat photos of it pinned to the wall in front of the table.

I congratulated him on his industry and he mumbled something about taking my advice. It was hard to hold a natural conversation there, knowing that everything was being monitored by James or Will or the FBI or the landlord.

Outside, leaning into the wind as we hurried toward the subway, he explained: "If I do have to drop out of sight, I'll need money. Can't just buy a ticket to South Carolina and expect not to be followed. I can endure a certain amount of humiliation, to save my skin."

"You have a plan?"

"Several. Most likely, I'll leave all of my things here,

just take a book bag, go down to Penn and step on the tube to Los Angeles. Then go to Las Vegas by way of Denver. If I time it right, the whole thing will be less than two hours. In Vegas I can get a laundered identity for ten or twelve thousand bucks. Birth records, school, past employment; everything already inserted in some state's computers." I'd heard of that "service." There were thousands of nonexistent people in the United States, waiting for Nevada to supply them with bodies.

"The fingerprints won't match, of course, but I don't plan on getting in trouble with the law. And I won't have any credit identity, or any relatives. But that won't make much difference, where I'm going."

"You sound pretty sure you will be going."

"Seems likely." He put his arm around me. "Though I hate ... well, I'll be enrolling in the next quarter, but that's just to avert suspicion. Probably leave in a month or so."

"Leaving all your *books*?"

He nodded. "Everything. The rare books, I'll be mailing to my friend, two or three a week. I don't dare do anything that looks or sounds like packing."

"So you'll be gone by the time I get back?"

"Probably." We huddled together at the subway entrance. "Don't try to call or write. But if you can come, my friend's farm is on Route Five, Lancaster Mills. About ten kilometers outside of town. Perkins. But make sure you aren't followed; they'll be missing me by then."

"Route Five, Lancaster Mills, Perkins. I'll get there ... one of my field trips is to New Orleans; I can sneak away at the Atlanta interchange, on my way back."

"Good. Now, shall we try the museum?"

"Just tourists."

✦ ✦ ✦

We went to the Museum of Modern Art, where there was an exhibit of contemporary American drawings. Benny appreciated them, but most of them left me behind. Scrawls, thumbprints, inkblots, childish doodles. I guess my taste in art is like my tastes in music. Wrong century.

When I got home, there was a disturbing letter from Daniel:

Dear Marianne,

Although it would seem self-serving, I'm on the verge of asking you to cut short your year and head for the Cape while you can still get home. A very vocal minority is urging the Coordinators to pull up stakes, stop all shuttle service until the groundhogs come to their senses.

It's a complex situation. We do get a balance-of-payments benefit from allowing Earth tourism, but it isn't nearly as much as normal times, since we can't bring them up and back on top of the regular cargo.

There's no arguing the point that groundhogs who can afford vacations in orbit are the most powerful and influential Earth citizens. The argument is over what would happen if we did pull out—would the wealthy people tend to pressure the government into offering us a better deal? Or would the reaction be anger, "Let them stew in their own juices." The latter, I think, and I probably know groundhogs better than most.

One factor that influences the Coordinators toward moderation is the fact that you and a thousand other Worlds citizens would be stranded on Earth. (I think the actual total is about 800.) People are talking about boycotting for as long as five or even twenty years—withdrawing satellite power as well as transportation. The water situation is uncertain, but five years without imports wouldn't pose any great danger.

At any rate, the issue comes up for referendum next Sunday. I'm almost certain it will fail. (There's also the side issue of New New imposing its will on the other Worlds, implicitly, since most tourist traffic does go through here first. Devon's World would probably declare war—and come kill us with kindness.) Even if the issue were only political, I'd vote in favor of continuing negotiation. And the thought of you stuck there and me stuck here is just insupportable.

Years ago I read a story about a Swiss married couple. The husband had some medical problem, asthma or something, that required them to move into the mountains. Turned out the wife's heart wouldn't take the altitude. So she moved back into the valley and they spent the rest of their lives looking at each other through telescopes, waving. What a horrible thought.

John sends his love. We both talk about you all the time and look forward very much to your letters. I miss you terribly.

Love,
Dan

I did feel a rather strong pull orbitwards. Mainly because Benny was no replacement for Daniel (and John, for that matter). Second because I heartily wished I had never got mixed up with James's cabal, and would rather be forty thousand kilometers away than simply on the other side of the world. The possibility that shuttle service might be cut off ran a distant third.

I took news of the argument to Worlds Club after dinner, and for once I was the first one who had heard of it. Not the first one on Earth, though. Barry Rhodes called up the New New York Corporation at the Cape and found that only standby spaces were available from now until next Sunday.

"I'm tempted to go down there and wait," Claire Oswald said. "I don't fancy being a hostage here."

Some people mumbled agreement. The club chairman, Ian Carlson, shook his head and pronounced: "The thing to do is make a reservation for the week *after*. Then cancel it and make another, a week later. The referendum won't pass, this time." He lowered his voice. "But withdrawal is our only weapon against them. Next month, next year . . . it may become more and more likely."

I got an uncomfortable déjà vu feeling from that "our/them." Left one cabal to slip into another? Anti-Earth sentiment always ran high at Worlds Club meetings, but with an element of banter and self-effacement. Now, I could feel solidarity thickening around me. Us against them.

"I almost hate to bring it up," Sheryl Devon said, "but we're only looking at one side of the equation. What do you think the United States is going to do when they find out about the referendum? Applaud?"

"They wouldn't dare close the Cape," I said. "That's not U.S. soil. It would be an act of war."

"They wouldn't have to close it to cut off access," Ian said. "Just pass a law forbidding tourism to the Worlds."

"Turn our own weapon against us," Claire said. "Take the choice away while most Worlds people are still against withdrawal."

"It's against the New Bill of Rights," someone protested. "Article Six, Freedom of Travel."

I knew he was wrong on that. "No, the language of the article says 'state or foreign country.' New New York is neither, or at least they could so claim." That point had come up in Lobbies class. Nobody had ever tested the distinction in court, of course, since nobody had ever been forbidden access to the Worlds. "It wouldn't look good, though. The U.S. has made a lot of self-righteous noise about the restrictions other countries put on their citizens' traveling into orbit—"

Claire stood up, pale. "But they could call it coercion. Say we forced them into it."

"Say it was a temporary measure, until we came to our senses," Ian added.

There was a quiet chuckle and Dr. Wu, a white-haired

professor from Uchūden, primly hid a smile behind his hand. "Excuse me. You are not being realistic; you are not being sufficiently Machiavellian.

"You must realize that this conversation took place weeks or months ago? In the Privy Council of New New York? Decisions, that is to say, alternatives, are not put to referenda simply because of minority pressure. What your friend has written you, O'Hara, is the first visible move of a game that is more than half played. As the Lobbies must well know."

"Would you mind elaborating?" I said.

"Simply that the Privy Council and Coordinators have determined that this action will benefit New New York, no matter what the outcome of the referendum (though they must believe it will fail) and no matter what the States' response will be. Otherwise, they could have delayed the referendum until public opinion forced it onto the ballot."

"How could New New benefit from having the Cape closed down?" Ian asked.

"No doubt there are others wondering that tonight. I don't have the slightest idea," he said carefully, and then slowly looked from wall to wall. Total silence. It had never occurred to me that this meeting room might be bugged. Me, of all people. "And, excuse me, it is naive to think that the U.S. must pass a law to restrict tourism. At any rate, such a law would not apply to us.

"The reality is this: a state of embargo already does exist between the U.S. and the Worlds. It need only be extended to the Cape, which in the eyes of international law is part of New New York. The Cape does not manufacture its own deuterium. They buy it from U.S. Steel through a contract monitored by the American Energy Department. No fuel, no flights."

Claire's voice was shaking. "You mean the government of New New is willing to leave us all stranded here?"

"Possibly." Wu shrugged elaborately, an oriental marionette imitating an occidental gesture. "This is where we chose to be."

✦ ✦ ✦

Benny was waiting for me in my room; we had agreed that the dorm's lack of privacy was less unsettling than the ear under his bed. That I probably had one too was something we were aware of but no longer discussed.

I'd called him from the Liffey, and he had a fresh pot of tea waiting. I used a cup to thaw out my fingers and told him about the new developments.

" 'May you live in interesting times,' " he said. "Chinese curse."

"I feel more like cursing in American. *Damn* it. Of all the times to be going away."

"Where will you be Sunday?"

"London. That's Christmas Eve."

"At least you'll be able to follow the news."

"But I'll feel so isolated." I started pacing and slopped some tea on the rug. My first thought was that that was somebody else's problem; I only had the room for one more day. Feeling guilty, I got a washcloth and cleaned it up. "I feel isolated already," I said to the floor. "I won't know anybody in the class except Hawkings. And I can't really . . . talk to him." A tear surprised me. It fell on my hand still warm. I sniffed and wiped my eyes.

"Your period?" Benny said.

"I didn't know poets could count." I threw the cloth into the washbowl and looked at myself in the mirror. People with my color eyes shouldn't cry. They look revolting bloodshot. "That's not it. I'm a big girl, don't let hormones boss me around."

I stood behind him and massaged his shoulders. "I just wish . . . I wish I could go home for a week or two, I guess. You can't relax on this damned planet. Everything is so complicated."

He crossed his arms over his chest and took my hands. "I know something simple."

"You don't mind the period?" He'd made excuses last time.

"We'll make it an exclamation point." I pulled his hair for that and we wound up in a tickling match.

When I came back from the john, though, I was pretty much out of the mood, depressed again. But I worked hard at it, for Benny's sake. Besides, it's the second best thing for cramps.

29 ✦ Whom the gods would destroy, they first make sick

For hours I couldn't get to sleep. My mind was whirling; I couldn't stay on one worry for more than a few seconds, before another one would creep in.

I woke up choking. There was a puddle of sweat under my back.

"Benny!" I shook him, hard.

He came awake immediately. "What's wrong?"

"I—I don't know." I was panting, stuttering; it felt like I was being garotted. "Got, take me, infirmary." Sudden pang of nausea. I threw off the cover and staggered across the room to the washbowl. Vomited but no relief, retching. Benny draped his heavy coat over me and held my shoulders. I was trembling uncontrollably, going hot and cold in quick flashes. He turned on the light.

"We've got to get you dressed," he said quietly. I could hear him dressing himself, then gathering up my clothes from yesterday. The nausea abated a little. I washed out my mouth and tried to dress.

My knees buckled while I was getting into my jeans, and I fell halfway to the floor before Benny caught me. I couldn't do the buttons on my blouse, hands shaking so. Benny got them wrong but I wouldn't let him start over. A feeling of absolute dread growing: I was not going to make it to the infirmary. I was going to die.

We got my boots on and Benny waited outside the stall in the john while I shuddered through a few explosive moments of diarrhea. When we got outside, the cold air revived me a bit, and I leaned on Benny as we walked the two blocks to the Student Health Service. Halfway there, it all came back at once. I panicked and ran. Benny caught up with me and we lurched on together, his hand under my arm.

Then a blur: we got into the infirmary but I fell down while he was talking to the receptionist, they carried me behind a curtain and put me on a table, I tried to answer her questions but didn't make much sense, tried to keep my hands at my sides but they kept wandering in the air, finally my whole body was bucking in convulsions and a man came in and rolled me over and pulled down my jeans, I felt the cold hypodermic nozzle against my hip and a sharp sting when it went off. Then everything stopped, like a switch being thrown. I went limp. The man tucked my blouse back in and helped me roll over. "Rest for a while." I stared at the ceiling and reveled in the absence of symptoms, of desperation. What was it? Food poisoning? What had I eaten that Benny hadn't—the hot dog! On the street. Benny said they made them out of anything, carcasses of animals from the pound and the zoo. Spices covered any odd flavor. I kidded him about his weak stomach and said I liked the idea of eating hippopotamus. Not anymore. I sat up. I felt fine, just light-headed. Cotton in my ears. I watched the clock. I would look away for a long time and look back and only seconds had passed. I looked at all the bottles and instruments around the room and wished I had a book.

My hearing returned (or maybe I just started listening) and I realized there was a man in the area next to me, softly crying. Another man was talking to him very quietly. I felt sorry for their lack of privacy, only a draped sheet between us. I fidgeted, itching from the diarrhea, and wished this godforsaken planet had bathtubs. I unbuttoned my blouse and buttoned it up right. Got off the table and used a square of gauze to blow my nose, feeling vaguely guilty. We make hospitals into holy places and their appurtenances, icons. I dutifully got back on the table and the doctor came in.

"Are you feeling better?" She was a chilly-looking woman in her fifties, white hair pulled severely back over a permanent expression of disapproval.

"I feel fine. Was it food poisoning?"

"*Food* poisoning." She stuck a thermometer in my mouth and read it. "No, you had an acute anxiety attack. A small nervous breakdown. We've had a lot of them the past week. Aren't exams over?"

I nodded. It was all in my mind?

"You're worried about grades?"

"No ... it ... it's not school."

"Trouble with your parents? A man?"

"Partly. I guess that's it." No, actually, I'm afraid a group of wild-eyed revolutionaries is going to tie me down and force-feed me sleeping pills and booze. Then they'll kill Benny. Then the FBI will throw both our bodies in jail. Then the United States will blast the Worlds out of the sky. So what's new with you?

She rattled a bottle of pills that she had been holding out to me. I took it from her. "That tranquilizer you got will last a few hours. Take one of these before each meal, for the next month."

"Klonexine?" I read.

"It's a drug that inhibits the release of norepinephrine. Do you know what that is?"

"I was never strong in science."

"It's a hormone that, among other things, causes what happened to you, after a long period of stress. The pills will keep it from happening for a month. Do you fly?"

"No."

"Good. You shouldn't operate any vehicle, or participate in any dangerous sport, while you're taking Klonexine. Your body won't release adrenaline in case of danger. Otherwise, there are no side effects."

"Afterwards, when I stop taking it, will it come back again?"

"Usually not. If it does, I'll give you some more, schedule you for some—"

"But I'll be in Europe. Yugoslavia, I think."

She looked at me for a second and got another bottle out of a drawer. "Well, continue if you have to. But then we'll schedule some therapy when you get back, if you're still sick.

"Ultimately, you have to either adjust your personality so it will cope with the stress, or remove the sources of stress. Make up with your parents, ditch the boyfriend, whatever it is. If you take these pills for too long, a year or so, you'll never be able to function without them."

"I understand."

"Is there someone waiting for you?"

"Yes." She nodded and hurried out the door.

✦ ✦ ✦

Benny and I went back to my room and lay together for a few hours, talking quietly. I think the episode upset him almost as much as it did me. Not as deeply, though. Would I ever be able to trust my mind and my body again?

In the afternoon we walked aimlessly, down to the Village and back again. Benny tried to convince me not to worry—not because the troubles weren't worrisome, but because there was nothing to be gained by it—and he succeeded in some measure. We wound up in a flamenco club, watching the dancers and drinking brandy and coffee. That was probably a pharmaceutical mistake, since I'm not used to either, and I guess I was the most wide-awake drunk in the dorm that night. But it did bury the blues. Benny and I talked until early morning, mainly about the tour.

When I woke up he was dressed and putting on his coat. He said he hadn't wanted to wake me; he didn't like goodbyes. I hugged him close and whispered, "Route Five, Lancaster Mills, Perkins." He squeezed my arm and left without a word.

30 + 1,156 leagues
under the sea

The transatlantic tunnel is older than the U.S. system by some twenty years: slower, bumpier, noisier. It takes four hours to get from New York to Dover, and you learn not to let your tongue get between your teeth. I took the seat next to Jeff, but we gave up trying to talk after a few minutes. I was never so glad for hangover pills.

The train had a newspaper machine; I splurged on a complete (five-dollar) *New York Times*. Four hours was not enough time to read it all, even skipping sports.

Yesterday, while I was walking around in a numb haze with Benny, stocks worth ten billion dollars changed hands on Wall Street. Twenty people died in crimes of violence. The residents of Gramercy Park defeated a local referendum that would limit the size of personal pets. The Emir of Qatar and his entourage were scheduled to arrive on a state visit, coming by sea in a yacht that comprised half of the emirate's navy. Last-minute Christmas shoppers "thronged" the city (it was crowded enough unthronged; the population of Manhattan tripled every workday with commuters from all over the country). The "Entertainment" section listed 480 Stars in 48 different categories, ranked according to Gallup's daily poll. There was a birthday party for Major Tobias Klass, who at 142 was the oldest living veteran of the Vietnam war. Thirteen pages of referenda to be voted on in various localities. Advertisements covered exactly half of each page, and they were interesting, sometimes for their subtlety. They sponsored the only comic strips in the paper.

There was an interview with a broker who commuted daily between London and New York. She left her London residence at 8:45, caught the 9:00 tube at Dover, got into New York at 8:00, worked until 5:00, caught the 6:00 to Dover, which arrived at 3:00 a.m., allowing her five and a half solitary hours in London before starting over. She said she slept better on the tube than anywhere else, and it was cheaper than maintaining a separate residence in New York, appropriate to her social status. She couldn't find a decent flat for forty thousand a month?

The "Space" section had no mention of the upcoming referendum in New New. Maybe that had been covered in yesterday's edition. No editorials, either, which seemed strange. The Times was the most Worlds-aware paper in the city, maybe in the country. They did note that there was a face-to-face meeting between New New's Coordinators and the Church Council of Devon's World, the first such meeting in over a decade.

Every establishment on Broadway had a display ad in the "Classified" section. They were marvels of euphemism and double entendre. The individual "personals" were interesting, too: will psychoanalyze your cat, trade boxing gloves & equipment for books, seek male or female for Legendre triune, must be under twenty-five and broadminded; secrets of the universe revealed, fifty dollars, satisfaction guaranteed; make big money on your phone/ stuffing envelopes/in your spare time/and save your fellow men from themselves.

I had to admit that New York was a world more complex and exciting than all the Worlds rolled together. In the three months since I stepped out of Penn Station I hadn't gone more than twenty kilometers in any direction, but I'd done more and had more done to me than in twenty-one years in New New. (Actually, it may have been more than twenty kilometers when Benny and I took the floater up above the city. It looked so peaceful, a medieval vision of the Heavenly City, with all of the graceful post-Worlds skyscrapers seeming to float on the top of the cloud. What does it do to a person's outlook to live or work surrounded by that scene?) It occurred to me that this whirlwind tour might actually be a relaxing change, if I kept the right attitude.

It didn't start out relaxing. The Dover terminus was as big and crowded as Penn Station, with the same sort of determined mindless bustle, like a hive of frenzied insects each bent on his own mysterious assignment. We stood in a stationary knot around our luggage while the tour director went off to find somebody.

"Almost makes you homesick," Jeff said. Depends on where home is. The population density of New New is higher than any Earth city's, but you never see so many in one place. I'd gotten used to it in New York, and was ready for it in London, but wanted the rest of England to be slow-paced and, well, dignified.

The director came back and led us down a long slidewalk to the Bank of England, where we made credit arrangements and were issued Temporary Alien blinker cards. At least that was a touch of home; Britain had advanced beyond currency and coins.

Since our passports and luggage had been stamped and inspected aboard the train, we were free to be herded away. We went up three long escalators and stepped out into the night. (It was two in the afternoon, New York time; seven here.) It was very still, not too cold, and a light snow was falling. We filed down a dry raised sidewalk to where a bus, omnibus, was waiting. It was an eight-wheeled double-deck vehicle with a disconcerting number of dents, but brightly polished.

Dover's famous "white cliffs" were behind us, which didn't make much difference, since it was too dark to see anything beyond the parking-lot lights. We got aboard and drove through a couple of blocks of nondescript modern buildings, and then out into the countryside, which was probably very picturesque, but unfortunately was not visible. All we could see was a pool of light on the road and vague shadows on either side.

After a few minutes we turned into a driveway and slowly crawled up a hill. The road had a couple of centimeters of snow on it and, from the crunching sound, seemed to be only gravel underneath. A large old house sat on top of the hill, yellow light streaming out of small windows on the ground floor. It was made of stone, covered with dead ivy, and the guide said it had been used as an inn for nearly three hundred years.

Our hostess, a florid fat woman, met us at the door and silently counted the people as they filed in. We were given a packet of information and a bed number; women to the right, men to the left.

Our dormitory was a huge room with, I think, the highest ceilings I'd ever seen. Bunk beds along one wall, two footlockers across from each bed, linen folded neatly on each footlocker. It was cold and drafty.

I was first one into the john, and made a delightful discovery: a bathtub! It was in a little closet separate from the toilets, with a sign-up sheet on the door. There was nobody signed up for the next half-hour (only four women in the room before we invaded), so I put down my name and went back to the footlocker for a towel.

I locked the closet door and slid the blinker card into the paybox, two pounds for thirty minutes. About twenty dollars. I would have paid ten times that. The faucet coughed and began to splash hot water into the plastic tub. Slightly brown water, but it made a great cloud of steam. I undressed and stood in the water while the tub filled, loving the moist heat rising. When it was deep enough I sat into the delicious sting and leaned back. The water shut off and I lay there like a dormant reptile for half an hour. I'd brought the travel packet in but couldn't get up the motivation to reach for it. The tub started to drain and somebody knocked.

She started the tub while I was dressing—close quarters—and it turned out we were the same sort of outlanders, in a sense, as she'd come to New York from a farm in Kansas, and was also used to baths rather than showers.

Something was nagging at me. It would catch up in a few hours.

There were only a few people in the dormitory room. Most of them were on the back porch, smoking and talking. I would have joined them, for the talk, but didn't want to go outside with wet hair. The woman on the bunk next to mine asked whether I played chess; we hauled a footlocker between the beds and set up a board. She was good and I hadn't played in years; the end game resembled Pearl Harbor.

Her name was Violet Brooks and I liked the apologetic way she enveloped my troops and destroyed them. She was an undergraduate, a senior from Nevada. I was curious about that state but she didn't want to talk too much about it. Said it wasn't as bad as most people said, but she was never going back. No taste for anarchy. Not many jobs for English majors, either.

We went into the "common" room, which was warmer and had tea and coffee, and leafed through our information packets. Violet had been to England once before, as a girl, when her mother had brought her along on a business trip. But she had only seen London, and claimed a week was scarcely enough to hit a few high points. We had eight days for the whole country.

Jeff came in with a number of other men, all covered with snow and slightly redolent of brandy. They stood around the stove that was keeping the urns warm, talking loudly and joking. The hostess stuck her head in and gave them a dour look.

They had been engaged in snow sculpture. Violet and I stepped outside for a few seconds to view their handiwork. It looked like a cross between a fat woman and a mountain of snow. They called it "the Venus of Dover."

Violet and I, it turned out, were the only students along who were not citizens of the United States. So we were free to take a side trip into the Supreme Socialist Union, which would not admit Americans. We decided to look into it—China, at least, was a fascinating prospect—though I suspected it would be too expensive. (Violet had plenty of money; her mother ran a bordello.) No need to decide until February.

They had delayed dinner until ten, for our transatlantic stomachs, which made it only a couple of hours early. Bangers and mash, an authentic English meal, bland sausage with mashed potatoes. I didn't mind it, but Jeff said he finally understood why the British had roamed the seas to forge an Empire: they were in search of a decent meal.

A few warm beers afterward, and some excited talk about going into London tomorrow, and I went off to bed.

Lying on the hard mattress, under a heavy quilt, I started sweating although I wasn't particularly hot. Then dizziness and a sudden feeling of rootless horror—and I realized I'd forgotten to take the pill. The Klonexine from lunch had worn off.

I got the bottle from my bag and rushed into the john and washed down a pill. Then I sat in one of the stalls, sweating, teeth chattering, waiting for it to take effect.

I felt like crying out, or just crying, but managed to keep my jaws shut. And think, after a fashion.

I may have made a dreadful mistake. Lulled by the drug. I wasn't escaping anything, going east, just postponing trouble. I should have gone up instead. This world was no place for anyone with access to another. I should be down at the Cape, waiting for a seat. Going back to Daniel, to peace. Leaving this desperate planet to work out its own fate.

The pill did its magic, corralling all of the norawhatzis into a safe place. I could almost talk myself back down. I had pretty well cut myself off from James and his group. Benny was resourceful. The Cape would be there when I got back. I got very sleepy. The sheet was damp and cold, but I lay very still and it warmed under me.

I dreamed a montage: Benny held down and forced to take pills, my pills. Jacob's Ladder coming down, hitting New York. Violet looking at me with James's glass eyes. Jeff tying me up with padded ropes, naked, rampant.

31 ✦ London bridge

When we got off the tube in London I was set to immerse
myself in History and Culture—but the first sight was a
weird combination of anatomy and abnormal psychology.
The Lambs of the Eternal Eye.

There were about a dozen Lambs in a line, begging, as
we got off the train. They wore saffron robes and made soft
music with finger-cymbals and sticks. Their skulls had
been surgically removed from the eyebrows up, replaced
with clear plastic, a sight presumably more pleasing to
God's eye than to mine.

They had stationed themselves wisely, as their tin
plate full of foreign coins and currency showed. A blinker-
card economy is hard on beggars; they had to get to
foreigners before the Bank of England did, or on their way
home.

One of them carried a sign saying THE BRITISH RAIL SYS-
TEM DOES NOT ENDORSE THIS ACTIVITY.

London taxis have human drivers. Eight of us squeezed
into a cavernous black vehicle; Jeff told him the name of our
hotel. We emerged from underground into bright morning
sunlight and blue sky—garish after months of New York's
perpetual cloud.

The driver had an impenetrable accent (Cockney, I
later learned), and chattered constantly. We drove down

the Thames and sped by Parliament, Westminster Abbey, Buckingham Palace, Hyde Park—the Albert Memorial was almost majestic in its ugliness—and finally down into Kensington, where our hotel was. One man was trying to follow our progress on a map, and remarked that we were being taken for a ride in American idiom as well as British fact. I think the driver said this was the fastest route for this time of day.

When we got to the hotel and it was time to pay, I had to take over, as the only one used to blinker cards. The bill was twenty-one pounds; I tipped him three pounds, more for easy arithmetic than service. Inserted my card and punched it up, then passed my card around while the driver unloaded the luggage, telling everybody to punch three pounds, put the obvious end of their card into the obvious end of my card (all very sexy) and push the NOCODE button. One person gave me thirty pounds by mistake, and it took a while to sort that out.

The other two cabloads of people were already there, but presumably had not had as comprehensive a tour. The rooms had been arranged for in advance, but who was with whom had not been. Mr. Eppingworth, our director, noted that we had thirteen women and eleven men, and all of the rooms were doubles, and rather primly asked whether there were a lady and gentleman who would not mind? I thought about Jeff, maybe hesitating because of last night's dream, but another couple shot their hands up with the speed of lust. Jeff had glanced my way, not too surreptitiously, and that set off an obvious chain of thought:

I liked Jeff, but was more in need of a friend right now than a lover. He was too American to be athletically casual about sex; it would make him protective and intimate—and most of what bothered me, and I would like to talk out, were not the sort of things one would say to an FBI man, not even over a pillow. No matter how open-minded and thoughtful he seemed to be.

I could go ten weeks without the services of a man. Or

maybe one of the others would turn out to have a suitably casual attitude—or maybe one of the women? The thought surprised me. My two such experiences, on Devon's World, had not been pleasant, but then those people were *weird,* the women even more than the men. I needed arms and shoulders now, more than any other part, and women had as many of those as men, and had a more reasonable attitude toward tears.

I broke out of reverie in time to hear the last part of Mr. Eppingworth's warning about gambling. The lobby of the hotel, and its pub, had slot machines that could suck all of the credit out of your blinker card in minutes. If we had to try them, be sure the rate selector stayed at the ten-shilling mark. That reminded me, I'd have to study the monetary system again. I'd glanced at it, and remembered a pound was about ten dollars, but I didn't know a shilling from a doubloon from a pelican.

Violet and I chose each other for roommates; we had a half-hour to settle into our rooms before we met the tour bus outside. They were going to orient us to the city and then set us more or less free.

Violet set her suitcase in one corner and opened the drapes. The room was small and old—probably older than New New, it struck me—but neat and freshly painted. She bounced experimentally on the edge of one of the beds; it was some kind of old-fashioned design, with springs of metal.

"Bet you wish I was that blond chunk," she said, smiling.

"The big one? Jeff?" I sat down on the other bed.

"I saw you looking at him."

"He's a nice man. We had a class together last quarter .. and we've gone out a few times, dinner, sports. Nothing romantic."

"Not interested?"

I lay back on the bed. "I'm not sure. I don't want to get into anything complicated."

"Line obligation?"

"No, just another man. Maybe two. The only thing I've decided about my line is that I'd die a virgin before I'd join my mother's."

"Me, too," she said emphatically. "Brooks women never get anywhere. Too late for me to die a virgin, though, thank God."

"Figure of speech. You want me to introduce you to Jeff?"

"Too big." Violet was more than a head shorter than me. "I'd have to stand on a chair. But he is sort of fascinating."

"You'd make quite a couple. A federal policeman with the daughter of—"

"He's a cop? FBI cop?"

"That's another thing that makes it complicated."

"Oh, I see. You don't want to tell him about all of that dope smuggling."

I studied my nails. "Murder for hire, actually. I don't think he would approve."

She laughed. "Want to go downstairs and get something to drink? It'll probably be a long ride." Good idea.

We shared a pot of tea and our life stories, compressed. Her mother had bridled against the male-dominated Brooks line, but couldn't legally be separated from it under Massachusetts law, her husband-of-record having given no grounds for divorce. So she took her infant daughter and ran away to Nevada, where she capitalized on her beauty and skill, and became a successful courtesan (the highest evaluation conferred there by the Guild of Working Women). She did that for eight or nine years, investing her income wisely, and bought her own bordello in Las Vegas. Violet—named for the color of her eyes when she was born; they were deep black now—went to boarding schools in New England and rarely visited Nevada, since the child of any rich person was too tempting a target for kidnappers. Whose profession was not illegal there. Nothing was.

She was worldly and intelligent but also deeply troubled, at some depth she didn't have access to. She worshiped her mother but rarely saw her. She had never met her father, and "wouldn't walk around the block" to do so, which was something we had in common.

She painted and wrote poetry (and knew Benny's name) and didn't have the faintest idea of what she was going to do after school. She respected her mother's profession but didn't want to pursue it. She was majoring in English out of love for it, but didn't want to teach.

She said she envied me my ambitiousness.

The bus tour was an extended version of the cab ride, whisking us from place to place as fast as the traffic would allow. I guess the theory was that we should at least see the outside of everything. We did have a lovely lunch at a place called the Prospect of Whitby, a pub on the Thames that dates back to the Tudors. Five centuries.

It was more tiring than I would have thought; sitting, listening, and watching for eight hours. But it was fascinating. We even got to see King George, at quite a distance, as he was dedicating some public building. I'd seen him ten years before, when he passed through New New on his way to the Moon.

When we got back to the hotel, Violet and I decided to combine a little exploring with dinner, so we set off down Brompton Road in search of a reasonable place to eat. Wrong road. After we'd looked in a dozen or so windows and rejected the posted menus I felt I was imposing on her, since she didn't have to economize, and I told her I didn't want to feel responsible for her starving to death. But Violet said she'd planned to eat frugally, too, so she could spend on other things. Ten cheap meals in London would buy a nice dress in Paris.

We finally came across a street vendor with sandwiches and ale, which we consumed on the way back to the hotel (he also gave us friendly advice about restaurants; we should have gone north instead of south). A cold drizzle started, but we had been warned, and put on plastic capes and hats.

It was a lot different from walking the streets of New York. The traffic was heavier and faster. Berserk, that is to say. Evidently there were no robot vehicles, and driving was a competitive sport; pedestrians were obstacles thrown in to make the game more interesting.

But on the sidewalks and in the shops, the pace was slower and more polite than in America. No sense of being in the middle of a beehive. Kensington was mostly residential, though.

The police were of both genders, wore no armor, and appeared to be unarmed. There were hitters, we'd been told, but they were rather rare. London proper had only one-fourth New York's rate of violent crime. ("London proper" doesn't include East End, which is a walled-off lawless section run by a bunch of hooligans who call themselves the National Front.)

We picked up a bottle of madeira, against the chill, and went back up to our room to put up our feet and see what cube was like in England. Their major networks are also owned by the government, but the programming seemed more intelligent, and the commercials more witty and straightforward, not scary appeals to the subconscious.

Neither of us had had madeira before, sweet and strong. We drank the whole bottle and passed quickly from giddiness to sleepiness. We wound up sleeping together, innocently, like girls. I woke up at dawn with her naked body warm against me, and though it felt nice I was vaguely disturbed by the lesbian-ness of it, and managed to disentangle myself without waking her. I drank about a liter of water, which was a mistake, but did find the hangover pills, and left them out for Violet. Then crawled into the cold bed and waited for the dizziness to subside.

Violet wanted to spend the day visiting literary landmarks, and I tagged along, though I don't know too much about English literature (I would have, if I'd taken a full certificate in American Lit).

Dickens's house was fascinating because it was full of nineteenth-century memorabilia, and quite a bit of it was about America. Dickens had nothing but contempt for the young country, but he evidently wasn't averse to taking their money, giving readings. From there we went to Dickens's favorite pub and had a couple of literary pints, getting a start on tomorrow's hangover.

Samuel Johnson's house was a couple of hundred years older, the wooden steps worn round by centuries of trudging tourists, but it was more like a museum. Hard to be properly awed when I've never read anything of the gentleman's work. (Our guidebook was enthusiastic about *his* pub as well as Dickens's, a "chophouse" that had been in continuous use since 1667. But it was lunchtime, and the place was so crowded we literally couldn't get near it, a knot of beer-drinkers filling the alley in front of its door.)

The morning was bright and unseasonably warm, but the afternoon compensated with sleet and bitter wind. We decided it would be a good policy to spend the rest of the day indoors, and went back toward Kensington to wander through the Victoria and Albert Museum. We split up there, since Violet wanted to study the paintings and I wanted to spend a couple of hours with their marvelous collection of antique musical instruments. They were all functional, and you could listen with earclips to period music being played on them.

I was engrossed in a basset horn (which looks like a clarinet assembled by a cubist maniac, and sounds like a bad cold) and jumped when someone tapped me on the shoulder. It was Jeff Hawkings.

"Jeff! You scared me."

"I'm sorry," he said quickly. "You're the first person I know I've seen all day."

"What've you been doing?"

"Walking, riding the tube. Saw Scotland Yard. Waited in line for the Tower, but it got too cold." He shook his head. "There's so much . . . how about you?"

I gave him a quick summary of our literary day. "Sounds interesting," he said, smiling. "Have any plans for dinner?"

Violet and I were going to an Indian restaurant the sandwich vendor had recommended. He asked whether he and a friend could come along. I said sure, but for some reason thought the friend would be female, and felt a little twinge of disappointment, maybe jealousy.

The friend was male, and obviously brought along for symmetry, with Violet. At the time, I was amused, and a little flattered.

Looking back. What if I'd been in a different mood, and been annoyed by Jeff's directness? What if he hadn't gone to the museum, or hadn't signed up for the tour course, or hadn't gone to the University, or hadn't been born? Life would have been simpler, though I would certainly be dead.

32 ✦ Diary of a traveler (excerpts)

23 December. . . . the curry was pretty much like home, except for a side dish of vegetables, which didn't seem spicy at all, at first, and then ignited a few minutes later. Quenched it with a lot of beer and bread. Have to watch that; up to 52 kg. yesterday.

Worked off a few grams dancing. We went with Jeff and Manny to a place called the Denatured Alco-Hall, a dance hall in East Kensington. It was a big round room, garishly lit, with tables and chairs jumbled around a wooden dance floor. They were doing the Mash, this month's dance (fashions change more slowly here than in N.Y.). It's done in a circle, with no bodily contact other than hand-holding, but a rather complicated step that looks like the Big Apple we saw in Entertainment. The music was a half-century off, though, Beatles.

I would have preferred that Jeff hold more than a hand—in fact, by the end of the evening I felt like a bunny bitch in heat. Must have been the curry.

He seemed more interested in Violet, anyway, maybe not because of the reputation Nevada women have. If he were Worlds I would have asked him straight out and politely dragged him back to the room, ask Violet to knock loud and wait. But not here.

Just as well. I don't need yet another man complicating my life. (Why can't groundhogs see that it doesn't *have* to be complicated? Some of them can, I guess, but not Jeff. He's serious about everything. Strong, cool. Maybe smoldering. Wonder if anything will happen between him and Violet.)

Violet and I agreed this morning that it was a little cold to be sleeping in our skins, so we bought pajamas while we were wandering. Tonight she dressed with her back to me and slipped immediately under the covers. She's obviously bothered by last night. We were both pretty drunk; maybe she thinks something happened and she doesn't remember. Have to find some innocuous way to reassure her.

But god, I don't want to sleep alone tonight. I'm sitting here alone in the john, writing and fighting back tears for no reason. I'm going to take another Klonexine.

24 December.   What a wonderful place this is to be, on Christmas Eve. It snowed heavily all day, and if you squint a little you can be back in the nineteenth century, or the twelfth. Most of us went to Albert Hall, where a man portraying Dickens read a Christmas story. It was curiously moving, wistful. I would be glad to take religion if you could turn it off and on at will.

Jeff caught me completely off guard by giving me a present. It wasn't very fancy, a realtime currency converter (I'd seen his and admired it), but it threw me into a real dither. He rescued me by saying he knew my line didn't celebrate the holiday, and he didn't expect anything in return, except maybe a holiday kiss.

It was a casual, cousinly kiss, but I think we were reading each other furiously.

He didn't give anything to Violet.

25 December.   Stayed up late last night, watching the cube with the sound turned down to a whisper. The mid-

night news confirmed that the New New referendum had been defeated soundly, and there was no word of reaction from the Lobbies. But Congress won't be in session today.

Stonehenge was truly weird. I didn't really follow all the astronomical explanations, about why they lined it up the way they did, but it's marvelous that it was built at all, by prehistoric men. Some of the huge rocks were dragged from as far away as Wales.

We also saw the remnants of a Roman road, but it was not even 2,000 years old. Built yesterday.

Spent the afternoon in Bath, which was interesting. The town itself is beautiful, with an impressive cathedral and so forth, but the main attraction is the baths, both of them. They have the historic bath, that goes back to the eighth century B.C. (King Lear's father supposedly took a cure there) and is made over into a museum, and the Disney bath outside of town, which is a reconstruction of the Roman facility, lead-lined hot and cold pools surrounded by elegant tilework and sculpture.

Nudism strikes me as un-British, but it's part of the bath's attraction. All very homey to me, of course, but some of our group found other things to do. Jeff and Manny joined me and Violet, and it was a nice lazy time. Jeff does look startlingly like Charlie, except in penile particulars (I've never been able to look at an elephant without thinking of Charlie). Both Jeff and Manny were circumcised, something I'd seen only among Devon's World tourists. Manny is Jewish, but I wonder what Jeff's reason is.

Violet is spectacularly endowed and she moves pretty well when men are watching. Jeff and Manny got into the water fast, obviously to immerse their salutes. Pity.

(I'd like to be a man for a day so I could figure out their odd behavior. Erection is just an attractive reflex, but it dominates them so. Maybe it drains the blood out of their brains.)

The others ran from the hot bath to splash into the cold one, but that's a form of masochism I've never been able to understand. The dressing rooms were segregated; Violet and I sat under the hair dryers and discussed the two men. She likes Manny and I thought it was mutual. I told her I'd be glad to get lost for the evening, if she'd like to have the room, but look what happened.

On the floater back to London, Violet whispered something to Manny, then Manny whispered something to Jeff, then Jeff whispered something to Violet, and I was starting to feel really excluded, then Jeff brought the whispering over to me. He said that Violet and Manny wanted to spend the night together, and would I mind taking the other bed in his room.

Well, it was time to strike, of course. I told him I would very much mind taking the other bed, but could be cajoled into his own. He laughed, relieved, and said something about making the floater speed up.

He was really remarkable. A totally different person in bed, very warm and passionate and unselfconscious. And he has recuperative powers like Charlie's. We made love twice and went out for dinner, then came back and had each other for dessert. Then the goat poked me awake sometime after midnight (actually, that was a nice dreamy time; I don't think either of us was completely awake—succubus and incubus). It was a merry Christmas (written 26 Dec.).

26 December.   Jeff and I went to the Palace of Westminster to see Parliament in action. There was not too much action, really, since most of the members were on vacation.

We watched a debate in the House of Lords from the "Strangers' Gallery." They were discussing a bill that the House of Commons had passed, regarding standards of analysis for the regulation of dairy products. One Lord denounced the bill very eloquently and bitterly. Another asked him how many dairy cattle he owned; he admitted it was something over two thousand head. For some reason I had this outrageous vision of two thousand cows loose in the park, in New New.

I have to admit I was a little repelled by the obvious accumulation of wealth and power in the House of Lords. It seemed to me to epitomize the philosophical gulf between Earth governments and the administration of New New. No one needs that kind of wealth. No one who loves power should be allowed to administer to the will of the people.

But at least it's displayed openly here. The people who rule the United States do it behind the closed doors of board rooms.

Jeff is a changed man. Well, not changed, really; it's just that he wasn't truly himself all last quarter. He was grinding hard at school and working overtime every week, to accumulate leave. Also, he had been in love with a woman, proposed marriage and was rejected, about a week before I first met him. When he kissed me Christmas Eve it was the first physical contact he'd had with a woman since August.

We had a long and earnest talk in a Westminster pub. I told him all about Daniel, and how I felt about sex and affection. It looks safe. Right now he also needs a friend rather than a lover.

We went back to the hotel and sealed our bargain. I asked him about the circumcision, and he said it was a line tradition. A man's first son is circumcised; only first sons are eligible for membership in the elders' council—if they stay in the line long enough to be an elder. I told him I wouldn't stay in any line that chopped off a piece of my body when I was too young to have a say in the matter. He shrugged that off, and pointed out (speaking of barbarism) that at least he had never undergone voluntary mutilation, such as having his ears pierced.

I didn't pursue the argument, since I've never had a foreskin that didn't belong to someone else, and also didn't mention what I thought about a line that only allowed men to be leaders, though I suppose he knows me well enough to know what I'd say about that.

There is the obvious problem, that I'm not going to write down. I'll be careful.

(27 December–30 December: Stratford-on-Avon, Scotland, Wales, York and the Yorkshire Moors, Killarney, Limerick)

30 December.   . . . that it's easy to understand why John was so impressed by the Irish countryside. Even in midwinter it's beautiful; I'd love to see it in the spring.

We haven't seen much of Dublin except for the zoo, which is unforgettable. The regular part of it is impressive, more variety than the Bronx one, with the animals in environments that resemble their native habitats. But it's the O'Connor Laboratory exhibit that draws people from all over the world.

Research in genetic manipulation is legal in Ireland (though not on humans), and the O'Connor people have set up a display in the zoo to help finance their work. The ticket was fifty pounds, with student discount.

The ant is the thing that stays with me the most. It was the size of a dog, nearly a meter long. Swimming around mysteriously in a tank of pale blue fluid (it had to float, they explained, because its legs would not support its weight in gravity). There was a goat with two heads, with her two-headed kid. A hairless chimpanzee that looked like a grotesquely malformed old man. Dwarf bats like ugly little moths. There was a shrew that seemed normal but had been alive for fifteen years, ten times its normal life span. . . .

31 December.   If London is the place to spend Christmas, there's no place like Dublin for New Year's Eve. Oops, I should have labeled that January 1st. It's 2:30 a.m., and I am trying to control my handwriting here, after ten or twelve pints of good Guinness and one glass of

champagne, writing in a brightly lit hotel room with Mr.
Jeffrey Hawkings slung sideways over the only bed, snoring
like a dragon.

John never told me about writing your initials. You can
take your finger and write your initials on the top of the
foam on a glass of Guinness, and the letters just stay there
all the while. While you drink it down. Real Guinness, that
is to say, that you can only get here. Good thing I don't live
here, I'd weigh 100 kg. by now. Jeff was a little silly about
all the stout I consumed. In America, heroic beer consump-
tion is a male preserve. Ha! Who's awake, Jeffrey? Score
one for the slits.

Must watch the language. These Irish are wonderful
friendly people but they expect ladies, lie-dees, to be sort of
polite and nice. Maybe I shouldn't have sung the one about
the jolly tinker. Most of them knew it, though.

Girl, you are drunk. Will take a hangover pill and leave
the bottle in easy reach. Push Jeff on the floor. No, just lie
crossways over him. I could sleep on a fence.

2 January.   . . . after the basic tour, Jeff went off to visit
the headquarters of Interpol, the European equivalent of
the FBI (combined with the CIB, I guess). Violet speaks
some French, so I stuck with her.

Going from Dublin to Paris is almost as big a jolt as
going from the Worlds to the Earth. Not even considering
the language difference. Ireland is much like New New, as
John had said, in its pace of life, the automatically expected
friendliness and sharing. France, or at least Paris, seems
even more tense and fast-moving than New York City. (I
understand this quality is a modern one, of which old folks
disapprove.)

One thing was like Dublin, though. Violet has a hyper-
trophied sense of the macabre: just as she had to drag us to
St. Michan's there, here we had to go to the Catacombs. It
was good theatre; there's no lighting in the underground
tombs, and they give you a candle with your ticket. The

bones of six million people, ugh. Death is such an insult. . . .

French cooking is delicious but the restaurants are so expensive. As advised, we'll be snacking on bread, cheese, and wine in our rooms in the morning and evening, with just one meal out (if it were warmer we could take our bread, etc., out to one of the parks, which would be a homey touch—the parks are beautiful anyhow, in the snow).

The wine here isn't as good as American, not at the prices we can afford, but the bread and cheese are marvelous. I guess a girl who grew up on good goat cheese couldn't be expected to like the bland rubbery insult that passes for cheese in America. Here even the cow cheeses are good, and there are hundreds of different kinds. . . .

Jeff is totally romanced by the city, and I have to admit I wouldn't mind staying longer myself. A month or two would be nice.

(I wish he wouldn't let the romance go directly to his groin. He dragged me away from a perfectly good conversation tonight. Well, I could have said no. I like the attention. I like not having to be a therapist. It makes me feel like a girl again, with Charlie, all free and atavistic.

Is he still making up for lost time, I wonder? I swear he was born with an extra bone in his body, retractable.)

Picked up mail at AmEx. Several letters from John and Daniel and an incomprehensible poem from Benny. Not particularly good. No letter with it.

(3–4 January: Paris, Lyon, Nice)

5 January.   . . . I can't stop staring at the mountains. They loom on all sides, bigger than Paphos. Paphos would get lost in the snowdrifts between them.

The city itself is fascinating, though. The original Grenoble was completely destroyed in a "meltdown," back in the fission days. They didn't start rebuilding until twelve years ago, so the city is thoroughly modern, and preplanned down to the last centimeter. John would love it, all foam-steel and composites, graceful the way most Worlds architecture is. I think it's the first time since we came to Europe that I've been out of sight of some big grey cathedral.

Sad monument to the east, though. A perfectly round lake of black glass, still slightly radioactive. Over a hundred thousand dead.

Jeff took Violet skiing this afternoon. I might have gone along to give it a try, but they said there was no real provision for beginners here, and I don't want to finish seeing the world bound up in a body cast. The Klonexine wouldn't make it any safer, either.

So I wandered around town until the cold got to me, then set up camp in this coffeehouse to write letters. Daniel, John, Benny, and even a note to Mother.

I didn't mention Jeff to either John or Daniel. It was easy to talk to Daniel about Benny, since I knew he wouldn't feel threatened. Jeff might arouse some primal groundhog instinct in him. As if I could fall in love with a mudball cop.

6 January.   Last day in France, good to be back in Paris. It was a slightly cold day but no wind and lots of sun; too nice to stay indoors. Violet and Manny spent all day in the Louvre, but Jeff and I walked until dark, from Montmartre to the heliport and back down the Seine to the pension. Then rubbed each other's feet for a while. His are big and ugly and mine are getting there.

(Seriously, all of this walking is changing my shape. My slacks are getting looser around the middle and tighter around the thighs. Will have to take care that it doesn't turn to fat when I get back to 0.8 gee. Maybe give up handball for track.) (Back to 50 kg. tonight.)

Jeff and I split the cost of a European-language translator. It's a four-language box that has a large vocabulary but no grammar other than the sequence of words spoken, which can lead to accidental humor on both sides. But they're in common enough use that nobody has trouble understanding them. We got it for less than half price, from an English tourist at the heliport; presumably, we'll pass it on when we leave Europe.

We saw so much today. Better go find the map before I try to write it all down. . . .

33 ✦ Coda (code)

Once On It

At rest from thinking every day of you
(The rearmost poet of this weary age),
Regretting words I never can undo:
Aye! Never can undo this only page.

I don't miss you more than I'd miss breath
(Since breath's a ware that doesn't keep so well),
I'd rather conjure love to you than death:
Skin, though live, is covered with dead cells.

Since skin keeps coming back to stalk my mind
(I'll think of other organs by and by),
Please forgive the way this poem's designed:
The poet's got a skinny word supply.

Keep this letter as you travel on
(Crafting second letter after dawn),

—Benny

34 ✦ Try calling on the World for peace of mind

Nothing in Madrid prepared us for Nerja. Madrid was cold and just had normal city bustle; not many tourists this time of year. Nerja was sunwarmed and paved with tourists. (And the tour took us here because it was far less crowded than Málaga or Torremolinos.)

Not too many Spaniards, it seemed. Most of the chatter sounded Scandinavian when it wasn't English. Our language machine made interesting noises when we tried to eavesdrop.

I was impatient to get into the ocean, since it had been too cold for swimming at Nice. But first I had to rent a "bathing suit," contradiction in terms. A couple of bright scraps of cloth that barely hide nipples and genitals. I never felt so naked bathing at home. But it is erotic, in an adolescent, peekaboo way.

The water was rather cold but it was all right once you got numb. Jeff gamely stayed out with me for a few minutes, but when his teeth started audibly clattering I sent him back to the beach.

Salt water tastes interesting and its density makes you

feel buoyant. But it's hard to swim well when you're trussed up like something out of a Devonite fantasy. I tired pretty rapidly and joined Jeff on the beach. He toweled me dry and we lay down on the sand, wedged between two parties of Germans. You could have walked from one horizon to the other without stepping off human flesh.

"You look good in that," he said. "Especially wet."

I'd noticed the difference. "Feel like an ad for a Broadway parlor. I'll be scraping off eyetracks all night."

"Wish I could help." The hostel we were staying at was divided into male and female dormitories.

The wind shifted and we got a whiff of the Mediterranean, beyond the pollution boundary. That was some electromagnetic barrier a kilometer or so out. Our translator renders the Spanish term as "wall of shit," which is sort of an awesome image. I buried my nose in the towel.

We fell asleep and got toasted pretty well. Jeff woke me and we took a quick splash. The damned bathing suit had sand in it; there was no way I could get it all out without taking it off, which I was tempted to do in spite of all the signs saying you would be arrested.

It was a longish walk back to where we'd rented the suits. By the time we got there, between the sun, salt, and sand, I was burned everywhere my skin had been exposed and rubbed raw everywhere else. People pay good money for this.

Madrid AmEx had been closed Sunday, the mail part, but the tour director had had our mail forwarded today. I had letters from John and Benny.

John's letter was disturbing. Guarded language. He is not sure the Lobbies are acting in their own best interests. He is not sure of what the true sentiments of the American people are. (If they *have* any opinion one way or another. The Worlds can buy cube time to explain their problems, but the Lobbies can schedule dozens of sex and thrill shows in competition.) The situation is reasonably stable. He thinks. Our only useful threat is shutting down the power, and we've made the threat, and they've weighed it, and haven't yet closed the Cape. Negotiations, if you can give that word to it, continue. But it's hard to separate the information from the noise.

Benny sent another poem:

> *Deuce On It*
>
> Crafting second letter after dawn
> (Recall the last, I hope; it means a lot),
> And hope you'll keep this letter when I'm gone:
> I'd rather not be buried in a plot.
>
> Beware the ides of any month of Spring
> (Try calling on the World for peace of mind),
> Lay low. There's no use in bartering:
> All men who hold the goods are too unkind.
>
> Please be careful what you think and say
> (Stay within the bounds of common sense),
> Rough winds do shake the darling buds of May:
> Of May, the darling buds have accidents.
>
> I be afraid. Don't think that I'm untrue
> (Since no more letters fly from me to you),
> —Benny

It was posted in Denver. So he'd started running.

This poem was more straightforward, if a little scary. But the words didn't sound like Benny in either of them. Which could have been the form, of course. Every poem of his I'd found was traditionally minimalist; his using sonnets made me think there must be a code.

I hadn't found it in the first one. I'd finally given up, deciding he'd used too subtle a code. I'm no poet, after all; I haven't even studied that much poetry.

"Letter from Benny?" Jeff had come up behind me.

I jumped, and held the sheet against my chest. "He wouldn't want anyone else to see it. Personal."

He shook his head. "All I saw was that it's a poem. Wish I could do that." He sat down across from me. "Dinner?"

"If it's late enough. I want to lie down for a while." We agreed to meet here in the common room at eight.

I found the code in a few minutes this time. The repeated line, "Crafting second letter after dawn," was the key. Reading the second letter of each word didn't work, beyond "reef." But reading down, taking the second letter of each line, gave RENDER ALL TO FBI. I went upstairs and got the first poem, which translated to THEY DID KILL HER.

So we had been right. But what did he mean by "render all"? Had he gone to the FBI, or was he asking me to do it?

And what about the content of the poems? The first one didn't make much sense, beyond the coded message, but the second had some real information. "I'm gone: I'd rather not be buried in a plot" was clear, but the rest wasn't, other than a general sense of danger, foreboding. I suppose "I be afraid" meant "FBI raid." God knows what else was hidden in metaphor and rebus, though I should probably be careful on the ides of May. The fifteenth?

I took my pill early, and tried to get some sleep. Dreams kept waking me up, and the sunburn made it hard to find a comfortable position. I finally went down to the common room with a book.

Jeff was on time. We worked our way toward the beach in approved Spanish barhopping style. They have *tapa* bars, where small snacks are served with beer and wine. You have a drink and a snack and then move on to another bar. Some of the snacks were seafood; I tried not to think of what they'd been swimming in.

Most of the bars were crowded and noisy, standing-room-only places. It wasn't until we got to a relatively quiet one that he noticed I hadn't been very talkative.

"Is something bothering you?"

"Can't figure out which parts of this thing are edible." I'd gotten something that might have been a pickled fig.

"Is it Benny?"

I guess that was when I made the decision. I nodded.

"You know he doesn't have anything to worry about," Jeff said. "I'm quite—"

"That's not what I mean. Benny's the same kind of friend as you are." I bit through the rind. It was fibrous and sour. How to say it? "Benny's in serious trouble. His life's in danger."

He set the wineglass down without drinking. "Is he sick?"

"No ... or if he is, it's the least of his worries." I drank the rest of my wine all at once and signaled the bartender. He looked at his feet; men order here. "Why don't you drink that up and get us another?"

He did. "Who's he in trouble with?"

"We don't know a name." The bartender brought over a tray of food. Jeff, brave soul, took a shrimp; I stuck to the vegetable kingdom and selected a wedge of avocado. "A few months ago, Benny and I joined a ... well, a political action group. Slightly underground, but as far as we could tell not mixed up in anything really illegal."

"Communists?"

"Nothing so formal. Sort of radical antiestablishment, was all the people seemed to have in common. Some were communists, some plain anarchists, some even sounded like right-wing libertarians. Just people dissatisfied with your form of government."

Jeff concentrated on peeling the shrimp. "No name?"

"No, they used various 'front' names, but they were emphatic about not having a permanent name. Benny said that probably meant they did have a name, but we weren't deep enough to be told."

"Sounds possible."

"You know something about them?"

"No. Nothing from Washington. But you hear rumors."

He squeezed some lime over the shrimp. "A lot of politicians have died young lately. Conservative Lobbies, all of them." He looked at me. "Why the hell did you get mixed up with them? I can see Benny."

"Research . . . I was curious."

"Dangerous kind of research."

"It didn't seem so at first—more like a debating society with delusions of grandeur. But then there was a really suspicious coincidence." I told him about Benny meeting Katherine on the way back from Washington, and her "suicide." Then I showed him Benny's coded messages.

"You think Benny was more deeply involved than you were?"

"I know he was. At least, he was doing something he couldn't tell me about."

"Yet he went to the FBI. Or wants you to."

I nodded. "Can you check?"

"I'm not sure you really want me to . . . did you ever do anything illegal for them, yourself?"

"No, just some statistical analysis."

"Still, there might be trouble." He looked thoughtful. "I think I can get around it; there's no need to implicate you directly. Better wait till we get to Geneva, though. I can use the Interpol scrambler there."

"Scrambler?"

"Safe telephone system." He studied the two poems. "Speaking of that, have you called New New York lately?"

"No. It's terribly expensive."

"He might be telling you to. Why else would he capitalize 'world' here? 'Try calling on the World for peace of mind.' "

"Worth doing."

"You don't know this Katherine's line name or last name?"

"Nobody's. We went by first names only."

"What about the day she died. Can you remember the date?"

"I can get it from my diary." It was the day after we'd seen *Chloe*.

"The city might have done an autopsy. There will be a death certificate in any case, which could be useful. Is there anything else that might help identify one of them?"

I told him about James's bugeye prosthesis, and the address of the place we usually met. He made some notes while I tried to remember everything I could. It felt good to tell him. Benny had relieved me of a large burden. Maybe I *would* get into trouble with the FBI. I doubted that they would hold me down and poison me.

When I'd finished, he zipped the notebook shut and didn't say anything.

"You think I've been foolish."

"Not really. Naive, yes . . . you and Benny, too. What this sounds like is a handful of penny-ante thugs, fanatics with, as you say, delusions of grandeur. That doesn't make them less dangerous than a large organization, not to you and Benny. It makes them *more* dangerous. They don't have to answer to anybody."

He took a sip of wine and continued, quietly. "That Benny found the bug in his room is interesting. It could be that they were simply amateurish and low on resources. But you can get an invisible bug for less than a thousand bucks. It could be that they wanted him to find it."

"To test him?"

"That's right. And he did exactly the wrong thing, tiptoeing around it. He should have confronted James with it—been outraged. Instead, he gave them every reason to believe that he's spying on them."

"Well, he should be safe by now. I hope."

"You say he was going to Vegas for a dryclean, and then on to someplace secret. He probably will shake them that way, but it's not perfect. My agency could find him, for instance, and they may want to."

"How could the FBI work in Nevada?"

"We don't, officially. But it's an open secret that we have thousands of people there on retainer, so to speak. Some of them are in the laundry business. Benny doesn't know enough about the underworld to avoid them. I'd give you odds there's a file on him in Washington now, if there wasn't one before."

I had a sudden intuition that James and his gang might be just the opposite of what they claimed; might be a clandestine arm of the government set up to monitor and control dissidents. I didn't mention that to Jeff.

He put the notebook back in his purse. "Feel like walking?"

"Let's go down to the beach. I'm a little light-headed."

The streets were gaily lit and full of wanderers. But within a block of the beach, all the streetlights were out of commission; the beach itself was dark as the inside of a closet. And full of people.

We made love standing up under the sign SE DETIENEN PERSONAS DESNUDAS. To stay within the law we left most of our clothes on.

I like the clinging-vine position, but it's easier in low gravity. Afterwards, Jeff sat with his back against the sign and I lay down with my head on his lap. We panted to each other for a while.

"This gravity," I said. "It makes me feel like an old woman."

He stroked my damp hair. After a minute he said, "How old are you, Marianne?"

"Twenty-two." I'd guess Jeff to be ten years older.

"Must be the youngest post-doctoral candidate at the university."

"I'm only post-doc for their own paperwork. Hard to translate New New's certification."

He ran his large hand gently over my face, tracing its shape as a blind man would. "I had a . . . disturbing experience when I was your age. Nine years ago. I was starting my last quarter of undergraduate work, and found out I had missed one physical education credit. Signed up for a quarter of wrestling.

"It was frustrating. I was as strong as any man in my weight class, but I couldn't win a single match. Points, I'd get early points, but they'd always outlast me.

"I went to the infirmary, finally, and they said I was in excellent shape. Then I asked the wrestling instructor about it and he sat me down and told me the obvious: everyone in the class was a few years younger than me. Up until your middle or late 'teens, you're still a growing organism. Then there's a few years of stasis." He paused. "In your early twenties, you start to die."

"Hey, thanks. I needed cheering up."

He traced his finger around my breast. "The funny thing is, in my case he was exactly wrong. Exactly."

"How so?"

"Well, I kept getting weaker. Finally they sent me to a glandular specialist—the big clue was that my shoes were getting tight; my shirts seemed all to be shrinking around the shoulders."

"You were growing?"

"That's right. I had a rare form of acromegaly. Pituitary gland thought I was a kid again. That's why I'm so big. I actually grew eleven centimeters before medication stopped it."

I stroked him. "It must have been pretty short before that."

He laughed and returned the gesture. After a while he said: "Shall we do it like everybody else, lying down?"

"Me on top, though." I'd heard stories about the sand.

✦ ✦ ✦

The next morning I tried to call New New through the New York operator. I got a printed message advising me that all communications would be passed through a delay circuit and would be subject to censorship. Then a hard-looking male operator came on the cube.

"Name and Social Security number," he said.

"Sorry. Wrong number." I pushed off and looked up the number of the Cape shuttle office; punched it.

A tired man stared at me. "Before you say anything," he said, "be advised that this call is being recorded and traced."

"That's all right. I just want some information."

"Plenty of that."

"I'm a Worlds citizen touring Europe. I tried to call New New just now, from Spain, and got some blather about censorship. What's going on?"

"Harassment. As far as we can tell, that's all it is. You can sometimes get around the delay circuit thing by calling Tokyo. They can patch you into New New via Uchūden, if you get good operators; if the phase angle works out. I can compute optimum times for you, if you wish."

"No, it was just a social call. Say, if I were a U.S. citizen, they couldn't censor me, could they?"

"Not if you could prove you were calling another U.S. citizen. There can't be a dozen left in the Worlds, though."

"A dozen! What about tourists?"

He laughed bleakly. "Don't get much news in Spain, do you? The last tourist came back two weeks ago. We can't afford to send them anymore. It's another piece of harassment, but a more serious one. You know we have to buy our fuel now, since we can't trade with U.S. Steel."

"I know."

"Well, on December thirty-first, the government pulled the price controls off deuterium. Supposedly ... actually, there was a long list of applications for which the controls still apply. Virtually everything but space flight. We have to pay ten times the fixed rate—but the amount we can charge for a ticket is still fixed by law! We'd lose a fortune on each flight if we shuttled tourists.

"We have enough fuel stockpiled to get every Worlds

citizen home, with a comfortable margin. But it has to be orchestrated—do you have a reservation?"

"No, I don't. It's that critical?"

He nodded. "It's not just the shuttle. The tug that takes you through the Van Allen belts also runs on deuterium; it has to run with a full load of passengers. So we orbit five shuttle loads each Monday." He studied a sheet of paper. "The earliest I can schedule you is May fourteenth."

"I'll still be in school."

He shrugged. "If I were you, I'd take the earliest date possible. You can always cancel and reschedule—but if the situation doesn't improve, there won't be any more shuttles after mid-July."

"All right, put me down." I gave him my name and number. "And I think I will try to call through Tokyo. What are those times?" I wrote them down on the back of my diary, thanked him, and pushed off. Translated to Spanish time and found I could call in forty-five minutes.

Getting through to Tokyo was no problem, but the patch via Uchūden put purple blotches all over the cube. I tracked down Dan at the labs.

He peered out of the cube. "Marianne?"

"Yes, darling, we have to make it quick. Do you know about the fuel squeeze at the Cape?"

"Of course. Didn't you get my letter?"

"I've gotten several; nothing about that." *Damn* them. "They must be censoring letter transmissions."

"They are. You calling through Tsiolkovski?"

"Uchūden. I've got a reservation for the shuttle on May fourteenth. If things don't get better—"

"Can't you come home before then?"

I shook my head. "Earliest date. Have to push off. So good to hear you and see you."

As his image faded: "I love you." I bit my lip for not saying it myself. It was only a hundred pesetas a second.

35 ✦ Diary of a lover (excerpts)

13 January.   Jeff spent only a little more than an hour at Interpol. He said they had traced Benny—as they routinely do when somebody has his identity changed without taking the elementary precaution of bribing everyone in sight. He had gone to a farm in South Carolina, with the identity of Sheldon Geary.

As to James's bunch, he had only been told "not to worry." He said this probably meant that they were well infiltrated.

I'm glad Benny got away but wish that nobody knew where he was. Jeff didn't know whether the FBI was going to pick him up for questioning. He had broken federal law in being accessory to the forgery of his documents, but the agency rarely bothered to arrest people for that. It was more useful simply to keep an eye on them. . . .

Geneva isn't as pretty as Lausanne, but it's more impressive. All very neatly laid out and meticulously maintained. The weather field keeps it warm enough to walk around with just a light jacket, and the avenues are lined with green growing things. We went down by the lake and sat on the grass there, enjoying our picnic while a blizzard howled a few meters away. Swiss chocolate is remarkable. . . .

I'm trying to taper off the Klonexine. Less tension so less medicine. Violet taught me a trick. Open the capsule and divide the powder into two piles; refill each half-capsule and plug the end with a bit of bread. So I'm still taking them with each meal, but at half dosage.

Jeff has become very tender and solicitous since I dropped all my problems on him. I think he has a stronger mothering instinct than I do. Yet he has the most violent legitimate occupation in the world, and to stay alive must have a killing instinct equally strong. He's full of paradox, keeps surprising me.

(14 January–18 January: Berlin, Munich, Bonn, Rome)

19 January.   Pompeii is the most interesting place we've visited, in terms of history. I guess because of the ordinariness of it—old monuments are interesting, but they are monuments, culturally self-conscious, built for the ages. Pompeii was just an ordinary city, and what's preserved here are ordinary houses, shops, pubs, brothels. Walking down the streets is a mundane trip through time.

The Italian government had Pompeii thoroughly restored by the turn of the century, and they had the good sense to cover the city with a plastic dome, to protect it against the weather and the pollution that drifts down from the industry around Naples. So it looks just like a city of 2000 years ago, only slightly worn.

In the museum outside the city, they have plaster casts of people, animals, and vegetation, preserved when they were entombed by the swift fall of ash from Vesuvius. The eeriest is of a dog, fighting to free himself from his chain. The human figures are pathetic, sometimes gruesome, preserved with their expressions at the moment of death.

(Violet was fascinated by that, of course. She mentioned yesterday that she'd started school with a major in thanotics, studying to be a "death counselor." Sort of like a hypochondriac getting a job as a druggist.)

Back in our stuffy room in Naples, Jeff and I lay together in the dark for a long time, talking about death. He is matter-of-fact about it, and I think honestly not afraid. Just suddenly not-being. He was brought up in American Taoism, though he rejected it in his teens, and admits that the passive fatalism of that religion probably still affects him, or infects him. We were tired and made slow love with our hands.

(20 January–26 January: Athens, Salonika, Dubrovnik, Belgrade)

27 January.   They wanted us to go through Maghrib before the Alexandrian Dominion because Maghrib is so much more modern and familiar. At least women can show their faces. They don't execute criminals in the public square.

It is still the most alien place we've been. We spent late morning to early afternoon in Tangier, which used to be a major port. Now its main industry is wringing money from European tourists, being picturesque.

The foreignness is enthusiastic and unrelenting but it's not fake. At least not in the Casbah, the native quarter. At midday, with eight or nine people in our group, we felt isolated, alien, in danger. Sinister-looking people stared at us, scowling, measuring. Beggars showed us their sores and stumps. In the open-air market, meat was hanging in the warm sun, crawling with flies. A small mob formed when one of our people resisted paying a man after taking his picture. He paid.

The tourist part of town is all white beaches, colorful fluttering flags, music and dancing, high prices. For lunch I bought couscous, which had been so delightful in Paris, but here was an indigestible lump of yellow starch. Cheapest thing on the menu, though.

The train to Marrakesh was a fascinating antique. Polished wood and brass and agonizingly slow. We saw lots of desert and some camels, and herds of goats invariably tended by small boys who looked like they would rather be doing something else.

We came in at sundown (the agent probably planned that) and Marrakesh was heartstopping beautiful. It's an oasis, lush green after hours of desert, with the Atlas mountains behind it dramatic with snow, and all the buildings are red clay, more red in the setting sun. When we got off the train we could hear muezzins chanting from towers all over the city, calling faithful Muslims to prayer. There were evidently no faithful Muslims at the railway station.

The hotel was rundown but fairly Western, sit-down toilets. When Jeff and I tried to register together we were coldly asked to show proof of marriage. So I spent a quiet night with Violet, reading. We were advised that there was no inexpensive nightlife in the parts of Marrakesh where you could safely go at night.

The four of us set out early in the morning and, dutiful tourists, admired the Koutoubya mosque and the thousand-year-old walls that once protected the city from nomad invaders. Then we went to the Djemaa El Fna, which is the largest and most colorful market in Maghrib.

In front of the actual market was a large packed-earth square full of exotic entertainment—snake-charmers, acrobats, mimes, musicians. The musical instruments were mostly strings, types unfamiliar to me, and they weren't playing in anything like a diatonic scale. Or maybe some were and some weren't, which would account for the weird discords they seemed to hit on every other note. But it wasn't unpleasant.

Violet and I got tired of having every man we passed stare us in the crotch—Maghrib women don't wear pants—so we went into the first clothing stall and bought loose kaftans. We bargained for five minutes, passing numbers back and forth on a tablet, since the man didn't speak either English or French. We worked him down from 5000 dirhams to 2500, though we had to walk out of the shop twice to get the last 500 (a technique Violet had learned from a guidebook). Then we put the kaftans on over our western clothes and undressed underneath, the sight of which nearly gave the poor bugeyed man a stroke.

We met Jeff and Manny at the weapons shop next door, where Jeff was still arguing over the price of an intricately carved cane that concealed a sword. When we left with them, the merchant ran after us, waving the cane in a theatrical way, and agreed to meet Jeff's last price. Jeff paid him, but later wished he had cut the price again, to see what would happen. Manny said he thought it might be smart to do your experiments in bargaining etiquette at some place other than a weapons shop.

We didn't buy much else. We had been warned not to change too much money into dirhams, since you couldn't take them out of the country and it was illegal to change them into foreign currency.

It was more relaxed than Tangier's Casbah, and a little cleaner, but there were several times I was glad to have two meters of husky armed policeman as an escort. Violet and I got accustomed to the "Maghrib handshake." In a crowd, men were constantly gliding their hands across your buttocks, to make sure you had two. Violet was amused by it, but I thought it was a little disgusting. Once a man sidled up behind and touched me with something other than a hand; he got an elbow in the ribs for his effort. He growled something in Arabic but Jeff stared him down.

Most of the afternoon was delightful, though. We went past the shops into the part of town where people lived and worked, normally out of the sight of tourists. I was particularly fascinated by a man who was running a wood lathe by foot power, rolling the soles of his feet rapidly over a wooden axle (the feet had nearly a centimeter of translucent callus), the power transmitted by squeaking pulleys to the thing he was working on, a cane like Jeff's. He worked close to the wood, thick spectacles protecting his eyes. He never noticed us watching him.

There were tanners and dyers and weavers and coppersmiths and blacksmiths, most of them working in ways that hadn't changed for centuries. We stumbled on to one electronics/cybernetics dealer, which was jarring.

... had a long sleepy bath and then at 10:30, as prearranged, tiptoed down the hall and traded places with Manny.

... but it was so sweet just to be with him. I'm afraid I've fallen in love again. My only consistent talent.

(28 January–3 February: Fez/Meknes, Casablanca, Kisangani, Dar es Salaam)

4 February.   The Alexandrian Dominion comes as a cold shock after the friendliness and modernity of Black Africa.

At the Cairo customs station, all women were required to buy a chador, a shapeless robe that covers you from head to foot. Only your eyes are allowed to show. We would have to wear that whenever we were anyplace a man might see us.

On our way to the hotel, we passed a large public square, fountains and beautifully tended flower beds and topiary. On the fence around the square were impaled rotting heads and hands from recently punished criminals. For some reason they didn't look real.

Over the hotel desk there was a sign in several languages. I'll copy it down:

> THIS IS A HOTEL NOT A HOUSE OF PROSTITUTION. ADUL-
> TERERS WILL BE PUNISHED ACCORDING TO ISLAMIC LAW:
> IF UNMARRIED, ONE HUNDRED LASHES. IF MARRIED,
> DEATH BY STONING. *FOREIGNERS BE ADVISED.* THIS LAW
> IS STRICTLY ENFORCED.

Six days of this. Oh, well, I always wanted to see the Pyramids. . . .

(5 February–9 February: Alexandria, Mecca, Baghdad, Damascus, Ankara, Jerusalem)

10 February.   So good to be rid of that damned chador, and to see women's faces and bodies again. Three cheers for Krishna.

Delhi is the most crowded place I've ever seen, but the people are calm and good-natured. . . .

. . . bed was squeaky so we moved onto the floor. The rug seemed soft to me but it took the skin off Jeff's knees, large price to pay for not disturbing the sleep of our neighbors. So I got to be on top for the second round, doubly nice after a week of being debased for being a woman.

11 February.   We spent the afternoon in Khajuaho, at the famous Devi Jagadambi Temple, mostly. Thousands of delightful erotic sculptures, showing every possible way, and some impossible ones (Hindi demigods evidently could bend in ways that humans can't; they also had pretty impressive sex organs). Jeff said he was taking mental notes about the positions that didn't involve kneeling.

Several Muslim women were waiting outside the temple, while their husbands, or husband, enjoyed the sculptures. At least they can show their faces in Bharat, though they do have to wear a modified chador. Most of the men and women wear European-style clothes.

At a bookstall by the temple Jeff bought a copy of the Kama Sutra, illustrated with pictures of the temple figures. I decided I'd better get some sleep on the way back to the hotel. . . .

13 February.   . . . but our final impression of Bharat was marred by the incredible squalor of Calcutta. Our guide said it had never been worse, with some twenty million refugees fleeing starvation in Bangladesh. . . .

14 February.   Vietnam is America's only real ally in Southeast Asia, and wherever we go, we're treated with anxious friendliness. Not surprising, since they're surrounded by SSU countries, and only American military might keeps them from being overrun—especially by China, who's been trying to absorb them for thousands of years.

(I decided not to take a side trip into the SSU, since the transportation is so expensive it would eat up half my remaining travel money. Violet went into Kampuchea to see Angkor Wat, and will join up with us in Ho Chi Minh City.)

Hanoi is a tidy, earnest place. . . .

(15–17 February: Hue, Pleiku, Banmethuot)

18 February.   The Kampucheans were not very friendly to Violet. She was even spat upon. It wasn't simply racism, she found out. Many people believe that the independence of Nevada (and Ketchikan) is a hoax, and that visitors are spies. . . .

(19–22 February: Tokyo, Kyoto, Osaka, Hiroshima)

23 February.   Two days' rest before we go on to the last leg of our travels. Nothing to do on Guam but lie on the beach, swim in the warm water, enjoy each other.

And some time to try to straighten out my feelings about Jeff. I love him, all right, but it's not the kind of love I have for Daniel. In a way it's a more juvenile thing, like it was with Charlie, more hormones than brain cells. We both know it can't be permanent, and that makes it sort of romantic and wistful.

It brings me up short to realize that I've known him longer than I've known Daniel, in terms of together-time, and I probably know him better than I know Daniel.

I've never said anything about love to him. Who am I protecting?

(25 February–6 March: Manila, Papua, Darwin, Perth, Melbourne, Sydney, Anchorage, Fairbanks, Ketchikan, Guadalajara, Mexico D.F., Acapulco)

36 ✦ Kaleidoscope

After I got settled into the dorm, I went over to the bound-journals stacks in the library. My cigarette-paper diary was still there, but nothing else, no message from Benny.

Should have memorized the position of the papers inside the magazine. It seemed to me that they had been moved, but I couldn't be sure. (If somebody had read them, though, it was probably Benny. Find out in a couple of weeks.)

I called his apartment and the landlord said he'd disappeared, without paying rent. He'd confiscated everything in the apartment and was going to sell it after ninety days. I said I might want to buy some of the books. Will ask Benny.

Called registration and signed up for twelve hours of "directed reading" courses in history, politics, and economics. Then I walked down to Penn Station to buy my Americapass.

It felt good to be back in New York. Not to be coping with a new language and set of customs every other day. And I'd missed it. London is cleaner, Tokyo's bigger, Paris is more beautiful, and so forth—but no place has such exciting variety and contrast. Industry and decadence, opulence and squalor, tranquillity and violence, past and future. Old New York.

✦ ✦ ✦

Jeff and I had dinner together at the Vietnamese restaurant. Over dessert, I complained about the extortion of having to pay for a dormitory room that would be unoccupied four days out of five, while I toured the States.

"You could move in with me," he said.

"That would be fun," I said, "but no solution. They would triple my tuition; that's how they keep the dorms—"

"Not if we were married."

I dropped a little ice cream on my lap. "What? Married?"

"People get married. I love you."

"Jeff . . ." I got busy with a napkin. My brain was stuck. "Jeff, you, I thought you understood, I, Daniel and me . . ."

"I do understand. But you love me too, don't you? Some?"

"You know I do. But not *marriage*. After six months, you'll never see me again."

"I've been thinking about that. There are two solutions. One, we could get a mutual-consent divorce when it comes time for you to leave. 'Better to have loved and lost than never to have lost at all.' "

"I don't know that I could accept that." Marriage is sacred, if anything is.

He nodded. "I didn't think so. But you might consider it from an anthropological perspective. Marriages of convenience are very common here, you know; when you're among barbarians, it's safest to temporarily conform to their customs."

"I'm not much of an anthropologist. What's the other solution?"

He made a little tent with his fingers and stared down at it. "I could go back to New New York with you. Or join you later, after the shuttle's on a regular schedule again."

"You mean you'd give up the FBI?"

"There are police in New New. They could put my talents to use. Wouldn't they be almost compelled to take me, if I were the spouse of a citizen?"

"In normal times, yes. But, Jeff . . . you wouldn't like it there. Not after growing up in New York and living the way you have. It's too quiet and peaceful. Boring."

"I've thought of that, too. I think I've had enough excitement."

"But—"

"Now you're going to bring up Daniel." I was, as a matter of fact. He spoke formally: "I would be more than willing to join him in a triune marriage. That you love him is enough of a testimonial." He looked directly at me. "I'd rather have half of you than all of any woman I've ever met before."

"The men don't get half," I said, almost automatically, "the woman gets double." I covered my face with my hands. "Jeff, Jeffie, you have to give me time to think. Ever since I was a little girl I've been fighting the idea of joining a triune."

"But your family wasn't really—"

"I know. But all the other bastards around me were." A three-way marriage is fine for adults: stable tripod. Not so great for the children, though. They become manipulative.

"So we could start our own line, you and Daniel and me. And the Boy Scout troop down the block."

I had to laugh. "You overestimate me. Four or five would be plenty."

"Seriously, I don't want to rush it. I know you need time to think. Talk it over with Daniel."

"That presents a little problem. I haven't mentioned you to him, at least not our relationship."

"Do you want me to write to him?"

"No. Not yet." I stood up and dropped a fifty on the table. "Don't get up. I have to walk for a while."

"You shouldn't go out alone."

"Just to the dorm. It's not the Casbah."

"Still, be careful. Why don't you take my knife."

"I'm okay." I kissed him on the cheek and went out.

It had just started to rain, a steady cold drizzle, no wind. I put up my hood and was comfortable; the weather matched my mood. The cold black and double glare.

Jeff hadn't mentioned the third alternative, that I marry him and stay here. What would that be like? Marianne O'Hara, groundhog. I couldn't see it. Not even in this wonderful city. The Earth is closed space; history's mistakes endlessly repeating. The future belongs to the Worlds.

But could Jeff adjust? I turned the last corner before the dorm entrance.

"Aye there, sweetbuns." I froze. I'd seen enough cube to recognize gang talk.

Another voice: "So-o-o lonesome, she is. Oll alone t'night."

Three men stepped out from behind the shrubbery, blocking my path. There was no one else in sight. "Get out of my way," I said weakly. My hand curled around the spraystick in my coat pocket.

"W'd she knife us?" They were all corpse-white, heads and eyebrows shaved, dressed in tailored denim shirts and kilts.

"She w'dna. She sweet." The first one who'd spoken stepped forward. "Just a little front-to-front, sweetbuns." He lifted his kilt at me.

"Front-to-back, I like," said the pimply one.

"Front-to-top," said the tall one.

"All right," I said, trying to keep my voice level, "but it's not for free."

The front one laughed and turned to say something to his comrades. I pulled the spraystick out of my pocket and fired; the luminous jet spattered him from shoulder to ear. He gasped and then vomited explosively.

The smell was hideous. I held my breath and shifted aim. The pimply one tried to ward it off with his hands, but it didn't work and he fell to his knees retching.

The tall one very calmly reached into his pocket and pulled out a gun. He vomited a split second before he fired, which probably saved me. The bullet sang off the sidewalk and my right ankle stung from the fragments. I turned and ran.

I ran two blocks, to the dormitory's rear entrance, then rushed down the corridor to the public phone in the foyer. I called the police; they already had a floater headed here, responding to the gunshot. I sat in the lobby (after trying to scrub the rotten-egg smell from my hand) and in a few minutes an armored policeman came in. I told him my story and filled out a complaint form.

"Do you think you'll catch them?"

He nodded. "Blindfolded. But even if they'd had time to wash the smell away, that luminous paint adheres for days."

"Will I have to go to court?" That could really throw off my schedule. But worth it.

"Probably not." He looked rueful. "Not unless they charge you with assault."

I was dumbstruck. He elaborated. "There's no law against suggestive talking, nor 'accidental' exposure of genitals. If the tall one still has his gun, we can charge him for illegally possessing and discharging it. But it's probably in the sewers by now."

"They—they could have me arrested?"

"You assaulted them with a deadly weapon. Puke-O has killed people. The assault could be proven even if you hadn't admitted to it."

"But that's insane!"

"Sister, I couldn't agree more. But that's the way it works." He picked up his helmet. "Don't worry. They're probably too citywise to make a formal charge. If they did, it's true we'd have to hold you in jail for a couple of days—but because of your countercharge, we'd have them in jail, too. We could put them in cells where they'd be sure to have bad accidents."

Cold justice. "What you're saying ... if they don't charge me, they aren't going to jail?"

"No. We'll pick them up, take them down to the station for fingerprints and retina scans. Ask them some questions. Since they didn't hurt you, that's all we can do."

"They didn't hurt me?"

"I'm sorry, ma'am."

I sank back into the cushions. "This is the second time."

"You shouldn't be out at this time of night alone, unarmed. This isn't the nicest part of town."

I was getting tired of hearing that advice. "Then what the hell are police for?"

"Sometimes I wonder." He put on his helmet and spoke to me from behind the mirror blankness. "There are eighteen thousand of us and sixteen million of you. We can't be everywhere. Will you be all right?"

"Yes. I'm sorry." He nodded and walked out.

Before he'd come I'd bought some tea from the lobby machine and used it to take a pill. Now I could feel the pill taking effect. I sipped at the cold tea and looked over the bulletin board for a long time, and then went up to my room.

I touched the door and with a sick feeling realized it wasn't locked. I pushed it open and slapped the light switch, expecting to find a burgled shambles.

"James?" He was sitting erect in the straight chair by my desk. How long had he been there in the dark?

He nodded slowly, glass eyes sparkling. "You weren't home. I decided to wait for you."

"How did you get in?"

"The door was open. You must have forgotten to lock it."

In a rabbit's rectum, I did. The Klonexine muted my anger/fear/frustration, but I still snapped at him. "Come back some other time. I've had an awful day. Three men tried to attack me."

"Together, or seriatim?"

"All at once. Less than an hour ago."

"You shouldn't be out this late without protection." I opened my mouth to answer that, but he reached under his left arm and slid out a small black hand laser, trailing two taut wires. "You see? Even I do, and I'm not one tenth as attractive as you are."

"Isn't that a laser?"

"Twelve shot."

"I thought they were illegal for civilians."

"Very much so." He held it out, in my general direction, a little too long for it not to have been threatening. He replaced it with a soft click.

"I thought you were about the most nonviolent of the group."

"That's true, even to tense: I was. There is no group now."

I didn't say anything. "Where is Benny?" he asked.

"I was going to ask you that." I sat down on the bed. "His landlord says he disappeared."

"He did, and most conveniently. Two days later there was an FBI raid. There was some violence and loss of life."

I don't know why that surprised me. "Who?"

"No one you knew. Two of us and two of them."

"And you think Benny, uh, reported you?"

"Either that, or the FBI picked him up and squeezed him. The coincidence of his disappearance can't be coincidence. I wondered whether he had called or written to you while you were traveling."

"He wrote me twice, poems. I'd be glad to show you the letters, but I didn't keep them." Memorized them, of course. *Please be careful what you think and say.*

"There wasn't anything in the letters about the fact that he wouldn't be here when you came back?"

"I can't say." Best way to lie is tell the truth. "The poems were very obscure; they might have said anything. There was nothing but the two poems."

He didn't react. After a couple of seconds I opened my mouth to fill the silence and he said, "Last quarter you had a classmate who was an FBI agent."

"Jeff Hawkings."

"Did he know Benny?"

"The three of us got together a couple of times, on the way to class. Only twice; I think those were the only times they met."

"It's a possibility, though."

"I can't see Benny—"

"You can never tell. The FBI can plant an agent in a neighborhood and let him act out a role for years, just to eventually infiltrate a group such as ours. No one is completely exempt from suspicion, not even me."

"Or me?"

"We checked on you, of course. You are what you claim to be." He put on his hat and stood up. "I would stay away from this agent Hawkings. He may want more from you than your friendship."

"I met him before I ever got involved with your group."

"Still, prudence. I'll be in touch." Don't be, I wanted to shout. He closed the door softly and the automatic lock snapped to.

37 ✦ Death of a poet

I left for Chicago in the morning. Jeff was going to be out of town for the next three days, on maneuvers with the squad he'd just been given. I wouldn't know how to get in touch with him even if that had been a good idea.

Chicago was a feint, of course; I was really headed for Atlanta and thence to Benny. But I did have a legitimate reason for going to the aptly named Windy City.

It was a biting cold, clear day, and the wind that rushed through the corridors between the kilometer-high buildings often gusted strongly enough to make you stagger for balance. I spent most of the day wandering through the art and science museums, which were not only edifying but also gave me many opportunities to make sure I wasn't being followed.

Then I spent a rather awkward evening with my father, who lives in Evanston, outside of the city. We don't have much in common other than physical appearance—the cube Mother has of him, in his late twenties, looks enough like me that we could be fraternal twins. So now I know what I'll look like at fifty: flabby and fading. That's a real comfort.

He was a nice enough man, though. Divorced eight years ago, living alone in a flat only a little larger than my dorm room. Sort of wan and resigned. He was glad to see me, but I think he would have been glad to see anybody.

Afterwards, I felt exorcized, in a way. If he were happy I think I would have been bitter.

I slept on the tube from Chicago to San Diego; San Diego to Seattle; Seattle to Atlanta. Then surface train and public floater to Charlestown and Lancaster Mills, where I drank tea for a couple of hours in an all-nighter, waiting for a U-Rent to open. Rented a bicycle for the last ten kilometers.

I felt exposed and obvious, pedalling down the rutted farm road. I didn't look up the two times floaters hummed by overhead. There was an unmarked mailbox just past the tenth milestone; I hooked the bike to it and picked my way down a muddy path to an old house that appeared to be made of wooden logs.

It actually was, about half logs and half cement, and it looked handmade. There was a cord hanging from a hole drilled in the door; I pulled on it and a bell rang inside. After several rings with no answer, I stepped off the little porch to peer through a cloudy window.

"Looking for someone?"

I jumped. He was easily two meters tall, but skinny. Cadaverous. Sharp features, dark sunken eyes, black beard stubble, rumpled faded work clothes, a double-barreled shotgun cradled in the crook of his left arm. He had come quietly from behind the house.

"Yes, I—I'm looking for Benny. Benny Aarons."

"No one here by that name." He scratched his stomach and the barrels of the gun swung around to line up on me.

"I might have the wrong farm," I said, and realized that was possible: I might have stumbled on some crazy recluse. "I'm looking for Mr. Perkins's place."

He looked at me for a long cold time. "You have the hair for it. You be Mary Anne?"

I nodded vigorously. "O'Hara. Where's Benny?"

"Supposing I knew this Aarons. Supposing you did too. Where did you meet him?"

"An English seminar at New York University. Dr. Schaumann."

"And where did you go, the first time you went out?"

"The Bronx Zoo."

He didn't move at all during this whole exchange. Neither did I. After a moment, he said, "Guess you're her." He let the gun slip and caught it expertly. "Let's go inside."

I followed him into the single large room. Where the walls were exposed, they looked the same as they did outside. Most of the wall space was covered with bookshelves, though, and paintings. One of Benny's pictures was hanging over the fireplace, where a large piece of wood smoldered. It was hot and stuffy.

He motioned me to a rough table with two chairs. "Sit. I'll get coffee."

I sat. "I really don't need any, thank you." He grunted and poured two cups from the pot that was sitting on a black iron stove. He took a bottle of whiskey off a shelf and poured some into each cup.

He sat down across from me and slid one cup over. He shook his head slowly.

The smell of whiskey and coffee will always bring back to me that feeling of helpless horror growing. "Something's ... wrong."

"Benny is dead," he said precisely.

I think my heart actually stopped. A wave of remorse and fear rushed over me, so strong I almost fainted. Perkins reached across the table and steadied me, hand on my arm.

"What happened?"

He let go of me slowly and eased back into his chair. "Not what they say happened." He raised his cup. "Better drink some."

It made me cough and finally brought tears to my eyes. Perkins gave me a surprisingly clean handkerchief. "What do they say happened? Who are 'they'?"

"The police, they say he killed himself."

"Benny would never do that."

"I know. And he doubly would never do it without he left a note. Wordy son of a bitch. Excuse me."

I blew my nose. "No, you're right."

"He was murdered. Now what the hell was going on? I knew he was in deep trouble but he wouldn't tell me a damned thing. He said I was better off not knowing. Was there somebody layin' for him?"

"I don't know." I didn't know who, at least.

He took a cotton bag of tobacco out of his shirt pocket and began rolling a cigarette. "This is what happened. About three weeks ago. I put on some mush to fry for breakfast and went out to the barn to get Benny. He had fixed himself a little room out there in the stable. Don't have horses no more.

"Well . . . he was hanging there. Long rope tied up on the rafters by the hayloft."

"My God!"

"Well, he didn't do it himself. Somebody marched him up to the loft and put the noose on him and pushed him off."

"How do you know?"

"You want a cigarette? I got some real ones around."

I shook my head. "How can you tell?"

"You really want to know. Well. I cut him down. It was cold in the barn and he was stiff. He didn't have no clothes on, that was the way he slept." Perkins lit the cigarette carefully and sipped his coffee.

"I guess I stood and looked at him for a long time. Then I saw there was something wrong, I mean something peculiar.

"His left arm was dislocated, popped right out of the socket. There was a big brown bruise on his left wrist, and another on his right shoulder. You know what a come-along is?"

"No."

"Well, you put somebody's arm behind his back and pull it up, like this." He reached around as if he were trying to scratch between his shoulderblades. "Then you grab his other shoulder and push. He has to come along with you. Police do it."

"That's how they got him up into the hayloft?"

"Right. And he must have struggled something fierce, to dislocate his arm and get those bruises.

"I showed that to the police and they agreed with me, at first. But I called them a few days later and they said the case was closed, suicide. Said the coroner said the injuries were caused by Benny trying to get loose from the rope, after he'd jumped. Said a lot of people have second thoughts like that. But that's a load. It just couldn't happen."

"Not Benny, no."

"Not anybody. How'd he bruise his right shoulder? Did he do it before or after he'd popped out his arm? It's a load, all right." He took a furious drag on his cigarette and it showered sparks over the table. "The question is, who?" I nodded.

He banged the cigarette out on the jar lid that served as an ashtray. "You know more'n you think you can tell me."

"I can't . . . I hardly know you." Then he read my mind.

"You think I might not be who I say I am?"

"That's possible."

"Well. I don't have a flier's license to show you. That wouldn't do anyhow, I 'spect." He got up and went to the stove for a refill; picked up the whiskey bottle and put it back down. "Want some more?" I said no. He sat back down and stared into his cup, as if gathering his thoughts.

"Benny and I were best friends in middle school. We're line cousins. My folks moved up to New York for a few years and we lived in the same line house as Benny." He waved at the hundreds of books. "He got me to readin'. I guess I was as good a friend as he had. Why don't you ask me something about him? Like I asked you."

"Believe me . . . you're better off not knowing anything."

"That just ain't so. I been walkin' around with a gun for three weeks. Better off if I knew what I might be up against."

"I don't think they'd bother you," I said without too much conviction. He just stared at me. "All right. Tell me about Benny's . . . love life. Did he have any homosexual experience?"

Perkins frowned and took his time answering. "If he did, he never told me about it. Wouldn't expect him to, though. I know he had a really bad time with a woman some years back, and hadn't seen many women until you came along. He told me a lot about that—say, I don't want to embarrass you."

"Sex doesn't embarrass me."

"Well, he was real confused about you because he had a hard time separating out the sex from the love. You know? Not the way most everybody does. Stronger, because he had nothing to go on, nothing good. And all of a sudden he had everything. He said there was nothing you didn't know, nothing you wouldn't do."

"He was wrong there. But the things I won't do would never occur to Benny."

He shifted restlessly. "What did he tell me that nobody else would know? . . . You, um, did it once in the women's locker room. You had to hide in a smelly little closet."

I smiled at the memory. "Why?"

"A whole gym class came in. Right at the wrong moment."

I nodded. The right moment, actually; I'd never seen Benny recover so fast. The situation must have fulfilled some obscure fantasy. "You're right. That's something not even the FBI would know."

He leaned forward, alert. "You suspect the FBI?"

"No . . . I was just—"

"I do."

"You think the FBI *killed* Benny?"

"Some part of the government." He rubbed at his chin

savagely with the back of his hand, sandpaper sound. "Look, Benny told me how he got here. He zigzagged all over the country for a day and then went to Vegas. Took off his beard and most of his hair and got his skin dyed, then got all new papers. Then he spent another three days constantly on the move, before he got here. No private person could have tracked him down.

"And look. How come they dropped the investigation, just like that? They only even interrogated me once, the day after he died, and I'm the only real suspect they could have. Somebody told them to get off it."

I hardly heard what he was saying, for the overwhelming rush of guilt. "What day did he die?"

"January ninth. Why?"

So I hadn't caused it; that was before I'd told Jeff. "Could we go outside? I—I'm having difficulty breathing."

He picked up the shotgun on the way out. It was still cold and clear. We went behind the house and walked between rows of dead cornstalks.

"I wanted to get out because I was afraid your place might be bugged," I said.

"If it's the FBI you're worried about, I might be bugged." He switched the shotgun to his right hand and buried his left deep in a pocket, for warmth. "They can get you while you're sleeping, do microsurgery. Leave a bug in your skull for the rest of your life."

"Come on ... that's just something you see on the cube."

He shrugged. "Why would the FBI be interested in Benny?"

How much to tell? "I think he was in touch with them. If he was murdered, it wasn't them who got to him." I gave Perkins a synopsis of our dealings with the sinister political action group. "Before Benny left, I think he tried to penetrate the group as deeply as possible, and then told the FBI all he knew."

"You think that would make him safe from the FBI."

When I didn't say anything, he continued. "That sounds paranoid, doesn't it? Well, you didn't grow up here. You don't have anything like the FBI in the Worlds."

I shook my head. "I have a friend who works for the FBI. He's a good man."

"I'm sure it's chock full of good men. But believe me, if they want to do something to you, they just *do* it. They don't have to answer to anyone."

Jeff had used the same phrase, in a different context. "What good would it do them? To kill Benny?"

"That's a point," he admitted. "You'd think it would be to their advantage to keep him alive and kickin'. They might could use him again." He pulled a dried cob off a stalk and threw it away, hard. "So what do you think?"

I tried to recall James's conversation the other night. "I really don't know. If that group were capable of finding him, I don't doubt that they'd be capable of killing him." We ran out of cornfield and started walking toward the barn. I tried to stifle a feeling of dread. "He told me where he was going. Maybe he told someone else."

"He said not. But it might be that somebody was listening."

"No, we were alone. Outdoors, in a subway entrance."

We went into the barn. I glanced up and was glad not to see a rope hanging from the rafters.

"This was his place, here." Perkins pushed open a plank door.

It was about the size of his room in New York. There was a single window with a sheet of plastic tacked over it. There was a cot and a chair, and two crates pushed together to make a table. The table was covered with a chaotic jumble of books and papers, grey under a film of dust. A wood-burning stove and a suitcase, and a drawing of me, pinned over his cot.

"I haven't touched anything. Is there anything here you'd want?"

That complicated funny man, all the pain and joy of

him, and it came down to this. I shook my head slowly but then took down the picture, rolled it up and put it in my bag. We left quickly.

"What about his relatives?" I asked.

"I haven't told anybody. Far as anybody knows, that was Sheldon Geary and he committed suicide. Anyhow, Benny's parents disowned him when he left the line. There's nobody—"

We surprised a large bird and it suddenly clattered into the air in front of us. Perkins dropped to a crouch and the shotgun roared. I was somehow face-down in the mud, the blast ringing in my ears.

Hands shaking, Perkins hinged the gun open and extracted the smoking shell. He got another from his pocket and reloaded. "Christ I'm jumpy," he said in a harsh whisper. "Sorry." He helped me up. "Do you have a change of clothes with you?"

"Back at the Atlanta station. Suitcase in a locker. But I'll be all right, it'll brush off when it dries."

"Well, let's get you inside." My teeth were chattering by the time we got to the door. He stared back at the field. "Even missed the god-damned bird."

Perkins handed me a blanket and studied the wall while I got out of my clothes and hung them by the stove. I suppose it was a potentially erotic situation, what with the tension and forced intimacy and his knowledge of my butterfly tendencies. But he just sat me down at the table and made a fresh pot of coffee.

"Look, you might be in as much danger as Benny was." He took a wooden box off a high shelf.

"I don't think so. I didn't get as deep into the organization."

"That might not make any difference. You were Benny's lover; they don't know how much you might know." He set the box down in front of me.

I lifted the lid cautiously. It was a small silver pistol and a box of ammunition.

"Take it, just in case."

"I'd never be able to use it." It was cold and surprisingly heavy, and smelled of oil.

"Never know until the situation comes up," he said quietly.

"I don't mean morally . . . I mean I wouldn't be able to hit the floor with it. I've never touched a gun before in my life."

"I could show you how to use it. Once your clothes—"

"No." I put the gun back and closed the box. "I appreciate the thought. But if it comes to shooting people I don't have a chance anyhow. It's not like the Greeks or westerns, where I'd want to take some of them with me. I don't have that gland." *Those* glands, I thought.

"Then what do you plan on doing?"

"I have to think . . . I have a pass for unlimited tube and rail travel for forty-five days. I might just keep moving around."

"That might be a good idea." He poured coffee and I accepted a cup, to warm my hands.

"What about you?" I asked. "Why do you stay here?"

"I've given that some thought. In the first place, I couldn't get far; don't have much money. Also, I'm out in the open here, nobody's going to sneak up on me. Mainly, though, if they haven't got me by now, they must not be especially interested.

"And this is the best time of year. No crops to worry about. I just sit in here and read. My reward for cracking ass nine months."

We sat for an hour or so, reminiscing about Benny. When my clothes were dry he brushed them off outside and brought them to me.

"Do you mind if I don't turn away? I don't see a woman too often."

"I don't mind." I let the blanket fall and dressed without hurrying, in front of his sad and hungry eyes. I normally might have done the friendly thing, but was too depressed and upset. I suspected he was, too.

Perkins walked me out to the bicycle and we exchanged awkward goodbyes. I assured him that I would come by if I was ever in the area again, but we both knew I wouldn't.

38 ✦ Storm gathering

When I got back to the dorm there was a hand-delivered note in my box. Not from James, to my relief, but from the Worlds Club. Special meeting tonight, about Cape Town, whatever that was.

I might as well go. I'd have to be in New York tomorrow, anyhow, when Jeff got back. I did some laundry and repacked my suitcase, then went down to the Liffey to read until the meeting started. I didn't want to be in my room.

Reading has always been an escape activity for me, whether the subject matter is light or difficult. This one was difficult but absorbing, an economic history of the United States from Vietnam to the Second Revolution. I immersed myself in it to keep from thinking, by thinking, though it should have been obvious by then that my academic career was over.

Traveling around the world, I wasn't really aware of the extent to which relations between the Worlds and America had degenerated, and the last three days had been so full of personal terror that I wouldn't have noticed if the Sun had started rising in the west.

There were only thirteen people at the meeting. Most of them had already moved to Cape Town, but had come back to New York to tie up loose ends. Everyone else was either down in Florida or home in the Worlds. They explained: Nine days before, the United States had put a temporary prohibition on the sale of deuterium for space flight, even at the astronomical price U.S. Steel had been getting.

Steve Rosenberg, from Mazeltov, explained it to me. "New New York found two more CC deposits on the Moon; they may be rather common. So they got a little aggressive. The Import-Export Board increased the price of satellite power. They gave the U.S. a schedule of monthly increases that would continue until the price of deuterium went back to normal. So the U.S. cut it off."

"Which was no surprise to the Coordinators," I said.

"I imagine not. But we have enough deuterium in storage to get everyone back, with some to spare. They're trying to get everyone back as soon as possible, which is why Cape Town."

I'd learned that Cape Town was a collection of tents and shanties inside the entrance to the Cape. Worlds citizens were going up in order of reservations, and they were up to May first. I could be home in a week.

But it wasn't quite as orderly and comfortable an evacuation as had been planned. They were using only one shuttle, the high-gee one, to save fuel. People were allowed only seven kilograms of baggage, including clothes. The rest of the payload was seawater.

"Why salt water?" I asked.

"Well, there are valuable chemicals in it, and salt for food. But mainly it's the heavy hydrogen: deuterium and tritium.

"We found out that all of the water U.S. Steel was giving us was 'light water'—all of the heavy hydrogen had been processed out of it. That wouldn't normally make any difference, since it's always been cheaper for us to buy heavy hydrogen from Earth, than to set up a plant to make our own. It's different now. Jules Hammond pointed out last week that there's enough deuterium and tritium in a tonne of seawater to boost forty tonnes to orbit."

"So we've built a plant?"

"It's not the sort of thing you can do overnight. But they're in the process. In a month or so, it's possible we'll be able to 'bootstrap' water into orbit, without using any earth-made fuel."

"Do the Lobbies know this?"

"Yes .. it should make them more cooperative."

I wasn't so sure.

The meeting was strained. A lot of talk concerned what to take along as your seven kilograms. I resolved to go naked and barefoot, so as not to leave my clarinet behind. Actually, though, I didn't have much beyond the clarinet and my diary. I'd feel guilty taking things that were just souvenirs. Some cigarettes for Daniel and some Guinness for John. Benny's picture. What of Jeff's?

When the meeting was breaking up, I mentioned that I didn't want to go back to my dormitory room, saying it had just been painted. The only one who wasn't going straight to the Cape was Steve Rosenberg; he offered me a couch.

When we were "alone" on the subway, he asked whether I would rather share his bed. I said I was in too complicated an emotional state for sex, and he understood. So I lay awake for some hours on his couch, mostly worrying about seeing Jeff, partly wishing I were in the next room. There's no better sleeping pill, and Steve seemed gentle as well as pretty.

39 ✦ I want to be
in that number

I tried to call Daniel the next morning but was told the
equipment was "not functioning." Went back to the dorm
and found a note, unsigned, saying there was an urgent
meeting that night, be at the Grapeseed at eight. I planned
to be a couple of thousand kilometers away.

I closed my account at the credit union and went to a
broker and converted most of the cash into twenty ounces
of gold, always scarce in the Worlds. Put two changes of
clothing in my bag, then loaded everything else into the
trunk, took it down to Penn Station and had it sent to Cape
Town. Then I met Jeff for lunch.

He was stunned at the news of Benny's death. He
couldn't argue with the necessity of my going to Cape
Town and getting home as early as possible.

"But marry me first," he said.

"You keep asking me that in restaurants," I said. "You
know I love you, Jeff, but . . . it would just make both of us
unhappy."

He shook his head and clasped both my hands. "A
symbol, that's all. It doesn't even have to be permanent. We
could get married in Delaware, make it a one-year renew-

able contract. Then when I get to New New York we can make whatever arrangement seems right."

A one-year contract didn't sound much like marriage to me. But it would make it easier for him to emigrate. "I guess there's no harm in it. Could we do it right away?"

"I have two days off. We could even squeeze in a little honeymoon, in Cape Town."

"New Orleans," I said. "I'm not going back without seeing it."

✦ ✦ ✦

We spent about an hour in Dover, thirty seconds of which was taken up by a bored notary reciting the marriage statute to us. Better than a Devonite ceremony, I guess, but not exactly moving.

It was a good time to visit New Orleans. The week before had been the annual sustained riot of Mardi Gras, and things were getting back to normal—a sustained wild party, that is to say.

Gambling and prostitution are legal in the old French Quarter; the gambling confined to one large casino but the prostitution is everywhere. It was handled better than on Broadway. To keep his or her license, a whore had to submit to a daily medical inspection. Prices were fixed by law, and any crime against a customer was cause for automatic and permanent revocation (a "ticket to Nevada," I found out they called it). Most of the whores wore conspicuous costumes—a "slave girl" in rags and chains gave me a shiver—but some wore regular clothes, with license prominently displayed. Many transvestites and people whose orientation was ambiguous or, more likely, flexible. Some gorgeous chunks of male meat that gave me unwifely urgings.

But mainly it was music. It wasn't pure Dixieland everywhere—in fact, there were even a few places with that mindless Ajimbo noise—and even where there was Dixieland, it was usually not the classical raucous polyphony, but smoother modern variations. But Preservation Hall had the real stuff, and Jeff dutifully sat with me for hour after hour there. He claimed to enjoy it, but I've seen his music collection, and it runs to urban ballads with a little light opera, no jazz.

In a spirit of evening things up, I went to the Casino with him, and watched him play for a couple of hours. He went in with five hundred dollars and said he'd play until he'd doubled it or lost it. He lost it, mainly on blackjack, though he dropped about a hundred on I-Ching, the rules for which I never did figure out.

We made love often and with some desperation, and walked the quaint streets saying obvious and important things. We ducked out of the rain into an antique store on Decatur Street, where my foolish mudball cop bought me a ring that must have cost several weeks' salary, a fire opal surrounded with diamond chips. Later, when he was sleeping, I slipped out and went back to the same place, and traded an ounce of my gold for a man's ring, a small gold nugget set in black onyx, and slipped it on his finger without waking him. Saying goodbye was very hard. Afterwards I sat in our room, my room now, for a long afternoon of staring and thinking.

Finally I had to get out, and I walked through the mist rain to a place on Bourbon Street, Fat Charlie's, where we'd heard some real Dixieland. It was a small place and not clean, sawdust on the floor, mismatched hard chairs tucked under random tables. But the music was loud and beautiful.

What changed my life was this: after one fine set I gave the waiter a ten and asked him to buy a drink for Fat Charlie, who was the group's clarinet player, and a good one. Fat Charlie brought the drink over and sat with me, and he was rather fascinated to find a Dixieland lover who was a woman, a white woman, a white woman from another World. When I admitted I played the clarinet, he was even more fascinated, and brought over his machine. He gave me a fresh reed to suck and asked me to "show my stuff."

I amazed myself. His clarinet was a century-old Le-Blanc, bored out for jazz. The sound was hard and bright and sexy. I did a few scales and intervals and then part of the wailing introduction to "Rhapsody in Blue."

I looked at the clarinet. "Incredible machine."

"How long you been playing, girl?"

"Thirteen years now."

"Be damned." He touched my elbow. "Come on up here." He led me to the platform, where the other band members were lounging, nursing drinks.

"I've never played jazz with a live group before."

"No problem. These fuckers won't be alive till the sun goes down." He gave a sideways signal with his head and the men picked up their instruments and did the reflex things with spit valves and slides and tuning pegs. The pianist did a sarcastic arpeggio. "Saints in B-flat?" he said to me.

"Sure." He was giving me the easy one.

Fat Charlie snapped his fingers like four sharp pistol shots and the drummer banged out a two-bar street beat introduction. We started clean and I went through the first verse and chorus almost automatically, not trying anything fancy. In this kind of pure Dixieland the cornet carries the melody and the clarinet rides an obbligato over him, subordinate but with more improvisational freedom than any of the others. After the first time around, each chorus is given to a different instrument, to improvise over a muted background of chords and rhythm. Fat Charlie gave me a nod for the second chorus; I closed my eyes and tried to forget there was an audience and waded right in.

It was good. It's been a long time since I had any difficulty with the mechanics of improvisation, anticipating the march of chords and choosing appropriate notes, but this was better than I had ever done—feeding off the other players, trying to get out in music something about losing Benny and Jeff leaving, and about going home, and all the wonderful and terrifying things that had happened over the last half-year. All in sixteen bars, sure.

The eight or nine people in the audience applauded my solo, and Fat Charlie smiled and nodded. While the drummer was doing his sixteen, Fat Charlie came over and whispered, "Last chorus all together, in E-flat, okay?" It's not my favorite key, but I managed to get through without too much pain.

Afterwards Fat Charlie held up two stubby fingers to the bartender and steered me back to the table. "Will you be in New Orleans awhile?" He said the name of the town as one three-syllable word.

"Only two days." I explained about Cape Town and waiting for the shuttle.

"How 'bout sitting in here a couple of times? The novelty'd bring in business and you know you'd enjoy it."

"I'd love to, if my lip holds out." You lose embouchure fast if you don't practice every day.

"We can switch off." The bartender brought over two drinks in tall frosted glasses. "You tried a julep yet?"

"No, I usually drink beer or wine." The cold sweet taste of it brought a double memory shock: mint tea in Marrakesh, with Jeff; bourbon in coffee at Perkins's rough table.

"You don't like it?" Fat Charlie looked at me with a worried expression. I guess I'd paled.

"No, I do. It—it just reminded me of something." I could almost remember something Benny had said about the force behind art.

He found a rumpled piece of paper and a pencil stub. "We don't have enough violins for 'Rhapsody in Blue.' You got other favorites?"

I could fake anything from "Basin Street" to "Willy the Weeper." But I gave him a list of nine or ten I was most familiar with.

"I'll call and have some handouts printed up. What's your name?"

"Marianne ... Mary Hawkings." I hadn't taken Jeff's name, but it didn't seem smart to put my own on handbills.

"You have a picture we can use?"

"Please, I'd rather you didn't." I couldn't think of a lie fast enough. "Don't ask me why."

"Sure, that's all right. Mystery woman from outer space. Give you five hundred a night?"

I would have paid him twice that, for the experience. "Fine. What time?"

"Eight or nine. We'll be playing till 'round three." He left to have the handouts made. I finished the drink and went out to walk off the nervousness. The rain had gone away.

So I had to come to Earth to be a soloist. There was a certain boy from school, a first clarinet, I wished could have been in the audience.

I went up on the levee to watch the sun set over the Mississippi and then went to a place Jeff and I had enjoyed, an old brick building by the levee that served only coffee and *beignets*, a kind of sweet fried bread dusted with powdered sugar, the coffee rich with chicory and heavy real cream. I felt so alive, so sad-and-happy, so full of expectation. I walked all of the Quarter, up and down and across, humming and whistling the songs I'd be playing, straightening out the melodies in my mind. In a Bourbon Street sit-down place, I felt like having a fish dinner, so I ordered crayfish, crawdads, and was nonplussed when the waitress brought out a large tray with a mountain of red-black insectoid creatures heaped on it. She showed me how to dissect them, a tiny pinch of meat in each one. Delicate taste.

For another hour I wandered up and down Bourbon Street, loitering in the doors of places that had music, stealing tricks. Then I went on to Fat Charlie's. I passed dozens of handbills with my "name" on them.

There wasn't an empty seat in the place. The bar was shoulder-to-shoulder and there were customers nursing drinks, leaning against the walls. Fat Charlie came out of nowhere and put his arm around my shoulders.

"This is a big crowd, girl," he said quietly. "They came to see you."

"I can't believe that—what, two hours? Three?"

"It's a small town. These're not too many tourists . . . like I say, you're something different. They come by to see." He handed me five crisp bills. "Here's some confidence. You go back in the kitchen and warm up a bit. Machine's behind the piano."

"What will I be playing, what order?"

"You just name it. We prob'ly know it."

Well, that was an interesting challenge. I picked up his clarinet and went into the kitchen, trying to think of the most obscure piece I knew. The kitchen was barely big enough for me and the cook, since the only prepared food they sold was fried potatoes with lots of salt. The cook was a little fat white man who never looked up from the potato slicer, but said, "Bottle's in the refrigerator."

I didn't usually eat or drink anything before playing, because of the saliva problem, but this wasn't exactly Mozart, and I was nervous enough to appreciate a little liquid courage. The bottle turned out to be bourbon, of course. I poured a couple of centimeters into a rather clean glass and drank it in one gulp. Shuddered from the fire and memory.

I worked out a little opening line for "Stavin' Change," which they couldn't *possibly* know. Feeling mischievous relieved some of the tension. Then I did fast and slow arpeggios, lowest note to highest, in all the keys we could possibly use.

Fat Charlie stuck his head in the door. "Warm?"

"Sweating." He led me out onto the platform, where the other five were waiting. Most of the conversation died down and there was a little applause.

He leaned against the piano and said, "Well? What's first?"

"You know 'Stavin' Change'?"

Five grins. "Tryin' to fuck us up," the trombone said to the banjo. To me: "What key? C-sharp minor?" The pianist reached all the way to his right and tinkled out the first line, *I'm gonna tell you 'bout a bad man*, in a ridiculously high C-sharp. "Maybe B-flat," he conceded. "About sixty?"

I nodded and Fat Charlie gave two heavy snaps; I just had time for a quick breath and started my intro, the piano and banjo automatically and softly behind. Then the trombone did a quiet vamp and the cornet took over the line, and I slid under him in sweet natural thirds and fifths, low register, and it was like we'd been playing together for years. They were so good.

I'll never have another night like that. I've played in a lot of orchestras and bands and quartets, and against my own recorded sound, but I'd never played with professionals before. There are no professional musicians in the Worlds, except for the cabarets in Shangrila. These cobs could do anything, with the precision and synchrony of a music box. If I'd asked them for the Pythagorean Theorem they'd take four finger snaps and roll into it.

And the audience loved it. I know I wasn't all that good, not within a light-year of Fat Charlie, but it was cute, like a bear riding a bicycle. They were "regulars," aficionados, and when we did pieces that had coon-shout lines, they'd sing right along with us. (Which was a good thing. My singing voice is very ordinary, and an alto in with all that gravel sounded ridiculous.) They applauded and yelled and threw coins on the stage and bought us drinks. I had five mint juleps but didn't get drunk; I was living so high and hard they just burned away. But by three o'clock I was staggering, drunk on fatigue and applause. The inside of my lips all numb pain and salt blood and my body felt like it had been squeezed through six bright hours of orgasm. Fat

Charlie walked me back to the hotel and gave me a big wet kiss and a rib-cracking hug.

I slept like a dead thing. The phone woke me up at about ten.

"Hello, no vision," I mumbled.

"Jimmy Hollis here." The banjo player. "You know you're in the paper?"

"What paper? What the hell are you doing up at this hour?"

"Shee-it. I'm *still* up." I remembered he'd offered me 'phets last night. "In the *Times-Picayune*. You a star, lady, a *star!*"

I put something on and stumbled down to the lobby and punched up "Entertainment" on the *Times-Picayune* machine. There I was, on the first page, red hair and blue denim and looking very intense. I bought another copy to send to Jeff.

I actually was, technically, a "star"—one of the 480 on the list compiled daily by *The New York Times*. I was number ten in the subcategory "Jazz, Traditional, Instrumental."

I hadn't even finished reading the article when somebody knocked on the door. I put my hand on the knob. "Who is it?"

"Newspaper. *Times-Picayune*."

I opened the door. "Look, I don't—"

He was a tall man with an ugly scarred face. He raised a small pistol and shot me in the neck.

40 ✦ Joyride

I woke up with my wrists tied to the arms of a floater seat. To my right, out the window, a desert was rolling by about a thousand meters below. To my left was the ugly man who had shot me. There was a pilot and nobody else. My bladder was about to burst.

"I have to pee," I said to the ugly man.

"So pee," he said.

"Winchell," the pilot said, "don't be such a prick. If she does, you have to clean it up."

"Don't count on it." But he untied me and I rushed back to the john. There was a small welt on my neck, anesthetic dart.

Urinating, I realized the bladder pain wasn't everything and, disgusted, found sticky evidence of recent intercourse. I cleaned up raging and went back to the man Winchell, standing in the aisle.

"You son of a goat," I said. "You raped me."

"Oh no. You didn't resist at all. I think you liked it."

For three seconds I glared at him, trying to remember everything Jeff and Benny had taught me. I balled my right fist and hauled back as if to hit him. He stepped right into it. He laughed and reached forward to block it and I did my damndest to drive his testicles into his throat. He oof'ed and turned pale and started to fold up, and I hit his nose as hard as I could with the heel of my hand. Nearly broke my hand, but he crunched and bled in a satisfying way.

"Very well done," the pilot said. He was looking at me over the barrel of a dart pistol. "Not smart, though. When he can stand up again he'll bite off your arm and stuff it down your throat. Very very bad person." He lowered his point of aim and shot Winchell in the back.

"Now. Are you going to be good, or do I shoot you another dose? It's not healthy to have two the same day."

"I won't hurt you. I don't know how to drive a floater."

He nodded. "Sit up here, where I can keep an eye on you."

I strapped myself in next to him. I was still trembling with rage, and with something else, something I couldn't identify. "Who are you? What's going on?"

"I'm a free-lance pilot. Winchell's a free-lance muscle —all the way to the top of his skull, muscle. We snatched you for a guy named Wallace."

"Kidnapped?"

"That's right. Two hundred thousand up front, plus five percent each, of whatever he finally gets."

The desert must mean we were headed for Nevada. I thought about what Violet had told me about kidnapping. "But that's absurd. I don't have any money; nobody I know has any money."

He gave me a puzzled look. "Come on."

"But it's true. I'm from New New York; no one has private wealth."

"He must have some other reason, then." He shook his head. "Christ. No royalties."

"I don't see what you're complaining about. This doesn't seem like too much work for two hundred thousand dollars."

"I only get a hundred. It's the risk, not the work. Snatching's a capital crime in Louisiana, and in Louisiana they just walk you past a warm judge and take you out back and shoot you."

"Are we in Nevada?"

"Not yet. Wait till dark to cross the border." He lit a cigarette and leaned back to look at some dials. "Winchell, uh, raped you while you were unconscious."

"That's right."

"He is a low-life son of a bitch. I should have got someone else. It was real short notice," he said apologetically.

I stared out the window. "Twice in six months. I've been raped twice in six months." I was seized with sudden fury. "What's *wrong* with you groundhogs? *What the hell is wrong with you?*" I leaned over and was beating him on the shoulder and head with my fists, blinded with tears.

He shoved me away, not too roughly. "Hey! You want to kill us all?" We were much closer to the ground; he pulled back on the wheel and we rose to our former level.

"Here." He reached into his pocket and pulled out the dart gun. I braced for it, but he turned around and shot two more darts into Winchell. "He'll be out for a day now. And he won't be able to keep anything down for a week. I'd kill him for you, but people would think that was just to get his part of the advance. I'd have a hard time finding partners."

When I didn't say anything, he elaborated. "Listen, lady. I really am sorry. This is a business to me, and I normally work with good professionals. But it was a rush job; I was in New Orleans on vacation and got the call. I had to pick up a local. He had a good reference; I'm sorry he turned out to be a thug."

"What the hell do you call *yourself?*"

"Pilot. I fly merchandise and passengers under dangerous conditions." He turned on a radar screen and slid a knob back and forth. The scale of it expanded; a green dotted state line appeared at the top of the screen. "We're pretty safe now. A floater off autopilot isn't that unusual here, lots of tourists. We'll have to break a heavy police line to get into Nevada, though. They like to stop you on general principles."

"I can imagine."

"We might have some pursuit, though, if you've been reported missing. Is that likely?"

I weighed what to tell him, and decided it was in my favor for him not to be too nervous. "Not until about nine o'clock. I'm supposed to show up to play in a band."

"Seven here, won't be dark yet. That's not good. If someone suspects a snatch they'll put the border guards on alert." He banked the floater to the left and we started flying into the sun. "Think we better come in from the northwest. Let you see the Rockies."

I was still trembling. "I feel sick. I've never hit anybody before."

"Pretty good for a first try." He reached across me and opened a small compartment in the dash. "Look in the first aid kit there. Should be some Dramamine and tranks. Water back by the john."

I took the pills back, stepping over Winchell, resisting the impulse to kick him a few times. The pilot asked me to bring him a sandwich and a beer from the refrigerator.

My bag was on a shelf below the refrigerator. I checked and the Puke-O was missing. But the nineteen gold pieces were still sewed in the bottom lining.

I got myself a sandwich, too, and we ate in fairly companionable silence.

"You've already got your hundred thousand?" I asked him.

"That's right. Cash in advance."

"And you don't think you'll get any more? Five percent of nothing, I mean."

"That's possible. Wallace didn't say why he wanted you snatched. There are other reasons than ransom."

"If you turn this thing around and take me to Atlanta, I'll give you thirty-eight thousand dollars in gold."

He laughed, didn't look at me. "Not for a million, lady. I have a reputation to protect.... Besides, Wallace might possibly get angry, and have me killed. I'd never fly again."

"That's just what I'm afraid of. A friend of mine was

murdered and I think whoever did it wants to get me, too."

"Impossible," he said. "Roundabout, anyhow. If I wanted somebody murdered in New Orleans, I'd just go down to the waterfront. Ten thousand shitbags who'd stick a knife into you for the price of breakfast at Brennan's." He drummed his fingers on the wheel. "How do you come to have so much gold stashed away?"

"It's for New New York. They use it in electronics. Do you know anything about Wallace?"

"Never heard of him before yesterday. But that's Las Vegas. People come and go."

"He couldn't be the government, could he? U.S. government?"

"What, are you a spy for the Worlds? This is getting deep."

"The Worlds don't have spies on Earth. That would be like Philadelphia sending spies to New Jersey."

"Wouldn't count on that being true anymore. From the news, it sounds like things are getting pretty rough. You ought to be glad you're on Earth. Present circumstances excepted."

"Sure." Present circumstances included an awful lot besides a little kidnapping. I yawned hugely. The tranquilizer was getting to me.

"Go ahead and take a nap. But if you hear a loud chime, that means you have a half-second to get your arms on the armrests and make sure your head is straight up-and-down on the headrest. This baby can do eight gees on evasive maneuvers." I got into that position and decided I could sleep that way.

✦ ✦ ✦

When I woke up, it was dark. "How close are we?"

"About two hundred kilometers from the border. We're flying by radar, about ten meters off the ground." I could see shadowy landscape flashing by; we were evidently in some sort of a valley, following the twisted course of a river.

"How much longer?"

"Twenty-some minutes. Less if we have to goose it."

On cue, a voice said, "OREGON STATE POLICE. YOU ARE FLYING WITHOUT LIGHTS." It seemed to come from everywhere in the floater. The chime went off and I braced myself. "PLEASE IDENT—"

A loud roar and the scenery around us was suddenly lit up by bright blue light. The land fell away as acceleration crushed me back into the seat, as if a fat man had plopped down on my lap and was pushing back with all his might. I could feel my face distorting, the skin of my cheeks stretching back, eyeballs exposed to cold air. My ears popped painfully. The floater was shuddering violently. Then we were suddenly weightless.

"Stay braced. I have to do some things to amuse their radar." His right hand played over a keyboard. We were higher than the tallest mountains, but falling.

"What about Winchell?" I didn't dare look back.

"He's not the one I'm being paid to deliver. Hold on." The blast kicked in again and we were diving straight down. We flashed down the side of a mountain—sharp pain in my ears like somebody poking fingers down them. "Yawn," the pilot said; I did and they popped again. As the ground approached we leveled off with a violent surge, chin jammed down against my neck, sharp pain in back and breasts and elbows, and then we were just flying again, but very fast. I leaned forward and realized we were still accelerating slightly.

"You do this often?" I asked.

"Often enough to be good at it. That's why they called me." He tuned the radar. There were three bright spots drifting down the screen, dimming. "I'm not worried about the Oregon cops. But they'll have warned the border guards. Big border, though; they might not have time to get into position."

"If they have?"

"Probably try to shoot us down." He grimaced, looking ghoulish in the green light from the radar screen. "Haven't got me yet."

"Why don't you contact them and tell them there's an innocent person aboard?"

"All that would do is give our position away. Don't worry. I'll be coming in at cactus level, five or six times the speed of sound. We'll just pop over the horizon and zip! We're in Nevada."

He really didn't seem to be very worried. But then maybe he was insane.

He studied the radar screen with increasing tension as we zigged and zagged, following the configuration of the land. After a few minutes he clicked a switch and leaned back.

"That's it. We're home."

"They can't follow us in?"

"International incident." He pushed a button. "Control, this is Baker eight-four-seven-six, coming in with a snatch. I need a pattern for Vegas, two-four, seven-nine, section OL."

"Congratulations," it answered. "Who's the snatch?"

"Marianne O'Hara, alias Mary Hawkings, registered with Landreth Wallace."

"All right, we'll notify. You've got the pattern. Endit."

"You know my real name?"

"All I know is you've got two names." He let go of the wheel, lit a cigarette and leaned back. "Can I give you some advice?"

"Sure. This is all new to me."

"First of all, don't try to escape. You don't know how to drive a flyer, so the only way out of Vegas is the tube. You have to pass Security to get out, and they'll know who you are. They can be pretty rough."

"I can walk out. Across the desert."

"No. Not only is it too hard a hike, but they'd pick you

up before you got five kilometers from the city limits. Just not very many people out there.

"And be cooperative. This Landreth Wallace, from the few minutes I talked with him yesterday, seems to be a nice enough fellow. Older man. But he is a desperate criminal, by definition, and in Nevada he can do anything he wants to you, even kill you. So don't provoke him."

"You mean I should start getting a taste for being raped."

"Not exactly . . . but I thought you Worlds girls were, well, liberal about that sort of thing."

I'm not a "girl," but at least he didn't call me a spacer. "Oh sure. We have rape contests all the time."

"Seriously. He's a criminal but isn't necessarily a violent or unreasonable man. I'm a criminal, too, and I haven't laid a finger on you, right?"

"Maybe you just don't want to wind up like *him*." I looked back and gasped. Winchell was crushed up against the lavatory door, lying in a thick pool of blood.

"Christ." The pilot unbuckled and walked back, took a quick look, and returned, shaking his head. "Dead as a rock." He buckled in and turned on the radio. "Control, this is Baker eight-four-seven-six again. I need clearance for a fast manual approach."

"What's the problem, Baker?"

"Dead passenger. May only be a couple minutes dead."

"Just a second . . . you're clear at two thousand meters. Take her to West End. Lose your snatch?"

"No, muscle. Endit." The acceleration kicked in, not as hard as before.

"I don't understand why you want him revived," I said. "Won't you get twice as much if he stays dead?"

"Not necessarily. Might just save Wallace a hundred grand. Have to take it before the guild." The roar got louder as we rose, and he shouted over it. "Probably I would get the money, but it sure wouldn't look good on my record. Be that much harder to get muscle I could trust."

Honor among thieves. We could see the glow of Las Vegas long before the first buildings came over the horizon.

I'd seen pictures of the city, but they were nothing like the reality. A glimmering fairyland of graceful but garish buildings; bright ghosts of holo advertisements, as large as the buildings themselves, hovering in the air.

We decelerated hard and floated down to the landing pad on a hospital on the outskirts of the city. Two orderlies were waiting with a stretcher; the pilot popped the door before we set down.

They rushed in and strapped the body onto the stretcher. "Who's going to pay?" the female orderly asked.

"Landreth Wallace. But he's under an Assassin's Guild guarantee."

"Okay. You want to fill out the forms?"

"Have to make a delivery. I'll be back in half an hour, or maybe Wallace'll come out."

"We can only give him maintenance treatment, without a signature. He's losing a thousand brain cells a second."

"Then he's already a hundred thousand in the hole." He unbuckled. "Christ. O'Hara, Hawkings, come along with me. Don't try anything."

So my introduction to Las Vegas was sitting in a hospital waiting room while a criminal signed forms to save the life of a man he detested. It got more interesting, though.

41 ✦ Reunion

Landreth Wallace's house, or place of business, was very
near the hospital; we spent less than a minute in the air.
The pilot turned me over to a silent man who was armed
prominently with two pistols. He led me from the roof
down a winding staircase to a small room with a chair, a
bed, and a cube.

"Mr. Wallace is out," was the only thing he said. He
turned on the cube and sat in the chair.

I sat on the edge of the bed. The show had to do with a
naked woman creeping through the corridors of an old cas-
tle, armed with a dagger.

"Do we have to watch this?" He waved his hand, evidently giving me permission to change the station; at least
he didn't shoot me when I started punching the button.

Prime-time cube involves various permutations of vag-
inal fluids, semen, and blood. I found a public-service station, and we spent the next twenty minutes being in-
structed in the use of compost in home gardens, with a
special emphasis on cucumbers.

A man in his seventies or eighties came into the room
and dismissed the guard. I turned off the cube, much wiser
in the ways of cucumbers.

"You were assaulted. I do apologize. The man was an
amateur."

"I doubt it. That word means 'lover.' " Past tense. "Is he dead, then?"

"I don't know. It no longer concerns me. He has guild coverage."

"This guild must not have very strong entrance requirements."

"It does, actually. But he was from out of state, an associate member. For that, I believe you only have to show evidence that you have committed a murder." He sat down.

"And you belong to the kidnapper's guild, I suppose."

He smiled slightly. "There is no such thing. To the best of my knowledge."

"But you do belong to something."

He looked at me for a second and inclined his head. "Pardon me? I don't think I understand."

"You must have had some reason for kidnapping me."

"Money."

"But I don't have any money. Nothing like as much as you paid those"—I searched for a word—"shitbags who abducted me."

The word appeared to offend him. "Please. Whether you personally have money is immaterial. There are very few individuals with fortunes large enough to meet your ransom.

"I shall explain, so far as I can. An unstable situation exists between the United States and the Worlds. Various ... people ... would benefit from a total severance of relations.

"Last night a decision was made, and analysis of various sources indicated that you are the most prominent Worlds citizen currently residing in the United States."

"Because of my music?" I was incredulous.

"I really don't know the details. Aren't you some sort of musical star?"

"But that's something that changes daily."

"Nevertheless, yours was the name chosen. I offer my personal regrets, if only for the selfish reason that I should find it easier to deal with a man.

"To sum up the situation. We have demanded that New New York pay fifty million dollars for your release."

"Impossible."

"And we have indicated that it would be a generous gesture on the part of the governments of the United States and Louisiana to help with the payment."

"That doesn't seem likely, either."

"We realize this. Much more than fifty million is at stake."

"Who are these 'people'?"

"If I told you more, you would have to die, whether the money were paid or not." He pressed his fingers together and said calmly, "I may myself die, for my knowledge. But it is an exciting thing to be involved with. Excitement is rare at my age."

"What happens to me if nobody pays?"

"The threat is that you will be killed. Actually, your life, and the payment, are trivial. If the desired objective comes about, you will probably be released." He stood up slowly. "At any rate, don't entertain any illusion about escaping. There are more than forty armed guards in this house. Even if you could escape from this room, you could only get to the roof. There are several people on guard there."

"It seems like excessive caution, against one unarmed woman."

He stood with his hand on the doorknob. "Nevada is a difficult place to do business. We don't want you kidnapped from us." He favored me with a wan smile and left.

Was it possible the door was unlocked? I went to try it, but before I reached it, it opened. A young man came in, carrying a tray of food. He didn't seem to be armed.

"Hello. Dinner time." He set the tray on the bed and then went into the bathroom, and returned with a small folding table. He uncovered the tray and there were two of everything. Bowls of chili, bottles of beer, utensils.

"I take it you'll be my companion for dinner?"

"Your companion for everything. I'm supposed to keep an eye on you."

"I thought this place was escape-proof."

He attacked his chili like a starved man. "It is. I'm supposed to prevent you from committing suicide, that's all."

"Suicide? God, what a crazy world."

"Well, you have to admit it would screw things up." He pinched open his beer, and then mine. "My name's Kelly, Kelly Chantenay. You're Mary? Or Marianne."

"Neither. O'Hara."

He nodded pleasantly and kept eating. I tried the chili and it was bland but palatable. "What do you do when you're not preventing people from committing suicide?"

"I'm a bodyguard. Kelly Girl."

"You were just rented for the occasion, then?"

"Most of us were. Except for that talkative cob who was down here with you, he's Mr. Wallace's regular bodyguard. He's a real joke, Two-Gun Pete. Americans."

"Landreth Wallace isn't a Nevadan?"

"No, he's from Washington. The city."

That was interesting. "He works for the government?"

"At the office they said he was a 'financier,' that's all I know. Sounds like a Lobby to me. They're all a bunch of crooks."

I tried not to laugh with my mouth full. "Was your name Kelly before you went to work for Kelly Girls? Or did you change it to accommodate them?"

"I get a lot of kidding about that. I should have known when I signed up with them that everyone would call me Kelly Boy. I'm going to change my name to George."

"They'll still call you Kelly Boy."

He laughed. "Well, it's worth it. They're the straightest outfit in town. And anyone who pays me two thousand dollars a day for sitting with a beautiful woman has my unswerving loyalty."

Well, he was a gallant liar. "That's a lot of money."

"Union scale. But I kick back two hundred to the clerk who picked me, and another four hundred to the union, for each day. It's still better than the States. I'd be paying more than half my income in taxes."

We ate for a while. "Are you actually trained in preventing people from killing themselves?"

He shrugged. "A bodyguard has to know all kinds of things."

"I could inhale a mouthful of chili." Sure. "Choke myself."

He pulled a knife out of his pocket, evidently sharp. "Tracheotomy."

"Drown myself in the shower."

"I'll be sitting on the pot, watching. If you want to bathe with an audience, that is. You can go without; I won't complain."

"Speaking of going . . ."

"I'm afraid so. I have to be with you every minute."

"That's right. I could braid a rope out of toilet paper and hang myself." Actually, he would probably be more embarrassed than I would. Violet told me that they have separate toilets for men and women here.

"You could flush yourself down the drain and escape," he said, deadpan.

"What happens when you have to sleep? Crawl in with me?"

"I won't sleep. Not for five or six days, with pills. If it goes longer than that, I can knock you out for twelve hours, painlessly. And I wouldn't crawl in with you. The carpet's soft."

"The last man who knocked me out raped me. More than once, I think."

"That's terrible." I told him about Winchell. "He'll never get another job, I can guarantee that. You want him killed?"

"What, would you do it?"

"I'm no scab. But anybody in the Assassin's Guild

would do it for pocket change. They have a reputation to protect. I wouldn't be surprised if they get to him in the hospital, just on principle."

It seemed likely. All of my rapists die in hospitals.

He went on. "They shouldn't let associates into their guild. It really waters it down. Americans are such animals, anyhow."

"I know some nice ones." Was I hearing this? From a Nevadan?

"For women your age, the second leading cause of death is murder after rape or sexual battery. They're *animals*."

"Women never get raped or murdered in Nevada." He said something in reply, but I didn't hear it. The tranquilizer I'd taken on the floater was wearing off as fast as it had taken effect. Rising sense of helpless terror. I snatched up my bag and emptied it on the bed, grabbed the bottle of Klonexine.

My hands were shaking so badly I couldn't get it open. I held it out to him. "Please. Open this goddamn thing for me."

He studied the label for a maddening few seconds. "Open it!" I felt like grabbing him by the shoulders and shaking him. He figured out the top, pinched and turned, and handed it back to me. I shook out three capsules and washed them down with the dregs of my beer. Then I curled up on the bed and trembled and sobbed.

Then my head was on his lap and he was stroking my hair gently, trying to say reassuring things. I reached around and held him tightly, awkwardly, his belt buckle pleasantly cold against my forehead, and in a minute the triple dose hit me like a velvet club.

✦ ✦ ✦

I woke up, groggy, to the sound of the cube: a news announcer had just said my own name. Kelly Boy was watching the program intently and hadn't realized I'd awakened.

It was a good thing I'd overdosed on Klonexine. I was flattened out and didn't come apart when I heard the details of Wallace's terms.

They had twenty-four hours to come up with fifty million dollars. If they didn't pay, one of my ears would be sent to the New New York Corporation at the Cape. Another twenty-four hours, the other ear. Then they would start on the fingers.

Kelly heard me sigh. "They didn't tell you about that?"

"I guess it didn't seem important."

"Don't worry. It won't hurt." He fingered a penstick clipped to his pocket, evidently the thing he could use to knock me out. "Just don't look in a mirror until you can have it built back. I had the end of my nose shot off last year. It wasn't so bad."

"Fingers, though?"

"That would be pretty expensive," he admitted. "Nothing like fifty million, though."

I wondered who else was making that calculation. "How close are we to twenty-four hours?"

He checked his watch. "Another thirteen. You want a pill?"

"No. Is there anything around here to read? I really do hate the cube."

He searched drawers but all he could come up with was a deck of cards. He taught me how to play gin rummy, and I had some talent at it. One thing Klonexine is good for is concentration. Nothing mattered but the cards. When breakfast came, nothing mattered but the scrambled eggs. Since there was nothing I could do about the situation, I kept myself thoroughly flattened out. I deliberately did not keep track of time.

I was dozing when lunch came. The man who brought it looked vaguely familiar, from the back. He turned around and it was Jeff.

"New guy?" Kelly said.

"Right." Jeff set the tray on the table, reached inside his shirt and pulled out a laser.

"Don't shoot him!" I said quickly.

Kelly raised his hands. "I'm not armed."

"Is that true?" Jeff said. He didn't look at me. He was frozen in a half crouch, holding the laser with both hands, aimed at the center of Kelly's chest.

"Well, he has a pocket knife. And that spraystick in his breast pocket is some kind of anesthetic, knock-out gas."

"You're pretty calm," Jeff said.

"Doped."

"Has he hurt you?"

"No," I said. "I'm a *bodyguard*," Kelly said in an injured tone.

I rolled off the bed. "Why don't I take his own spraystick and put him under?"

"Don't go near him," Jeff said. "He might use you as a shield." He gestured at Kelly. "Turn around. Put your hands on the top of your head." Jeff walked over to him and put the laser against the base of his skull.

"Don't twitch. Don't even breathe." He reached around carefully and took the spraystick from Kelly's pocket.

He stepped back. "Okay. Turn around." As Kelly was turning around, Jeff discharged the spraystick into his face; he wilted sideways.

"Let's move. We may not have much time." Before he opened the door, Jeff took my arm. "Maybe you better keep your eyes closed for a minute. I don't think you want to see what's in the hall. I'll guide you."

When he opened the door there was a smell like roast pig. I did open my eyes, and what I saw bothered me slightly. It was evidently the man Kelly had called Two-Gun Pete; at least he had a gun in each hand. There was a charred slash from the center of his chest to the middle of his face, oozing blood, and the top of his head had exploded. There were bits of his skull scattered down the hall, like chips of white pottery, along with most of his brains and one eyeball. My reaction to this gruesome sight was a testimonial to Klonexine: "What a mess. Did you have to kill many others?"

"Nobody else, not yet." We hustled toward the spiral staircase that led to the roof. "We gassed the guards up above and found the circuit box; cut off the power to the elevator. I tossed a couple of gas grenades down the fire stairs after I took care of that one."

At the top of the spiral staircase was a man in a black jumpsuit with a mirror helmet. Jeff gave him a signal with his thumb. He opened a door and shouted *Go!* I was surprised to see that it was night.

We got to the roof in time to see that man jump into a single-seat floater. There were three other small ones; they rose a few meters and took off rapidly in four different directions. One of them drew some hand-laser fire from the ground, but it didn't seem to have any effect.

Jeff's floater was larger, with two seats. We stepped aboard and he helped me strap in, a complicated net that slipped over the head and attached itself to the seat at hip level.

The transparent canopy slipped into place and, with a hydraulic sigh, the seats unfolded themselves into beds. I started to say something lewd, but Jeff snapped "Keep your arms in!" and we were suddenly roaring straight up, with much greater acceleration than the kidnapper's floater had managed. My ears popped loudly and I saw purple blotches and bright blinking stars. It was hard to breathe and I had aches in places where I never felt pain before or since. I was barely conscious when the acceleration abruptly stopped, and the beds became chairs again.

"You all right?" I nodded. I didn't think anything was broken. He touched his throat and said, "Well done, boys. All units return to Denver."

We were at a high enough altitude that the Earth's curvature was obvious. Las Vegas was a beautiful splash of light, slowly receding. The snow-capped mountains glowed faintly under a gibbous moon.

"I don't know what to say. They were going to cut off my ears."

He patted my hand. "What good is a husband who won't look after his wife's ears?"

"I'll never say anything bad about the FBI again."

"Don't count on it." He looked suddenly grim. "This was not an FBI job. Strictly private enterprise."

"Oh, I understand. The FBI can't work in foreign countries."

"Actually, we do, under various guises. We certainly have a lot of people in Nevada, which is how I found you so easily. But when it gets back to the Bureau there'll be hell to pay.

"What happened, I told my squad I was going to borrow some of the Bureau's equipment and try to come unsnatch you. I asked whether one of them might want to come along, as a friend not a subagent, and protect my back. All of them volunteered. Good bunch.

"So I checked out the vehicles and weapons from the Denver office, supposedly for a training exercise in assault tactics. The vehicles are all 'ghosts'; they look like commercial sport floaters. We painted over the license numbers. Right now we're headed for a rendezvous point in a Denver suburb, a private garage where we'll scrub the paint off."

"You've taken an awful lot of chances. With your career, I mean, as well as the danger."

"I'm not going to have a career with the Bureau much longer."

"It may be some time before you can get to New New."

"That's not what I mean. When I got back from New Orleans, I tried to pull the file on Benny. Couldn't. It was tagged 'Secrecy Class Five,' which means it's only accessible to a couple of dozen people.

"I'm good up to Class Three; if Benny had been just a

double agent, I could have gotten his file. There's a lot more going on. I think that farmer was right: the Bureau killed him.''

"Why?"

"I don't know. But here's the clincher. I looked to see if there's a file on you. There is; it's Class Five, too.

''This morning my supervisor called me in. There was a woman with him, from Internal Security. She asked me about you and Benny. I gave her a mixture of truth and bullshit. Evidently they don't yet know we're married, and I don't think they know I called in about Benny from Geneva. It must be part of his file, but the thing is almost a hundred thousand words long. It's not likely she read it all. But she might, now.''

"What will they do to you?"

"I don't know. What I should do is go back to Vegas and get a dryclean, then go down to the Cape and wait. But I don't have the hush money. That's what got Benny. A straight dryclean and the Bureau has a file on you in five minutes.''

"How much does it cost?"

"Oh, hell. Twenty-five, thirty thousand.''

"I've got it." I picked up my bag and ripped out the bottom lining. I held out a handful of gold coins. "Take it."

He hefted them. "I've never seen so much gold.''

"They told me it was the best thing I could bring back to New New. Credit per se isn't worth much, with the embargo on. The gold is valuable as a metal, for electronics.''

"How much is this worth?" I told him, $38,000. He handed back two coins and put the rest in his pocket. "Looks like we're making a hobby out of saving each other's life.''

"You think the FBI would have you killed?"

"I don't know anymore."

The radio chimed. "Ground yourself," a bored voice said. "Arizona State Police."

He put his hand on the stick. "I could outrun them . . .''

Instead, he touched his throat. "You guys have vision?"

"Channel Nine."

Jeff punched something on the dash, took out his wallet and held it open in front of a lens. "FBI business, all right?"

The radar became a flatscreen, a man in uniform peering intently. "You're coming out of Nevada. Is it that kidnapping?"

He used a voice I'd never heard. "Do you want to have your job tomorrow?"

The man stared for a second. "Understood. I didn't see you."

"Four other vehicles without numbers. Some of them may come into your airspace."

He smiled. "I sure don't see them on the scope."

"Thanks. Endit."

"Good hunting."

Jeff switched the screen back to radar. "No love lost between Arizona and Nevada." He punched some more buttons and let go of the wheel. "Game plan. When we get to the garage, we call a cab for you. You go straight to the tube station and take the first one out. Anywhere. Then transfer to Atlanta."

"I don't want to desert you."

"You won't be. Don't worry. I'll get my squad straight, have my second turn in the equipment, and then go back to Vegas. Take me six, maybe eight hours for the dryclean. No surgery, just a wig and a beard. I'll meet you at Cape Town, sovereign territory, should be safe for both of us.

"You've been in the news, so you might be recognized. Play dumb—'A lot of people say I look like her'—but if you get cornered, say you were rescued by five people who said they'd been hired by the New New York Corporation. I don't think New New York would deny it."

"All right. But isn't it dangerous for you to be going back to Denver? If the FBI's after your hide in New York, don't you think the word may have spread?"

"There's a chance," he admitted. "But there's no big

staff in Denver, and only one person on night duty. No one in New York knows I'm gone, though I'm supposed to meet with my supervisor in about twelve hours. I'll be on my way to Cape Town by then."

"You don't expect any trouble in Las Vegas?"

"Well, I did kill a man there, which is something they don't like outsiders to do."

"He was an outsider himself, if that makes any difference."

"It might. But it's not really worth worrying about. The only people who could link me to that murder are your bodyguard, who has troubles of his own by now, and my informer, who's an FBI agent herself."

"Does the murder bother you?"

He shook his head. "Just a little. I tiptoed down the staircase with a gas grenade in my left hand and laser in my right. When I saw the man in the hall I tossed the gas grenade, but I was never any good with my left hand. It bounced off the wall and fell short. The guy jumped out of his chair and drew two guns.

"It was like the last time. His reflexes versus mine. I won again, but it doesn't have the feeling of victory. And I never want to do it again."

"You won't have to. There aren't any guns in New New York."

"Wonderful." He stretched. "We're almost an hour from Denver. Long night ahead of us both; we ought to nap."

I had one of those strange Klonexine dreams. A small glass dinosaur was in the floater with us, jumping around, clacking its jaws. Finally Jeff caught it, pulled back the canopy, and threw it out. I woke up when that happened.

"Denver," Jeff said. It was beautiful at night, the golden lights in graceful geometry spreading out to the horizon.

While I was gazing, the lights went out, every one.

42 ✦ What happened behind their backs (1)

O'Hara didn't cause it. It happened because of a defiant credit transfer, and because of unusual industry on the part of the Third Revolution, and because of a multitude of minor factors, one of which was a difference of opinion as to who should ransom O'Hara. But initially it was the credit transfer.

In their first payment since New New demanded the rate increase, New York State defiantly paid at the old rate. At the same time they sent to New New York, both in orbit and at the Cape, a seven-page brief defending their right to do so. Coordinators Markus and Berrigan turned the brief over to the one person in New New who was an expert in American contract law. Then they announced that the solar power satellite needed maintenance, and they switched it off, at exactly five o'clock in the afternoon, Eastern time.

New York State had not been quite honest when they claimed that New New's powersat supplied only ten percent of their electricity. The real figure fluctuated between forty and fifty percent. When the satellite was turned off, everything went out of kilter.

It was a bad time for a blackout. People who left work a little early were stuck in darkened subways; others, in frozen elevators or abruptly inert office buildings—some facing an hour-long descent down lightless fire stairs. A few dozen died of heart attacks.

There was an interstate power net that kept the Eastern Seaboard operating smoothly. New York tried to suck power out of it, but it was too great a demand, all at once. There were blackouts and brownouts and crippling power surges from Boston to Norfolk.

Under the best of conditions it would have been the next morning before everything got straightened out. But conditions could hardly have been worse.

In an office building in Washington, the man who had requested that O'Hara be kidnapped considered the chaos around him. He went to a very private telephone and called three people. Then he went upstairs and discreetly murdered his boss, the Director of the Federal Bureau of Investigation. By midnight he was sitting in a well-appointed bunker under the hills of West Virginia.

Exactly at midnight, several hundred thousand acts of sabotage were carried out. They ranged in magnitude from the snipping of a cable in Des Moines to the detonation of nuclear weapons in Washington and Chicago.

The Third Revolution began at midnight and was effectively over by 12:01, though the fighting would go on until it was no longer relevant. It happened a month early. The original plans called for April 13th, Good Friday, but the confusion over the power loss was too good an opportunity to pass up.

Their slogan, "Power to the People," was not original but it did have a certain ironic force: in the sense of being able to turn on a switch or plug something into the wall, most of the people would never have power, ever again.

43 ✦ The beginning of the end

"What the hell is going on?" Jeff said quietly. On the dash of the floater a red light blinked several times and then glowed constantly: EMERGENCY POWER.

Jeff brought the floater down to treetop level, searched, and drifted down onto a baseball diamond. "It's not just Denver," he said. "The carrier wave this thing runs on is federally maintained."

We tried all the civilian channels on the flatscreen and got nothing but a white square, until we found a Canadian station. It was from a French province, but a simultaneous translation in English slid along the bottom of the picture:

... OF A SCALE UNPARALLELED IN THE COUNTRY'S HISTORY. AT LEAST TWO ATOM BOMBS HAVE EXPLODED, IN WASHINGTON AND CHICAGO. THE SABOTAGE APPEARS TO HAVE BEEN DIRECTED MAINLY TOWARD POWER GENERATION AND TRANSMISSION SYSTEMS, AND COMMUNICATION. THE GROUP RESPONSIBLE HAS IDENTIFIED ITSELF AS LA TROISIÈME RÉVOLUTION *CORRECTION* THE THIRD REVOLUTION AND CLAIMS TO HAVE OVER A MILLION MEMBERS UNDER ARMS. THE REVOLUTION'S LEADER, WHO CALLS HIMSELF PROVISIONAL PRESIDENT, IS RICHARD CONKLIN—

"My God!" Jeff said.

—WHO IS ALSO THE ASSISTANT DIRECTOR OF THE FEDERAL

BUREAU OF INVESTIGATION. A STATEMENT FROM HIM IS FORTH-
COMING.

IT IS NOT KNOWN HOW MANY OF THE COUNTRY'S LEADERS
SURVIVED THE DESTRUCTION OF DOWNTOWN WASHINGTON. THE
SECRETARY OF DEFENSE HAS DECLARED A COUNTRYWIDE STATE
OF MARTIAL LAW, ORDERING ALL MILITARY PERSONNEL TO RE-
PORT TO THEIR UNITS, INCLUDING THE SEMI-CIVILIAN NATIONAL
GUARD.

The message was repeated, and we were urged to stay
tuned for further developments. Jeff turned it off.

"I don't now how far we can get on emergency power.
Probably not as far as the Cape. Have to try, though."

"How long do you think the power will be off?"

"Depends on how thorough they were. Suppose they
actually destroyed all of the country's major generators? A
couple of thousand people could do the trick, with moder-
ate training." He typed out directions for the autopilot and
we drifted up off the grass with barely perceptible acceleration.

"We can't make new generators without energy. We
can't do *anything*. Get food to cities . . ."

"I wonder if it's the group Benny and I were involved
with."

"Probably. And with Conklin at the head of it, going to
the Bureau is what got him killed. What I wonder is how
much of the Bureau is involved? How much of the police
and military?"

For hours we watched the screen, cruising slowly to
conserve power. We got an outline of the catastrophe's di-
mensions.

New York City was in chaos, a three-way firefight
among police, looters, and revolutionaries. From most
cities, there was no communication at all. Satellite photos
showed that Pittsburgh and Los Angeles were in flames.

Canada, Mexico, and Nevada had all closed their borders. The revolution was condemned by most of Common

Europe but cautiously endorsed by the Supreme Socialist Union.

There were more than ten thousand people caught in the interstate tube system. Rescue operations were under way, but most of them would suffocate. Thousands had died because their floaters' failsafes didn't work.

New New York denied having anything to do with it, but the timing of their turning off the powersat convinced at least one commentator that they were part of the revolution.

"That's not possible, is it?" Jeff asked.

"I can't see it. Nobody's much interested in Earth politics except as it affects the price we get for steel and electricity. This 3R gang isn't going to help the market any.

"Besides, the Worlds are all pacifistic. We're too vulnerable to get involved in revolutions and wars."

"You're involved in this one, I'm afraid." It would be two days before we found out how catastrophically true that was.

44 ✦ What happened behind their backs (2)

The U.S. military had game plans for everything, even revolution. They even had plans for what to do in case parts of the military were on the other side.

What they didn't have a game plan for was the case where the man ultimately in charge of personnel allocation, a four-star general in the Pentagon, happened to be on the other side. Thus whole regiments, even divisions, were composed entirely of 3R members. They were all dispersed—"night maneuvers"—when the revolution started.

There were also game plans, of course, for retaliation. You could push a button and wipe out Cuba, or France, or the entire Supreme Socialist Union. A short-tempered and prejudiced man, who could only have been overruled by people who were vaporized by the Washington bomb, pushed the button for Worlds.

Nearly two hundred missiles leaped from the sea toward forty-one targets in various orbits. It was bloody murder.

The killer missiles were not nuclear. They were in essence giant shotgun shells, each blasting tonnes of metal shrapnel in east-to-west orbits calculated to intercept each World's orbit as the World rolled west to east, the schrapnel impacting with meteoric velocity.

The missiles were rather old, dating back to the 2035 SALT XI agreement. But they had been scrupulously maintained, and most of them did their job well.

Most of the smaller Worlds, such as Von Braun and the twins Mazeltov/B'ism'illah Ma'sha'llah, were instantly and utterly destroyed. Devon's World had a huge chunk torn out of its side, and the ninety percent of the population who were not at that time inside the hub or spokes all died of explosive decompression.

Some of the Worlds had up to thirty minutes' warning. Three quarters of Tsiolkovski's population survived, since it was made up of a series of airtight compartments: they'd had enough time to calculate the direction from which the brutal salvo would come and move nearly everyone to the other side. Uchūden braced itself for death, but the cloud of metal missed it by hundreds of kilometers. The nimble Worlds Galileo, OAO, and Bellcom Four were able to dodge in time.

Only one person died in New New York: a shotgun can't do much against a mountain. A few scraps of metal smashed through the observation dome, and one of them killed a janitor. Air loss was insignificant.

But the fifty missiles aimed at New New York hadn't been intended to penetrate the hollow rock. What they did do was reduce most of the solar panels to ribbons and disable the heat-exchange mechanism. If it couldn't be repaired, a quarter of a million people would cook.

It took only three days to fix, though, and the loss of the surface solar panels was no problem. The powersat that had serviced the Eastern Seaboard hadn't been a target, and it was easily pressed into service.

In the Worlds, fourteen thousand people had died in the first hour. Another five thousand would die over the weeks to follow, because New New was the only large

World with its life support systems intact. Shuttles brought a constant stream of refugees from Tsiolkovski and Devon's World, but there were only so many shuttles and they could only move so fast.

Nineteen thousand dead is not a large number in historical context. Three times that number died in the first hours of the battle of the Somme, for a scant kilometer of worthless mud; fifty times as many in the battle for the possession of Stalingrad; 2500 times as many during World War II. But the Decimation, as it came to be called, would be more important historically than any of these affairs.

It was not a "catalyst," for a catalyst emerges from reaction unchanged.

It was not a "pivot," because the forces had already been in motion for a long time.

It was an excuse.

45 ✦ Sunshine state

We made it to Florida, barely. A red FAILSAFE ENGAGED light blinked on and we descended rapidly toward a soft-looking pasture. Jeff steered us past a red barn and silo.

"We're a little north of Gainesville," he said. "If we can find a vehicle, we can get to the Cape in a day or two."

We landed hard. Before I could draw a new breath, Jeff had slid the canopy back, grabbed a weapon from behind the seat, and vaulted out. "Get out quick," he said.

It took me a while to untangle myself from the safety net, and then I just sort of dropped over the edge, lacking commando spirit. It was hard to feel too threatened with the dawn reflecting prettily off the dewy grass, birds cooing, clean country smells.

Jeff was peering over the floater's stern, looking at a farmhouse about fifty meters away. "Wonder if—"

There was a loud gunshot and, at the same time, the fading whine of a bullet that must have bounced off the floater. I cringed down.

"Not smart!" Jeff shouted. Another shot; no ricochet. Jeff aimed toward a tree (curious bell-shaped foliage) and a laser blast stabbed out. The middle of the tree burst into flame.

"That happens to your barn in five seconds," he

shouted, "and then the silo, and then the house. Come out with your hands over your heads."

"What the hell do you want?" The shout cracked on "hell."

"Don't you worry about what I want," Jeff said. He fired again and a haystack burst into flame. "Worry about what I've *got!*"

A white-haired man came out of the farmhouse door, followed by two younger men and a young woman. They stood on the porch with their hands in the air.

"Come on up to the floater," Jeff shouted. "'We won't hurt you." He made a patting motion to me. "Stay down," he whispered.

They walked up the incline toward us, having a little trouble on the slippery grass. Jeff didn't move. When they were in front of us, he said, "Put your hands down. Move together, shoulder-to-shoulder. Now shuffle to the left . . . there." They formed a human shield between him and the farmhouse.

He stood up and handed the laser rifle over to me. "Stay down, O'Hara. If there's a shot, burn everything." I wasn't even sure which button to push. Jeff stepped around the end of the floater.

"I have to assume you left someone back there," he said, drawing the hand laser from its holster. "He better not peep. You want to go back and tell him that?" He kept the laser pointed at the ground.

The farmer stared at Jeff steadily, maliciously. "Ain't no one down there. We all there is."

"Sure." Jeff leaned back against the floater. "This is government business. If you cooperate with us, we'll forget those two shots. Understandable, the way things are."

"The way things *are*," the farmer said, still staring, "is that we got no guv'ments, or maybe two. Which one might you be from?"

"The legitimate one." He showed his badge. "I'm a field agent for the Federal Bureau of Investigation."

He laughed. "That don't mean shit. It was you and those goddamn spacers got us into this."

"Not true. Richard Conklin's a traitor, but most of the FBI is loyal. We're trying to straighten things out. We need help."

The man kept looking at him, silently but not as maliciously. "Look at it this way," Jeff said. "If we'd meant to do you harm, you never would've got out the first shot. You'd be roast meat by now, if that's what we wanted. Isn't that true?"

"That's right, Pop," the young woman said.

"You shut up," the farmer said mildly. "What kind of help is it you want?"

"Food, water, and transportation. We can pay."

"What we hear on the cube, your dollar ain't worth bumfodder. Food's worth plenty."

"We can pay in gold."

"Gold." The farmer took a step forward.

"Get back." Jeff raised the weapon halfway.

"Sorry. Just wanted a look at your machine. Never seen a Mercedes before."

"It's a special police model. Got us all the way from Denver on fuel cells."

"Now, that might be worth somethin'. Once the power net gets up again."

Jeff hesitated. "I could kid you about that, but I won't. It's not mine to barter, even though we'll have to leave it here. It's government property and it has a tracer signal embedded in the fuselage. If you tried to drive it you wouldn't get ten kilometers."

The farmer stroked his chin. "You just said the right thing, I think." He half-turned, and shouted down to the farmhouse. "Maw! It's all right. They jus' cops." He shrugged at Jeff. "Left the ole lady and the baby down there. Didn't know what the hell you was up to."

"How far you got to go?" one of the young men said.

"The Cape. New New York Corporation."

"Why you want to go there?" the farmer asked.

"Bring them something they aren't expecting," Jeff said, smiling.

The farmer nodded. "Can't do you no good there. Floater's down in a soybean field five plat away." He glared at one of the boys. "Goddamn Jerry comin' back from a night on the town. Got a pigfart tractor—"

"Methane," Jerry translated.

"—get you into Gainesville. You might could pick up somethin' there."

So for one gold coin we got a knapsack full of dried meat, bread, fruit, and cheese, and several jugs of well water, and a ride into Gainesville. The "baby," who was ten or eleven, traced us a copy of their map of Florida. Jeff had him draw in the areas that were state parks and recreation areas; if possible, we wanted to find an overland vehicle, so as to avoid roads and towns.

They traded me a change of clothes—I'd been abducted in a bright red kaftan—and Jeff changed into his FBI uniform. We took from the floater a first-aid kit, compass, burglary kit, and enough armament to start our own revolution.

The tractor ride was at top speed, about equal to a fast walk. Both of the sons came along with us, armed and alert. Martial law evidently wasn't working too well in Gainesville.

"Americans aren't really bad people," Jeff said, nearly shouting to be heard over the hammering engine. "But we've been trigger-happy for three hundred years. There are four hundred million firearms registered in the various states, and probably just as many unregistered. Two per person, and you can bet every one of them is greased up and loaded today. The people *and* the firearms."

I was maintaining the national average. Ten-shot laser pistol stuck uncomfortably in my belt, riot gun on my lap. It was similar to Perkins's shotgun but worked on compressed air rather than gunpowder. It kept shooting as long as you held the trigger down, eight seconds per cassette. I was certain I could never use it.

The farmland gave way to lowrise suburbia, then highrises and malls. Whole blocks were burned out. There were squads of soldiers at some intersections; they saw Jeff's uniform and waved us on.

The city proper was a mess. Nearly half the stores were gutted, shoals of glass on the sidewalks and streets. Other stores were being guarded by conspicuously armed men and women.

The boys had a city directory. They took us first to Honest Ed's RV Rental, which was a smoking ruin, and then to Outdoors Unlimited. It was unharmed, and a fat man with a hunting rifle lounged in the doorway.

"You rent cross-country vehicles?" Jeff shouted.

"Got three," he answered. We unloaded our gear and the boys backed up to the intersection, and roared away with obvious relief.

"We need something that'll get us to the Cape and back," Jeff said. "About five hundred kilometers' range."

"That's no problem. Problem is, will you bring it back."

"I have no reason not to. This is FBI business—"

"I can read." The three letters were prominent on Jeff's right breast pocket.

"If I don't make it back, you can bill the government. I'll write you out a statement, good for the replacement price of the vehicle."

"Now that's just it. The money situation is really confusing. I've been doing business by barter, all day."

"I have some gold. Four thousand."

He shook his head. "My cheapest one's worth twenty times that. Tell you what. Your statement, the gold, and one of your lasers."

"That's against the law."

"Not much law around, you may have noticed."

"Let's see the vehicles."

None of them was a floater. Jeff selected one with six

large wheels; he verified the charge in the fuel cells and checked the manufacturer's handbook. There was plenty of power for the trip.

He wrote out the statement and signed it, then gave the man two gold coins and his laser pistol. The man asked for the holster, too. Then he handed over the keys.

We started for the door. I heard a soft *click* and turned around. The fat man was standing there with a fading smile on his face, the pistol pointed in our direction. Jeff was already halfway to him in a smooth *balestra*. He gracefully kicked him on the chin. He fell like a fat soft tree.

Jeff buckled on the holster and retrieved his laser. "It's not common knowledge, but the thumbrest on an agent's personal weapon is a sensor keyed to his thumbprint. Good insurance." While he was talking, he checked the fat man for a pulse. "Still alive." He found a tube of liquid solder and squeezed a few drops down inside the barrel of the hunting rifle. Then he searched the man's pockets for the gold and the statement. "We're felons, now. Let's go."

The RV's motor was a quiet hum. The seats were soft and deep. "Ah, sportsmen," Jeff said. He pushed a button and the windows rolled up. He said the glass had to be shatterproof but he didn't know whether it would deflect a bullet. He told me to keep the riot gun very visible.

We sped through the streets of Gainesville with only one incident. We both saw the silhouette of a man with a rifle, standing on the roof of a building across the street. Jeff slewed the RV to the left and we passed under him driving along the sidewalk, horn blaring to warn pedestrians. If he shot at us, I didn't hear it.

Jeff zigzagged through the city, following his compass. We were stopped several times by military and police roadblocks but didn't have any trouble.

We got on a "truck road" south of Gainesville, a straight smooth ribbon of concrete, and Jeff got the RV up to 150 kilometers per hour.

"If we dared to stay on these roads, we could be at the

Cape in a couple of hours. But there's bound to be trouble . . . ambushes, hijackers. Soon as we get out in the country we'll head straight southeast, toward the Ocala National Forest." We were going through an area of small factories and shabby lowrise apartment buildings.

The road curved and Jeff slowed down abruptly. "That's trouble, for sure." About a half-kilometer ahead, a truck was lying on its side. At least four people were milling around it, and at least one of them was armed. Jeff turned onto a gravel path marked "Service Road," that led behind a concrete-block factory, evidently abandoned. There was no fence in back, just a tangle of brush, taller than the RV.

"Hang on," Jeff said. He slowed down and did something with the levers mounted by the steering wheel. The motor's pitch dropped to a loud growl and we crawled into the brush.

It wasn't encouraging. There was nothing to see but green, in every direction. We'd go a few meters and fetch up against something immovable, back up and try a few meters in another direction. After a half-hour of this, we were suddenly in the clear: Jeff knocked over a wooden fence and we were speeding over a manicured pasture.

"Horse farm." He pointed to a group of the animals staring at us from a safe distance. "We'll be all right if we can keep away from buildings. One farmhouse per day is plenty."

Every kilometer or so, we'd slow down to break through another fence and take a new compass reading. We had to detour around a large lake (the RV would function as a boat, but Jeff said it would be very slow and too tempting a target), but then shot straight south across farmland to the Ocala National Forest.

The forest was full of trees, no surprise. Jeff weaved around while I tried to make sense of the bobbing compass, telling him to bear right or left, averaging rather south of east and east of south. But it seemed safe; we encountered a few jackrabbits and armadillos, but none of them was armed.

We came upon a sand road that bore directly southeast, so decided to chance it. We were able to maintain a speed of thirty to forty kilometers per hour, slithering through the woods. Green shade and silence on both sides. I guess we got complacent.

Suddenly a metal cable jumped up from the sand in front of us. Jeff tried to stop but we slid and slammed into it. Out, he said, and kicked open his door and dived. But I was tangled up in the seat restraint again, and this time it almost killed me. Just as the buckle clicked free, a bullet smashed through the windshield and peppered my face with glass fragments. I felt a hot splash of involuntary urine and broke a fingernail getting the door open, fell to the ground and crawled behind a tree, blasting the riot gun in various directions.

46 ✦ What happened behind their backs (3)

Almost every nation on Earth denounced the United States for its cruel assault on the helpless Worlds. Every country in Common Europe withdrew its diplomats (though most of them were on their way home already), and even the Alexandrian Dominion asked for a formal explanation of the action.

The Supreme Socialist Union announced that a state of war existed between their countries and the United States, until such time as the legitimate revolutionary government was installed. Systems were unlocked and thumbs hovered over buttons.

More than a century before, the combined weapons systems of the United States and the Soviet Union (now one-third of the SSU) had grown to the point where they could completely exterminate a planet of eight billion souls. Since no planet in the Solar System had anything like that number of people, they did the logical thing. They signed papers agreeing to limit the rate of growth of their weapons systems. A few misguided idealists on both sides suggested that it might be wiser to stop the growth of the systems, or even dismantle a few weapons. But more practical men prevailed, citing the lessons of history, or at least current events. The "balance of terror" worked, first in the short run; then in the long run.

When South America blasted itself back to the nineteenth century in a nuclear round robin, the major powers made sage and pious remarks and quietly congratulated each other on their mutual sanity. When the Soviet Union was bloodily preoccupied with its Cultural Consolidation, the United States did not take advantage; neither did the resulting SSU attack the United States during the year of vulnerability that followed its Second Revolution.

For one and a half centuries after the primitive pyres of Hiroshima and Nagasaki, the systems and counter-systems grew in complexity and magnitude. More and more agreements were signed. Peace was guaranteed so long as the systems worked.

The systems broke down on the American side on 16 March 2085. The same madman who had tried to kill the Worlds sat at a console under a mountain in Colorado. He turned forty keys and played a magnificent arpeggio on the buttons beneath them.

47 ✦ Firefight

There were a few seconds of silence after my spree with the riot gun. Then two shots, pause, two more. They were on Jeff's side, but he didn't fire back. I hoped it was because he didn't want the laser to give away his hiding place.

The silence stretched on. What if he were dead? Then so was I. I was pretty well hidden, behind a tree and a fallen log, but the man who was shooting (I assumed he was a man) must know about where I was. But then he also knew I had the riot gun. Maybe he would leave. Could I find my way to the Cape alone? I could take the compass out of the RV and walk southeast, maybe a week—

"Don't move, bitch."

He was hardly two meters away, crouched behind a tree. All I could see were his face and a hand gripping a large pistol. On the word "bitch" we both fired. He missed me. I thought I'd missed him, too, but then he stood up from behind the tree, gaping at the shredded remains of his hand, bright blood pulsing. He said "Oh" softly and started to run. A green laser pulse hit him at chest level and he fell to the ground, skidding.

I stood up trembling, trying to control sphincters. Jeff shouted, "There's another—" and I felt a sting on my neck and heard a gunshot. I slumped down beside the RV and put my hand to my neck; blood streamed down my arm. I felt myself fainting, put my head between my knees, and fell over sideways. I was dimly aware of gunfire, and green laser light, and some orange light, too. I passed out.

I woke up with Jeff spraying something over my neck. He pressed a cotton pad against the wound, and took my hand.

"We have to move. Can you hold this in place?"

Half the forest was in flames. I nodded dumbly and let him put my hand over the bandage. He lifted me up and put me inside the RV, slammed the door and ran around to his side. It was getting hot.

We backed up away from the flames and took off through the woods. "It's not a bad one," Jeff said. "Flesh wound. We ought to have it stitched up, though." When we were well away from the fire, he stopped long enough to tape the bandage in place.

"You feel up to navigating?" he asked. "I don't think we ought to follow that path anymore."

"Let me out first."

"Need help?"

I got the door open. "No, I've been doing it for years." I squatted behind the RV and relieved myself. All very rustic, with the sweet pine smoke and leaves to clean up with. Then I politely threw up for a while, on my hands and knees, everything in proper order, wouldn't be nice to do everything at once. Jeff must have heard me being sick; he was holding me for the last of it, and had brought out a plastic jug of well water. I rinsed out my mouth and held on to him while the dizziness passed, not crying, his shirt front salty between my teeth. The taste of him calmed me.

I pulled up my pants and buckled them. "Let's go. I can navigate now."

"Are you sure?" I was suddenly, helplessly furious at his professional calm.

"Doesn't anything ever get to you?"

He shook his head slightly. "Not while it's happening."

He walked me back to the RV door. "Let's get to Cape Town and have a nervous breakdown together."

There was a loud *boom* and something silver flashed overhead, leaving a solid-looking column of vapor behind.

"Christ," Jeff said, "I hope that's not nuclear."

48 ✦ What happened behind their backs (4)

Both sides had defensive screens of automatic lasers and antimissile missiles, and they were remarkably efficient: not one bomb in thirty found its target. There were lots of bombs, though.

Nearly two billion people died in the first ninety minutes. In a sense, they were the lucky ones.

One missile containing a biological agent, the virus Koralatov 31, went off a few seconds too early, and dispersed its deadly aerosol into the jet stream over Lincoln, Nebraska. It didn't infect anyone for several days. But in the weeks and months and years to follow, it would settle and thrive all over the world.

Only deserts and the poles were safe. No one would know that.

49 ✦ Cape Town

We only missed the Cape by about forty kilometers, over-shooting it to the south. We crossed the Indian River by moonlight, churning through the water at an agonizing crawl. There was a bridge in sight, but we'd had one ambush too many.

Merritt Island. Lights off, we sneaked north up darkened residential streets. All along the eastern horizon the sky was red and boiling grey; we supposed it was a forest on fire.

This was the first part of Earth I ever saw, close up, gliding in on the shuttle. So full of industry and promise.

A green-white flash dazzled us, followed by a low rumble, like thunder but deeper and more sustained.

"That would be the Cape's defensive net," Jeff said. "Someone's shooting at them."

"I don't suppose the 3R has missiles," I said. "It's the States after us."

"Probably." We had talked earlier about the possibility of the SSU taking advantage, starting The War that everybody always capitalized with their voices. Or of there possibly being a connection between the SSU and 3R.

"Do you think they'll be all right? The missiles won't get through?"

"I don't know. Those lasers must have been twenty

years old when New New York bought the Cape." He reached over and patted me on the breast, not taking his eyes off the road. My shirt was stiff with caked blood. "You know there may be no one there. Or the army or the 3R might have taken over—you could probably take the place with a squad of riflemen."

I hadn't let myself think of that, but it was obvious. What could they fight back with?

We found out a half-hour later. We ran out of residential area abruptly and, guessing, headed east along a road that was suburbia on one side and mangrove swamp on the other. Heading toward the fire. We came to a northbound road with a fence and someone fired a laser pulse over our heads.

A bright searchlight blinded us. "GET OUT OF THAT VEHICLE AND IDENTIFY YOURSELF," said a greatly amplified voice.

I saw Jeff take the handlaser out of its holster and stick it under his belt behind his back. "Keep your hands out in front of you," he said. "Be calm."

We walked toward the searchlight. "FAR ENOUGH."

A small woman armed only with a clipboard came out of the glare. "Are you Worlds citizens?"

I nodded. "New New York. Marianne O'Hara."

She riffled through the pages. "Root line?"

"Scanlan."

"Who are you?" she said to Jeff.

"He's my husband," I said.

"Not Worlds?"

"No, I'm an American citizen. I do want to emigrate, though."

"Don't blame you. I can't wait to get out of here myself. But you know," she said to me, "you'll have to wait until the war's over. If you want to stay with him, you'll have to stay here."

"She's going," Jeff said.

"Are you the one who was kidnapped?" I said yes. "They didn't treat you too well." To Jeff: "Drive past the gate about a kilometer, and there'll be a road to the right; that's Cape Town. There's an aid station in the middle there."

"Wait," I said. "There's room for one more man, isn't there? He's my *husband*."

"There isn't even room for you," she said without inflection, "or me. Haven't you heard?"

"Heard what?"

"The States tried to blow the Worlds out of the sky. There's nothing left but New New. And it's going to be crowded with survivors from the others."

I was stunned speechless. "So no groundhogs," Jeff said.

"None. There's one last flight going out at nine-ten this morning. Every shuttle leaving. And you'd be smart to be far away; the defensive lasers shut down a couple of minutes later. We want this place blown to pieces. We don't want the U.S. to have a launch facility."

"You ought to sabotage it yourselves," Jeff said—unrelenting professional. "The U.S. won't hit it once they see you've pulled out."

"You don't know." Her eyes glistened and her voice broke. "It's total war. The whole fucking planet." She said Whole. Fucking. Planet.

I staggered and Jeff grabbed me around the shoulders. "You can last until nine-ten?"

"Everything's automatic," she said. "So far, so good. I don't know what we'll do if they send soldiers."

Jeff reached back and handed her his pistol, butt first. He turned a switch on the side. "We have other weapons in the RV; you're welcome to them."

He gave them the riot gun and the grenades and the knee mortar and the subsonic claymore. We kept the laser rifle and my pistol, just in case.

Cape Town was a mess. Paper everywhere, a lot of it American currency. Piles of clothing, books, household effects. Fancy vacationers' tents mixed in with lean-tos of cardboard and scrap wood. Knots of people huddled around small fires.

We followed signs to the aid station, a graceful modern building that had once been a duty-free shop. The one doctor was asleep on a cot, snoring; a nurse helped me up onto a table and gave me a shot, then cut away the stiff bandages. I faded out while he was asking me what had happened.

✦ ✦ ✦

I woke up in the back seat of the RV, my head on Jeff's lap. The sky was getting bright. "What time?"

"Almost seven," he said. "I'll have to go soon."

My neck was tight and sore from the stitches. I pulled myself up to a sitting position and closed my eyes until the dizziness went away. "I'm coming with you," I said. "I can't abandon you here."

After a long silence, he whispered "Bullshit," and kissed me. He opened the door. "Think you can stand up?"

"I'm serious, Jeff."

"I know you are. I've had more time to think about it, though." He helped me out onto the crushed grass. The swamp air was cool and musty. We were less than a kilometer from where the nearest shuttles were waiting.

"Look at it this way," he said. "The war can't go on very much longer. I have weapons, transportation, a uniform; chances are I'll make it through.

"Let me keep the gold. As soon as possible, I'll get to Tokyo Bay, Zaire, Novosibirsk—wherever they're still launching. And I'll buy passage."

"It may be years before they let anyone up."

"Now suppose you did come along with me," he continued. "We wouldn't get into orbit any faster—and the two of us together would be a lot less likely to survive the next couple of weeks, than I would be, by myself. 'He travels swiftest who travels alone.'"

"You've got it all figured out."

"Pretty much."

"Except how I'm supposed to live with myself, letting you—"

"Don't be sentimental. Melodramatic. We have to be practical."

It wasn't a setting conducive to practicality, the space ships poised against an impossible magenta sunrise, my mind a confusion of gratitude, fear, guilt, and hope. I knew he was right but my will was paralyzed.

"Here." He took me by the arm and turned me around; opened the RV's front door. My trunk was on the seat. "I got your things while you were sleeping. Can you choose out seven kilograms' worth?"

"Already have." I unlocked it and lifted out a plastic bag. "Last day I was in New York." Almost nothing practical: a carton of French cigarettes and six bottles of Guinness, a clarinet with two dozen bamboo reeds, a diary, a drawing. A shamrock frozen in clear plastic, that Jeff had given me on New Year's Day.

He closed the trunk and heaved it into the back. "Better get you aboard. I've got a long way to go in two hours." He slid over to the driver's seat and switched on the motor. "Come on."

I sat down and eased the door shut. "Don't we have to find out which one . . ."

"You're going in Number Four, the low-gee one. Because you're injured." The vehicle bumped across the uneven grassland. He unbuttoned his shirt pocket and passed over a folded sheet of paper. "They let me do your manifest for you."

I stared at it without reading it. "How far do you have to be?"

"I don't really know. Some of those old missiles have a blast radius some tens of kilometers. Just want to get as far away as possible and be behind something solid, at nineten."

We lurched up onto the tarmac and Jeff sped toward Number Four. There were a few dozen people waiting at the lift entrance at the base of the shuttle, many of them propped up on crutches or sitting in wheelchairs, clustered around a small fire.

He eased the RV to a stop a little beyond the crowd and leaned over and kissed me. He was gentle but his arms were hard and trembling. "No words," he whispered hoarsely. "Just go."

50 ✦ Looking backward

It's been more than twenty years now and I still remember so vividly how lonesome, how guilty I felt at that moment, Jeff's car shrinking away down the tarmac, the smell of ozone from its motor dissipating, the people talking behind me. The silly sound of beer bottles clanking together in my bag, when I went to join them.

Even stronger is the memory of hearing his voice again, a few years later, barely audible through crashing static. He not only lived through the bombs but was one of the few people with the glandular quirk necessary to survive the plague. The acromegaly that made him so big. So he lived, at least for a while, though from what we know about life on Earth now he might have been happier dead.

My husbands and I were talking about Earth at dinner; about Earth and food. There was no city where all three of us went, since Daniel rarely left New York and John never visited there when he was in the States. Daniel mentioned a place in the Village, the New New Delhi Deli, where Benny and I occasionally went for lunch. Kosher and Indian take-out, spicy and cheap. And now thoroughly lost, except in our memories. So many of the memories are tastes and smells; I'd even like to smell the thick city air again, not to mention the sea and the jungle.

Musty swamp and sharp smell of things burning, the

morning I left. I don't remember any sense of the enormity of what was happening. I was so numb, with medicine and from the quick succession of personal shocks, that I sort of missed the end of the world.

Not the End, really, though it may have been the end as a world. When I was a girl, you heard a lot of talk about a future when most of humanity lived in the Worlds, tens of billions of happy people, with the Earth a minor backwater, a historical preserve. It seemed inevitable, since the Earth's population was declining and ours was increasing; since our fortunes were expanding and their horizons were closing in on them. But we saw it as happening through slow evolution, not sudden catastrophe. Not war and plague.

Old Jules Hammond had a particularly offensive program last week, with a so-called historian who tap-danced over European history in the relentless pursuit of edifying parallels to our present happy situation. Interposing the Black Plague between medieval darkness and Renaissance light. The World Wars between the dehumanizing Industrial Revolution and the freedom of the Space Age and Cybernetica. It bothers me that this sort of slap-happy propaganda is socially useful, maybe necessary, and that I'll have to acquiesce in it or even actively use it.

It's not as if I will be the first leader who ever turned her back on the truth because her people needed the comfort of fantasy. If everyone shared my sense of loss we would be paralyzed, doomed.

I have to put it behind myself literally. Live only with the present and the future. We have no real past. We live in a hollow rock surrounded by nothing. Outside of this bubble of life, night that goes on forever.

But this is true: it's only in the night that you can see the stars.